Atlas Arcane

Ultra Meridian Series: Book 6

Theo Mann

Invisible Publishing Company

Ultra Meridian Series

Contents

Chapter 1

"**A**nother twenty Stalwarts coming out from Macron Calypso!" Kuman called from the station behind Sheriff Mace Davenport's chair on board the stolen Stalwart-class gunship, *Tenacious*. "The Reserve Wing isn't messing around this time!"

"When have they ever?" Davenport called back. "Bring the fleet about to return fire!"

"The cavalry is coming out from Helios Sanctus, too," Yogro interjected from his side of the *Tenacious's* bridge. "They're demanding the return of their fugitives."

"Tell them to suck my......" Davenport broke off when a gunshot glanced across the *Tenacious's* flank. "Engage and drive the cocksuckers back to Hell where they belong. Babcock! What can you tell me about where that Ziprothil is?"

"I'm working on it!" Babcock shrieked from his own station. "It's moving around all over the place. No! I got it! It's at the Pegasus Mine. No! It's leaving the Pegasus Mine!"

"Who is it leaving with?" Davenport called over the crash of more gunfire.

"We got a few bigger problems than finding the Ziprothil!" Kuman interjected. "Fourteen Stalwarts are breaking the line! They're coming after us—this particular ship!"

Davenport turned his attention back to the battle and saw that the situation was becoming critical. The Reserve Wing never had been in the habit of playing nice, especially not where Davenport and his friends had been concerned.

Now the Reserve Wing Stalwarts were getting downright biblical, but he should have expected that.

The fleet of alien warships that once served Calyx Elkanon surrounded the *Tenacious*, but the Reserve Wing wasn't taking that lying down.

A solid rank of Stalwarts advanced to drive the alien fleet back. Daggers and Nitrols swarmed in from both sides trying to break the fleet's position and get inside Davenport's perimeter.

The escaped prisoners from Terminus Anathema and combined alien fleet stood firm and the gunfire shooting back and forth between the two sides escalated to deafening explosions. The Reserve Wing couldn't break through, but the alien fleet couldn't break away, either.

"Find that Ziprothil, Babcock!" Davenport ordered. "We need to know where to go when we get out of here."

Davenport almost went back to coordinating the battle, but he stopped when Babcock turned around and met Davenport's eye. "I'm sorry, Davenport. The Ziprothil is on a Reserve Wing Nitrol heading for Atlas Arcane. The Nitrol is traveling in convoy with a squadron of Daggers en route to rendezvous with more Stalwarts. They got it. The Reserve Wing got the Ziprothil."

A chill went up Davenport's spine. "Is there any sign of.....?" He broke off. He couldn't ask the question.

He got Dice and Fiddler back. All the rest of his people had vanished into space and now the Ziprothil was gone, too.

The Ziprothil wasn't just gone. The situation would have seemed bleak enough just because of that.

Now Admiral Joyce had the Ziprothil, the Ithium, and the chip that would turn both substances into a catastrophic doomsday weapon that could wipe out the whole Confederacy. That dirty rotten bastard.

Davenport's resolve solidified to ice-cold granite. "Track that ship and get us out of this battle. We're going after him. Break the line, Kuman. Duni, as soon as the Howitzers punch through, gun it and overtake that Nitrol. I don't care what it takes. We're getting that Ziprothil if it's the last thing we do."

"These Stalwarts might have something to say about that!" Kuman yelled over the noise of more gunfire coming from all directions.

"Then break through the Daggers!" Davenport ordered. "Wheel about and cut through. Bring the fleet in to block the Stalwarts' gunfire while we break away!"

"You'll need more than one Stalwart to take on the Reserve Wing!" Yogro countered. "I'm cutting twenty of our ships away to come with us."

"Do whatever you have to do! Just get out from behind these Stalwarts and overtake that ship! Stand ready to sprint, Duni!"

The *Tenacious* and a body of alien warships spun sideways and laid into the Daggers and Nitrols attacking from the port side. Duni throttled the *Tenacious* forward and the alien fleet overran the Daggers to break through.

The rest of Davenport's force charged the gap and laid into the Reserve Wing line. The fugitives from Calyx's prison empire struck a Stalwart at the far end of the line and the Stalwart exploded right on top of the *Tenacious*.

The concussion hurled the *Tenacious* sideways and more explosions boomed all around the ship. Something detonated behind Davenport's chair and Babcock flew away from his station.

"Get us through, Duni!" Davenport bellowed. "Get us through now!"

Duni punched the throttle and the *Tenacious* rocketed out of the battle. The ship burst into clear open space and Duni spun around to gun it in pursuit of the Ziprothil.

Another twenty of Davenport's fleet broke through at the same time. They surrounded the *Tenacious* and they all fired their engines to support the ship, but at that moment, the Stalwarts coming from Macron Calypso charged into the battle and hammered the *Tenacious* with more gunfire.

Davenport opened his mouth to order the fleet to break this line, too, but the same thing happened. Dozens of alien vessels tied up the original Stalwart line to give Davenport a chance to break away.

Now these new Stalwarts pivoted sideways and blockaded Davenport's group from escaping. The new ships formed a second blockade to hold the alien fleet here.

"We can't get through!" Kuman called. "What's Plan B?"

"To hell with it!" Davenport countered. "Scatter our ships and reconverge to encircle the Reserve Wing!"

"That's gonna be risky!"

"Don't tell me it's risky!" Davenport snapped. "Just do it! We can't go anywhere with these assholes trapping us like this!"

The order translated down the alien line. The two flanks that had been locked in battle against the Reserve Wing scattered in an instant.

The Stalwarts, Daggers, and Nitrols whirled away trying to acquire their targets, but the defenders broke apart too quickly and left the Reserve Wing with nothing to shoot at.

The plan worked beyond Davenport's wildest dreams. His fleet blasted outward in all directions. The Reserve Wing vessels all turned outward to follow their targets. The Reserve Wing formed a perfect circle.

The alien ships skidded into reverse and came howling back with a vengeance. They caught the Reserve Wing with its pants down, closed in an outer ring, and attacked to drive the Reserve Wing into a defensive huddle.

"Ha ha! It worked!" Yogro crowed. "Eat it, you bastards!"

"Finish them off!" Davenport ordered. "Cripple the Reserve Wing so they can't come after us?"

"Do you want to break away now?" Duni asked from the pilot's station. "We got a clear shot to catch up with the Ziprothil."

Davenport opened his mouth to answer when Kuman interrupted. "Another fleet is coming in hot and heavy! You thought you had problems before! Here they come! Brace for....."

A crushing smash struck the *Tenacious* and slammed the ship into the alien ring encircling the Reserve Wing. An overwhelming tide of ships blasted into the battle and drilled Davenport's fleet straight into the Reserve Wing ranks they'd just been fighting.

"What the hell is going on?!" Davenport bellowed. "Who's attacking us?"

"They belong to Yuki Duetis—Rizarth Hudan's old syndicate." Kuman attacked his controls. "The wires are buzzing with the news. Yuki is dead and Rizarth's daughter has taken control of the syndicate."

"What the hell is she doing coming after us?" Davenport countered. "Can you locate her in the swarm? See if you can hail her."

"I'm not picking up any indication of which ship is leading the charge. There are too many....."

Another bone-crunching impact struck the *Tenacious*. Davenport couldn't see or hear anything for a second as the ship's controls flickered off and then on again.

When the confusion cleared, he had to steady himself when he saw the state of battle outside.

Rizarth Hudan's old syndicate brought a massive fleet of ships that Davenport didn't recognize. Rizarth's people surrounded Davenport's fleet and the Reserve Wing. Rizarth's people fired into the crowd regardless of who they hit.

The incoming fleet hammered Davenport's group backward until his ships got mixed up with the Reserve Wing. Davenport's people and the Reserve Wing joined forces against these new invaders, but even with all those ships working together, no one could overcome the attackers.

The combined mishmash of Davenport's alien fugitives and the Reserve Wing retreated before the onslaught. The rear flank split apart to let them retreat and then Rizarth's squadron struck with a vengeance.

They spun inward toward the middle, launched a brutal onslaught on the former prisoners' position, and cut straight through Davenport's line to drive the defenders apart.

Reserve Wing Stalwarts and Daggers got caught in the same sweep. Both fleets bumped into each other trying to get away from Rizarth's assault.

The *Tenacious* skidded to starboard surrounded by Reserve Wing vessels all doing their best just to stop Rizarth's squadron from destroying them all.

Rizarth's squadron split the defenders in half. Davenport's group still couldn't defend itself, but Rizarth's squadron pulled the same maneuver again to cut the two halves into fourths.

"They're cutting us apart!" Kuman yelled over the concussion of gunfire. "They're dividing and conquering!"

"What the hell am I supposed to do about it?!" Davenport countered and another punishing shot slammed the *Tenacious* aside.

"We're receiving communications from Rizarth's flagship!"

"You said you couldn't identify his flagship!"

"One of them is hailing us. They're demanding we turn over the prisoners."

"What prisoners?!" Davenport fired back. "We're all prisoners!"

Kuman shook his head and then looked up. "He's demanding to speak to you."

"Put him on."

The communications link finally connected and Davenport found himself looking at another giant Hidion. "Who are you and why are you attacking us?" Davenport demanded. "We've never had any conflict with Rizarth Hudan's organization."

"Who I am isn't important," the Hidion countered. "You're holding an Adik prisoner on board your ship. We demand that you return him immediately."

Davenport frowned. "We have a lot of Adiks on board. They're our friends. We aren't holding any of them. We helped them escape from Terminus Anathema....."

"This one was not a prisoner at Terminus Anathema. His name is Dice. We demand that you turn him over immediately along with the female human that was flying with him when you captured them."

"I'm telling you we didn't capture them," Davenport fired back. "I can bring them here to tell you in person if you want."

"I do not want to hear from them in person whether you captured them or not. Prepare to be boarded to hand them over or you can prepare to be boarded when we take them by force. The choice is yours." The Hidion cut the signal.

"They're arming their weapons for another onslaught," Kuman reported. "If they attack again, we won't be able to stop them from crippling us, boarding us, and doing whatever else they want with us."

"Like hell we will," Davenport muttered. "Tell him he'll have to destroy the ship with Dice on board. We'll never hand him over."

Kuman tried to answer, but more gunfire cut him off. Rizarth's squadron reacted to that message with surgical precision, nailed the *Tenacious* with another strategic barrage, and drove the Stalwart farther away from the ships surrounding it.

The *Tenacious* returned fire, but too many of Rizarth's attack vessels surrounded the Stalwart. Duni couldn't break away nor could the *Tenacious* overcome these numbers.

A flank of twenty of Rizarth's vessels split apart from the rest of the squadron. Those twenty herded the *Tenacious* away from any other ship that might be able to guard it.

Davenport's throat went dry when he saw what the squadron was trying to do. They were coming after him and no one else.

Chapter 2

"The Ziprothil is on a Nitrol heading for Atlas Arcane!" Coon reported from his station in the gunship's rear. "The Nitrol is rendezvousing with more Stalwarts. They're too far ahead. We lost the Ziprothil, too."

"Get out of the controls, Coon!" Rodeo called from the cockpit. "We're leaving Chorion Osiris. You need to withdraw now in case we need you later."

"I'm going!"

Healey glanced over at Coon's station. His filaments had been completely intertwined with the ship's controls while Bandit launched the gunship into space.

Now Coon withdrew his filaments and went back to manning his station the old-fashioned way. "That is so cool!" Jace commented from his seat next to Coon.

Coon shot him a grin. "Almost as cool as yours." He nodded at Jace's copies. They filled the rest of the gunship's seats behind the Chorion Team.

"Can you locate any of our other people?" Rodeo asked.

"Whoa!" Laub breathed. "Check out the disaster at Terminus Anathema!"

All eyes turned to the prison—or what was left of it. Alien warships from Ekol Thaine's old empire floated in orbit and bombarded the prison to a hellscape of explosions.

The scanners picked up random groups from dozens of species overrunning different parts of the prison, getting into gunfights against other groups, and breaking apart to either advance or retreat.

The territory inside the prison changed hands multiple times in the few minutes it took Bandit to get within scanner range. "Can you pick up any human life signs?" Healey asked.

"There are humans in almost every group down there," Rodeo replied. "We wouldn't be able to find Davenport unless we went down there."

"We are NOT going down there," Axel interjected. "Forget about it."

"Communications with the prison are down, too," Rodeo replied. "We can't contact anyone to find out if Davenport is even still alive."

"What about the others?" Healey asked. "Can you track anyone else? What about.....?"

He cut himself off when he saw the reports from Helios Sanctus. The station had been catastrophically damaged. Dice and Fiddler weren't there anymore anyway.

Bandit must have been thinking the same thing. He had set a course for Helios Sanctus when he left Chorion Osiris, but he turned away when he saw the state of the station. The crew wouldn't get their questions answered there.

He flew past the station, but he had to veer away a third time to avoid getting pulled into a massive battle between the Reserve Wing and multiple criminal forces all locked in deadly combat.

Healey scrambled over the controls trying to identify them all. "Who's fighting who?"

"Yuki Deutis is giving them hell," Rodeo observed.

"It isn't Yuki," Coon called. "The wires are saying Yuki's dead."

"Hold up!" Healey interrupted. "The records indicate that Dice and Fiddler left Helios Sanctus in a stolen Reserve Wing Nitrol."

"That doesn't help us," Rodeo fired back. "There are Reserve Wing Nitrols all over the place!"

"This Nitrol isn't in battle. The Reserve Wing Stalwart *Tenacious* took the Nitrol on board. The Reserve Wing must have recaptured Dice and Fiddler."

"That's the *Tenacious* right there—the one fighting Yuki's people," Bandit observed.

"Get behind the *Tenacious* and see if you can board it. We'll retake Dice and Fiddler while the Reserve Wing is distracted."

Bandit swooped into the battle, but he had a hard time even getting near the *Tenacious* with all the other ships zooming back and forth, firing in all directions, colliding with each other, and detonating under hellish gunfire.

"Rizarth's squadron is going after the *Tenacious,* too!" Healey reported.

"Good," Rodeo countered. "The more the better. Then no one on board will see us sneaking in through the back door. Get your itchy fingers working, Coon. I need you to crack the Stalwart's hold."

"You got it!" Coon called. "Just tell me when. I won't go in until you get in position."

No one said anything for a minute while Bandit did his best to work his way through the battle. Rizarth's squadron carved the defenders apart, locked up everyone in different parts of the battlefield, and plastered everyone else away from the *Tenacious*.

Rizarth's squadron forced the Stalwart back into a corner by itself. Dozens of Rizarth's ships pivoted in reverse to aim their guns outward from the group attacking the *Tenacious*.

That ring of ships blocked anyone else from getting near the Stalwart, but Rizarth's squadron only guarded the *Tenacious* against Reserve Wing and alien warships that might be able to help the *Tenacious*.

Bandit hurtled around the battlefield and skimmed into position by the *Tenacious's* cargo hold. Coon's fingers hung poised over the controls waiting for Rodeo's word.

"Now, Coon!" Rodeo ordered. "Get in, open the hold, and get out!"

Coon went into a trance as his filaments snaked into the gunship's controls. The *Tenacious's* hold opened, but at that moment, another ship blasted out of the confusion and skidded into place right in front of the hold.

The new ship was a Phoenix-class frigate and it opened fire on the Chorions' gunship. "Return fire!" Bandit ordered.

Healey and the other Chorions spun their cannons around to blast the Phoenix out of the sky, but just then, the ship's communications systems switched on. "Rodeo! It's me—Lyons! What are you doing here? Why are you trying to get on board this Stalwart?"

"We picked up that this Stalwart captured Dice and Fiddler," Rodeo replied. "We were gonna go on board and try to free them while the ship is distracted by the battle." He frowned. "What are you doing here?"

"We were just about to do the same thing."

Rodeo cocked his head to one side. He didn't look at what he was doing anymore. "You're alone. It's just you and Emmett."

"Come on board with us," Lyons told him. "We can find Dice and Fiddler together. My people will tie up the Stalwart crew so they don't come after us."

"Your people!" Bandit asked. "What do you mean?"

"You must not have been reading the wires. I killed Yuki and took over my father's empire. This fleet is operating on my orders. We tracked Dice and Fiddler to this Stalwart. Now we're here to get them back." She took one look at their stunned expressions and tightened her lips. "Come on board. We'll need to work together to find Dice and Fiddler and retrieve them from Reserve Wing custody."

She cut the signal. "Um.....what the hell just happened?" Bandit squeaked.

"She killed Yuki and took over her father's empire," Rodeo breathed under his breath. "Jesus!"

"You better do what she says and land in the hold," Healey suggested. "You don't want to piss that lady off."

Bandit gulped and eased the gunship forward. The Phoenix was already setting down inside the hold.

Bandit landed next to the Phoenix and Healey and the Chorions unloaded. They met Emmett and Lyons outside. "Where are the girls?" Rodeo asked.

"Let's move out," Lyons snapped. "We don't have a lot of time." She raised her XQ and then noticed Jace standing there. "Who's he?"

"He's another Chorion," Healey replied. "He can help us. Spread out, Jace. We're looking for an Adik and a petite human female with brown hair and brown eyes. They should be together wherever they are."

Jace nodded. "No problem."

He set off toward the stairs and the rest of the crew followed. Healey didn't ask where the Armageddon Core was. He saw right away from Emmett's and Lyons's expressions that it couldn't be good.

No one had any time to discuss it first. Healey and the boys grabbed their weapons from the gunship and started climbing the stairs. Lyons pulled out a card showing scanner readings of the ship.

"There must be fifty Adiks on this ship," she grumbled. "How the hell are we supposed to find one?"

"Are any of them in close proximity to a human female?" Rodeo asked.

"Are any of them in close proximity to a Chorion?" Emmett asked. "The records indicated that Dice and Fiddler left Helios Sanctus with a Chorion."

"That's right," Lyons exclaimed. "I forgot about that. Here he is. He's in this crew lounge and there's a Chorion in there with him." She frowned at the readings. "In fact, there are five different Chorion life signs in there with him.....and one human female."

"Let's go," Healey ordered. "Surround that lounge, Jace."

"You bet."

Jace burst apart into dozens of copies. They all ran up the stairs with the crew following him, but the party had to pause more than once. Gunfire from outside kept jostling the ship and knocking everyone into the walls.

"Can't you call off the assault?" Healey yelled to Lyons over the noise.

"The assault is the only thing stopping the crew from coming after us, remember?"

"Not for long!" Emmett pointed at her card. "We got company!"

"Stand by to defend that lounge, Jace!" Healey ordered.

Jace didn't answer before the group made it to the right landing. He burst into the corridor beyond and his copies spread out to flood the Stalwart's deck.

Lyons, Emmett, Healey, and the other Chorions turned toward the lounge where Dice, Fiddler, and their Chorion companions had been just a minute before, but the lounge was empty now.

Lyons consulted her card again "They're on the move! Someone must have tipped them off that we're here!"

"How could they?" Rodeo demanded. "We just got here!"

More gunfire startled everyone into spinning around, but this didn't come from outside the ship. It burst right out in the corridor.

The group hustled back out there to find Jace's copies in a full-blown firefight against a bunch of Hidions, Zihori, Adiks, Zalvao, and a bunch of other aliens Healey couldn't see from here.

They advanced from every side and boxed the group in near the lounge. The copies returned fire and the *Tenacious* crew dropped dozens of copies all over the corridor.

"Fall back!" Lyons ordered. "We gotta fall back and overtake Dice and the others! Come on, Marshall!"

Rodeo, Axel, Emmett, and Laub moved in front of the party. Lyons, Healey, and the other Chorions fell behind Jace's protection, but the group still had to battle their way to another stairwell at the far end of the corridor.

The copies multiplied themselves again and twenty of them surrounded the group at the center. The copies pivoted to face another squad of the *Tenacious* crew blocking their way in that direction.

The copies rushed straight into the crew's guns. The copies opened fire, but their main defense relied on just taking the hits, losing dozens of copies, and overrunning the crew by sheer numbers.

They attacked the crew and the copies used hand-to-hand combat techniques to disarm the crew, kill them, and leave everyone lying on the floor.

One of the copies pushed the stairwell door open and herded everyone else inside. "Go! Move!"

"Dice and Fiddler are five floors above us!" Lyons reported. "The crew is all down here. Dice and Fiddler are unguarded."

"Except for those Chorions," Emmett pointed out. "They must be guarding the prisoners."

"Not for long," she muttered and raised her XQ. "As soon as we find them, they'll be dead and we'll get Dice and Fiddler back."

Chapter 3

"We're being boarded!" Kuman reported. "Two ships are hacking our cargo hold! One of them is a Phoenix-class frigate from Rizarth's fleet. The other is a gunship belonging to Typhon Elexor."

Davenport spun around in his seat. "Typhon Elexor! What are they doing all the way out here? They never leave Ultra Meridian."

"It's only one gunship," Yogro pointed out. "The hack is coming from there."

"The Phoenix is firing on the gunship!" Kuman went on. "No, wait! They're both moving in and the crews are joining forces. They're heading on board."

"They're after Dice!" Davenport shot out of his seat. "Duni and Babcock, you take over here. Kuman, you and Yogro come with me. Get our crew down there to intercept them. Locate Dice and move our people in to stop these assholes from taking him and Fiddler."

Davenport grabbed his weapon and stormed off the bridge. No one was going to board his ship and steal his friends while he had anything to say about it.

Kuman took a scanner from the ship's controls. Davenport raced down multiple decks to the crew lounge where Dice, Fiddler, and Jace were staying, but when he, Kuman, and Yogro joined up with more of the crew to defend the lounge, the *Tenacious* crew walked in on dozens of armed men guarding the lounge instead.

The crew broke out into the corridor and wound up walking into gunfire bombarding the walls. Three of Davenports' crew went down right there and Yogro got hit. He bellowed in pain, dragged himself to the nearest wall, and fired around the corner to bombard the intruders.

"Who the hell are these guys?!" Davenport roared to Kuman.

Kuman stuck his head out once and immediately pulled it back. "It's Jace! It's that guy Dice and Fiddler brought on board."

Davenport took his turn darting around the corner and cursed when he pulled his head back. Kuman was right. Every man out there was one of Jace's copies.

"Son of a bitch!" Davenport spat. "I knew we shouldn't have trusted that guy."

Kuman checked his card. "Dice and Fiddler are falling back to the medical deck! The intruders are pursuing! Look! Jace is surrounding Dice and Fiddler. He must be working with Rizarth's people to capture Dice and Fiddler."

Davenport checked the card. "Let's double back and cut them off. Come on!"

He gave orders to the rest of the crew to hold the copies here. Davenport, Kuman, and three Zihori dove back into the stairwell and raced down to the medical deck.

They came up against another army of copies here, but they all seemed to be fighting each other instead of anyone else.

Davenport waved Kuman into another corridor. They followed Kuman's scans and circled toward the intensive care unit where they almost collided with Dice and Fiddler coming the other way.

"Thank God you're all right!" Davenport exclaimed. "We thought they got you!"

"Who?" Fiddler asked. "Who is it?"

"I don't know but....." Just then, Jace came running around the corner followed by four of his copies. Davenport raised his weapon and aimed it straight in the first copy's face. "Back off, asshole. I don't care if I have to blow you all away. You aren't coming near these people."

Fiddler lunged for Davenport and tried to pull his gun down. "What are you doing, Davenport? It's Jace. He's our friend."

"He's the one invading this ship! He's working with Rizarth Hudan's people to capture you two!"

"That's impossible!" Fiddler exclaimed. "He saved our lives on Helios Sanctus. We wouldn't be here now without him."

"I don't care what he did on Helios Sanctus!" Davenport snapped back. "He's up there shooting at my crew to stop us from stopping them from taking you! Rizarth's people demanded that we hand you two over to them and then they invaded the ship to capture you. Who do you think is up there shooting at us?"

Fiddler opened her mouth argue, but before she could answer, another group of Jace's copies backed around the corner. They were engaged in a brutal firefight against another group of copies advancing from the other direction.

The gunfire threatened to destroy Davenport and his friends. He grabbed Fiddler and pulled her and Dice out of the way.

"What the hell is going on, Jace?!" she hollered over her shoulder while the group retreated to a different part of the deck. "Why are your copies fighting each other?"

"I don't know!" he called back. "I can't explain it!"

The friends burst into another stairwell and ran up three floors to the engineering deck. Davenport steered everyone through the engine room and out the other side to a part of the ship where he hoped no one would find them.

Fiddler turned to Jace. "You need to withdraw your copies. Collapse them all inside you so they stop fighting each other."

He nodded. "Done."

She blinked at him and then waved that away. "Come on. Stay with us. We'll figure this out one way or the other."

"The intruders are still covering most of the ship," Kuman reported. "They have dozens of Chorions with them. Most of the intruders are Chorions."

Davenport frowned and grabbed the card. "Let me see."

He scowled at the readings, but it was true. Dozens of Chorion life signs filled every deck, but they weren't the only intruders. "Are you sure you collapsed your copies, Jace?" Fiddler asked.

"I'm certain. I always know where all my copies are."

"Something weird is going on." Davenport shoved the card back into Kuman's hand. "We gotta rejoin with the rest of the crew. We'll lead the intruders back into the crew's guns. We'll get you and Dice behind the crew line so the intruders can't take you."

"Why do they want us?" Dice asked.

"They didn't say. Did you ever do anything to Rizarth Hudan—anything that could make him your enemy?"

Dice shrugged and looked away. "I might have."

"What did you do?" Fiddler asked.

"Well....it wasn't Rizarth necessarily that I did it to. It was Yuki Duetis. He hates me."

"But Yuki is dead," Kuman pointed out. "This isn't Yuki demanding that we hand you over."

"Who is it?" Dice asked.

"His daughter," Davenport replied. "She killed Yuki and took over Rizarth's empire. She's the one sending out her people to capture you and Fiddler."

"Why didn't you say so?!" Dice roared. "Why didn't you tell me that in the first place?!"

He spun away and charged back out into the corridor heading back toward the battle.

"You can't go over there!" Davenport yelled. "You're running straight into their hands!"

"It's Lyons, you fool!" Dice bellowed over his shoulder. "Lyons is Rizarth Hudan's daughter! She thinks you captured me and she's trying to get me back! Don't you get it?! She must have tracked us here from Helios Sanctus and she sees that you took our Nitrol on board!"

Davenport stopped in his tracks and blinked at nothing. "Lyons....is Rizarth Hudan's daughter?"

"Come on!" Dice snatched Davenport by the arm and they all took off running.

They spun around a corner and ran full tilt into Lyons, Emmett, Healey, and the Chorions.

Fiddler charged into Emmett's arms. "Dad!!"

"Baby!" He crushed her into his neck, lifted her feet off the floor, and spun her around.

Lyons launched herself at Dice, dropped her weapon, and threw her arms around him. "You're all right!" she exclaimed. "I've been looking everywhere for you."

He laughed and hugged her. "I'm alright. You didn't have to go shooting up the place."

Davenport stiffened when a bunch of Jace's copies retreated around another corner. They were still trading gunfire, but they traded it with the *Tenacious* crew instead.

The copies turned around and slowed as they advanced closer to the rest of the group. "Jace!" Fiddler exclaimed. "I told you to collapse your copies."

"I did." Jace turned to face the copies. "These aren't mine."

The copies walked slower and slower getting nearer and nearer to the place where Jace stood next to Fiddler. Each of the copies looked slightly different from him.

One by one, the copies combined into one man and the last two copies came face to face—except that they weren't copies.

One wore brand new tan pants, polished leather shoes, a tight black t-shirt, and his hair had been cut neatly around his strong features.

The other copy wore rough, hand-sewn rags patched together from animal skins and the tattered remains of other garments. His hair had *not* been cut recently and the parts that had been cut looked like they'd been chopped unevenly with a dull knife.

"If he isn't one of yours, who is he?" Fiddler asked.

"Isn't it obvious?" Axel pointed out. "They're twins. There are two of them with the same ability." He turned to the last two copies. "Which of you is the real Jace?"

"I am," the one in nice clothes replied and turned to the other copy. "Who are you?"

The one in rough clothes flicked his hair out of his eyes. He did it exactly the same way Jace always did. "My name's Jericho. I'm your twin brother. I've been living on Chorion Osiris all this time—or everyone thinks I have. My copies left the planet to do jobs around the Confederacy. Coots never knew I left."

"Then how.....how did Jace end up in Helios Sanctus?" Fiddler asked.

"The Reserve Wing sent a team of hired Chorions to the planet to scout for people with useful abilities. They're always sending teams to Chorion Osiris looking for people they can use. They took Jace thinking he was the only one. They never found out about me."

Jace stared at him with wide eyes. "How do you know all that? Do we have a family on Chorion Osiris? I never knew about....about any of it."

"Our father Coots still lives there," Jericho replied. "I remember when they took you. Our mother raised us alone in the forest. I was crawling around in the bushes when the Reserve Wing team came. They killed her and took you away. Later, Coots came to check on us. He found her dead and took me to live with him in the mountains. I never told him what happened and he never found out. He always thought there was one of us. He's still living there with one of my copies."

"So you were the one Admiral Joyce hired to come after us," Bandit exclaimed. "It was you all along when we thought it was Jace."

"Everyone on Chorion Osiris calls me Jace," Jericho replied. "No one knows my real name." He turned to his brother. "Until now."

Jace burst into a huge grin. "I never thought I'd find you!"

Jericho smiled more slowly, but eventually, he let it out and it lit up his whole face. "I never thought I'd see you again. I thought you might be dead."

Jace burst out laughing and grabbed his brother in a crude hug. Jericho tolerated it, but he pulled away sooner.

Davenport looked around. "Are there any other copies on the ship?"

Jace and Jericho both said, "No," at the same time. Then they did a double-take and stared at each other.

"Now what do we do?" Lyons asked. "Joyce has all three components."

"There has to be a way to stop him." Davenport turned to Kuman. "Get back to the bridge and start withdrawing our people out of the battle. We need to disengage from the Reserve Wing."

"I better go with you," Lyons added. "I'll give orders for my people to back off. We can join forces and go after Joyce, now that we have the firepower to do it."

Chapter 4

D avenport strode onto the *Tenacious's* bridge, but he had to stop himself from going near the captain's chair. Lyons approached it instead, sat down, and clipped over her shoulder, "Open a line of communications with my flagship."

"It's open," Kuman told her.

"Ignus—it's me—it's Lyons. I'm in command of the *Tenacious.*"

The same Hidion appeared on the screen and frowned at her. "How did you do that?"

"That doesn't matter. I'm taking command of this fleet. Break off your assault, bring our ships in line, and disengage from the Reserve Wing."

Ignus scowled at her and then at his controls. "If we disengage, they'll attack us again."

"No, they won't. Now carry out my orders. We're pulling back to Atlas Arcane."

"I don't like it," he growled.

"I don't like it, either," she replied. "There are larger considerations at work. Now disengage."

"Rizarth's squadron is pulling away," Kuman reported. "The Reserve Wing is re-grouping."

"How functional are they?" Davenport asked. "What can we expect if they decide to launch another assault?"

"Half their Stalwarts are crippled," Babcock chimed in from his station. "They won't be stupid enough to launch another assault."

"Send out orders to our fleet," Davenport told Kuman. "Tell them we're falling in with Rizarth's squadron."

"All our vessels are signaling acknowledgment," Kuman replied.

Davenport watched the Reserve Wing vessels retreat to the far side of the battlefield. Those that hadn't been as badly damaged glided to the front to defend their stricken sister ships, but none of them was holding together too well. They'd been beaten.

Now Rizarth's squadron came together with Calyx's fleet, the stolen ships the former prisoners took from Terminus Anathema, and a few stragglers left over from Ekol Thaine's dispersed empire.

All those ships drew in line and confronted the pathetic remnant of the Reserve Wing licking its wounds across the battlefield.

Emmett chuckled. "Not so big and tough now, are you?"

Lyons tapped the communications controls to open channels to all the ships around here. "Lay in a course for Atlas Arcane. I'm sending you identifying coordinates for a Stalwart carrying the Ziprothil. We shouldn't have any trouble following and intercepting it. Launch on my command. We can leave these idiots here to......"

"Ma'am!" Kuman interrupted. "The Reserve Wing contingent—they're arming for another assault! Incoming!"

A blast of cannon fire pelted across the *Tenacious's* nose. Then, out of some nightmare, the Reserve Wing contingent blasted out of position and reengaged with the syndicate force nearly ten times its size.

"I don't believe it!" Lyons snapped. "Finish them off! Put them in the ground!"

"Another fleet of Reserve Wing vessels is coming in from Helios Sanctus, Ma'am!" Yogro interjected. "We might have a problem!"

"Don't give me problems!" she countered. "Get rid of these assholes! Destroy every last ship!"

Rizarth's squadron rocketed out of position and locked with the Reserve Wing vessels that had been standing against the alien assailants to begin with.

That left Calyx's fleet and the escaped prisoners to confront the new Reserve Wing flank moving in from Helios Sanctus.

They met in a hail of gunfire and exploding ships. Three Stalwarts surrounded the *Tenacious.*

"We got more Stalwarts moving in from three directions!" Kuman yelled over the noise. "I don't think they were too happy about that bloody nose we gave them!"

"Where are they coming from?" Davenport hollered back.

"Close ranks!" Lyons ordered down the line. "Don't let them divide us!"

"It's too late!" Kuman told her just as a brutal smash rocked the Tenacious. The ship tipped up on one wing and more Stalwarts pounded the ship's underside to knock it completely over on its side.

Davenport pitched into Kuman's station and grabbed on to stop himself from rolling into the opposite wall.

Babcock didn't hold on in time. He somersaulted past Lyons's chair and fell over Breeze who was rolling around the floor with nothing to check him.

"What's the problem?!" Lyons roared. "Why can't we drive them off?"

"There are too many Stalwarts, Ma'am!" Kuman bellowed back. "They're overrunning us!"

"Bullshit!" she roared back. "Why aren't the three fleets closing ranks like I said?!"

"They can't break through! The Reserve Wing is pulling the same trick on us that you pulled on them before."

She groaned in frustration, but the three fleets couldn't fight their way back together. The incoming Stalwarts blasted to the center of the battlefield and seized control of the middle ground. None of the smaller groupings could fight their way back to reclaim it.

Davenport floundered back to Kuman's station. He tried again and again to give the order to close ranks, but Davenport could already see all three fleets trying to do just that and failing.

The Reserve Wing had sent in enough new, fresh Stalwarts to tip the balance in their favor.

The Stalwarts couldn't overcome the combined rebels' firepower, but the Reserve Wing didn't have to.

The Stalwarts just had to hold the three fleets apart so they couldn't join forces. That was the tipping point. All three fleets had to stand together for their advantage to hold.

Howitzers boomed up and down the line from all three fleets. The Reserve Wing returned fire in kind, but they hit enough enemy ships that they would tip the scales in their own favor pretty soon. Davenport had to act.

Kuman woke Davenport from his thoughts. "We got another fleet moving in!"

Lyons groaned. "Not another one! Aren't there enough Reserve Wing vessels here already?"

"They aren't Reserve Wing! They're coming from......they're coming from Nyx Anonyma."

Davenport's head shot up, but he didn't have time to answer before the new fleet bombed into the battle with guns blazing. Hundreds of ships flooded the battlefield and swept the Reserve Wing aside in seconds.

Stalwarts exploded all over the map and a few Daggers collided with the incoming fleet to burst on the ships' hulls.

Davenport gulped. "Is that who I think it is?"

The communications system flicked on and he found himself looking at a hideous alien with multiple jointed appendages and quivering pinchers surrounding its mouth.

"Davenport!" the creature husked. "I thought I'd lost you."

"Ekol!" Davenport gasped. "We thought you were dead! We saw you go down on....."

The words died in his throat. Vorax Summa. Davenport and the Chorion Team had watched Ekol Thaine's ship go down in flames on Vorax Summa—the same planet where Admiral Joyce planned to release the Ithium.

"These pesky Reserve Wing ships won't bother you again," Ekol rasped. "I see some of my people are flying under your banner."

"I took them in because they had nowhere else to go. Your empire has been in disarray since everyone thought you were dead."

"That's all over now. I hear you've taken over after Calyx Elkanon's death. That's perfect. I'd much rather negotiate with you."

Davenport opened his mouth to answer, but Kuman interrupted. "Another group of ships moving in. There are only eight of them, though—and they're small. They don't pose a threat to us and they don't belong to the Reserve Wing."

"Then we can destroy them just as easily." Ekol turned to some of his bridge staff. "Destroy those ships."

"Stop!" Davenport called. "Don't shoot! Hold your fire! It's the Wide Patrol! They're with the Sheriff's Service. Send out orders to every ship on the field to hold their fire."

"The lead ship is hailing you," Kuman reported. "The ship in question is designated *Vindicator.*"

"I know who it is. Open the line."

The screen switched. Ekol vanished and Davenport found himself face to face with Sheriff Deacon Pritchard.

"Sheriff," Pritchard began.

"Sheriff," Davenport replied.

"Good to see you back in the saddle," Pritchard went on. "I was wondering if you wouldn't mind if I come over and have a few words with you and your crew."

Davenport raised his eyebrows. "You want to come over—alone—and have a few words with me and my crew? Which crew—the one that escaped from Terminus Anathema?"

"You know which crew I mean." Pritchard held up a computer device and read off a series of names. "I have warrants to arrest you, Marshall Lawrence Healey, Emmett Duncan, Kay Hahn also known as Fiddler, Sabrina Lyons, the Adik known as Dice, and the Chorions known as Rodeo, Bandit, Alla, Axel, Laub, Wolf, Breeze, Coon, and Jace." He put down his device. "You can see that the Patrol doesn't pose a threat to you and I'm sure you won't consider one man coming over to your ship unarmed as a threat, either. I want to talk to you—that's all."

"One man?" Davenport repeated. "You're coming alone?"

Pritchard shrugged. "If you allow it, I'll bring Treese with me. That's all. I just want to talk."

"And you'll come unarmed?"

"I said I would and I will. If you agree, the Patrol will stand off here and wait for me while I bring the *Vindicator* into your hold."

Davenport glanced around at his friends. He didn't have to ask if Pritchard was sincere. Deacon Pritchard was possibly the one person outside Davenport's own crew that he never questioned.

He also didn't have to question whether Pritchard would be able to arrest the crew if he wanted to. The Wide Patrol might have a reputation as some of the biggest badasses in the galaxy, but no way could eight ships as small as theirs stand up to all these alien criminals.

That was the weird thing about it. The Wide Patrol came out here knowing they'd be massively outgunned. They didn't stand a chance—which meant they never intended to fight at all. Pritchard really did just want to talk.

Lyons turned around. She, Emmett, Fiddler, Dice, and the Chorions exchanged glances, too. Dice shrugged. "You might as well give him a chance to say his piece. I guess we owe him that much."

"Yeah, we do." Davenport turned back to the screen. "All right, Sheriff. You can come over and you can bring Treese with you if you want to. We'll meet you down there."

Kuman cut the channel and Davenport and his crew all looked around at each other again. Something had changed. Davenport didn't have to say a word. Pritchard showing up like this ended something. Davenport just didn't know what it was yet.

Chapter 5

Davenport and his crew assembled in the cargo hold and watched the *Vindicator* float in to land. The ship set down next to Lyons's Phoenix and the Chorion Team's gunship.

Davenport had resisted the urge to come armed, but he owed Pritchard that courtesy, too. If Pritchard was coming unarmed, Davenport had to do the same thing.

Pritchard wasn't Davenport's enemy. Davenport already knew that. He couldn't start treating Pritchard as an enemy, but Davenport found it nearly impossible not to think of everyone as an enemy, even the people who'd stood with him the longest.

Lyons, Emmett, and the Chorions all came armed, but they didn't aim their weapons at the *Vindicator* or at Pritchard and Treese when they disembarked.

Davenport got the distinct impression that his crewmates were finding it equally impossible to put their weapons down or to lower their guard.

They'd all been on the run for so long and defended themselves against so many enemies. They couldn't stop now, not even in the company of friends.

"Stay here," Davenport murmured to his people. "Let me talk to him."

He stepped out across the deck and walked up to Pritchard. Treese stood a few inches behind Pritchard when Pritchard held out his hand to Davenport. "Good to see you again, Sheriff."

Davenport shook his hand. "I wish it could have been under better circumstances."

Pritchard waved that away. "We take what we can get, don't we?" He frowned across the deck at the group gathered by the stairs. "It looks like you lost a few people."

"Thanks to Admiral Joyce," Davenport muttered.

"It's a miracle any of you is still alive." Pritchard waved at the crew behind Davenport. "Do you mind? What I have to say is for all of you."

Davenport waved toward the crew, too, and he accompanied Pritchard and Treese over to the group. Davenport moved back into line with his people when Pritchard halted there where everyone could see him.

"You all heard me read out your names just now," he began. "I'm empowered to arrest you all on charges related to your continued assaults against the Reserve Wing and resisting all attempts to take you into custody before now."

"You got that right," Dice boomed. "You can count on us doing a whole lot resisting in the future, too."

"I know you will," Pritchard replied. "That's why I'm here."

"If you're here to arrest us, you can shove your arrest warrants where the sun don't shine," Emmett fired back. "How about you issue an arrest warrant for Admiral Joyce for murdering four innocent girls at the Pegasus Mine—and that's not counting all the times he's tried to kill all of us?"

Pritchard sighed and held up his hands. "Just listen to me for a second, will you? We can do this one of two ways. If I leave this ship, the Reserve Wing will send out bigger and bigger forces to attack you. This war between the Reserve Wing and you, Ekol, Calyx's people, Rizarth Hudan's squadron, the escaped prisoners from Terminus Anathema, and anyone else who comes out to join you will keep escalating and becoming more and more destructive. All of you will be fugitives for the rest of your lives. You'll never get justice—and what's even worse, you'll never be able to stop Joyce. You'll all be so locked up with this war that you won't be able to move around freely enough. He'll be able to use the war as a cover to go do whatever he wants—and no one will ever find out what you all sacrificed to try to stop him. You'll be branded as criminals and that's the way everyone will remember you."

Silence fell over the group. Davenport already knew what was coming. He didn't want to hear it. He wanted to do anything to stop it, but he couldn't. It had been coming for him all this time.

"I'm asking you—I'm begging you—" Pritchard went on. "I'm asking you for the sake of the whole Confederacy to let me take you into custody. I know better than anyone that everything you've done since the beginning has been for the sake of the Confederacy and I'm asking you to continue to do that now. The only way to stop Joyce is if everyone finds out what he's doing. I'll take you back to Atlas Arcane where we can present all the evidence in court. Once we do that, we can bring the rest of the Reserve Wing against Joyce. Most of the Reserve Wing is still loyal. He's only corrupted one branch of it. The rest will go after him, but we need some way to lay out all the evidence so everyone sees what he's doing. We can get him indicted and turn the rest of the Confederate law enforcement apparatus to bring him to justice—and to bring all of you to justice, too. No one deserves justice more than you do and this is the only way you're gonna get it."

Davenport couldn't move. He sensed the others glancing at him for some indication of what he would do, but he already knew.

He could throw Pritchard off the *Tenacious* right now. Davenport could keep on going the way he was. He could use Calyx's and Ekol's fleets to protect himself. Davenport could stay free for the rest of his life.

Fiddler finally broke the silence. "I'm going with Davenport. If he goes, I go. If he stays, I stay."

"Me, too," Emmett chimed in.

Davenport turned around to face his friends. He would have given anything to protect them all from this.

"I'm going in," he told them. "You don't have to. You can take all these ships and keep on running, but I don't want to run anymore. If I thought turning myself in would protect you, I would do it in a heartbeat, but Sheriff Pritchard is right. This is the only way we can catch up with Joyce in time to stop him. None of us is strong enough, not even if we all work together."

"I'm with you," Healey added. "This is the only way to clear our names. That's the most important thing to me—apart from stopping Joyce."

"Aw, hell!" Dice growled. "I really did not want to go back to jail."

Lyons patted his arm. "At least we'll be there together."

Davenport turned to the Chorions. "If you come with us, you boys all have to make a commitment not to use your abilities to break free. If you turn yourselves over now, you have to stay in custody and see this thing through to the end—and that includes you, Jace—and you Jericho."

"I'm, going in, too," Jericho replied. "Joyce tricked me into carrying out a hit on my own people. I didn't know what he was doing. Marshall Healey told me I could testify against him and that's what I'm gonna do."

Jace stared at him and then gulped. "I'll go where Jericho goes—and Fiddler. If they go in, I'll go in, too. They're all I have."

Davenport turned to the other Chorions, but Rodeo cut him off. "Don't even say it, man. We're all in this the same way we always have been."

Davenport turned around to face Pritchard. "We'll turn ourselves over to you, Sheriff. I only ask that you give us half an hour to hand over control of these fleets to our people."

"Of course." Pritchard waved toward the *Vindicator*. "John and I will wait for you down here. You can come back down when you're ready to leave."

The crew went back upstairs, but they all paused in the corridor before they went back onto the bridge. "I can't believe it's all over," Fiddler remarked.

"It isn't over," Dice growled. "It hasn't even started yet."

Lyons sighed. "Staying free sure does sound nice, doesn't it? I guess it was too good to last."

"What was so good about running, hiding, and fighting all the time?" Emmett countered. "Someone was bound to catch up with us sooner or later. We got lucky that it was Pritchard and not someone else."

"If he's right that we can get justice for the Armageddon Core, then this will be worth it," Davenport told them. "Not even going back to Ultra Meridian as a fully reinstated sheriff would mean as much as that."

"Then we better go face the music." Lyons turned to enter the bridge. "My people aren't going to be happy about this."

"No one is," Dice grumbled.

"I'm not," Alla added. "What kind of fool willingly hands himself over for arrest?"

"The kind that has used up every other available option," Davenport replied. "You go first, Lyons."

"Thanks a lot, pal," she sneered and strode onto the bridge.

It took a lot longer than half an hour for her to convince all of Rizarth Hudan's loyal followers to go under Ignus's command and agree to fall back to Acrolith Diastema.

She went to great lengths not to mention that the Wide Patrol was about to take her into custody and ship her back to Atlas Arcane to stand trial on dozens or possibly hundreds of criminal charges. That would not have gone down well at all.

Then it was Davenport's turn. He contacted Ekol first. "Are you out of your natural mind, Davenport?" Ekol snarled when he heard the news.

"Maybe, but I'm doing it. I'm only asking you to take Calyx's people and the escaped prisoners from the Terminus Anathema break under your protection. I'll arrange it on this end. If these people go out on their own, it will only cause more problems later and you might end up in a war against each other."

"I don't like it," Ekol growled. "I thought we had an understanding, Davenport—and you're taking the Chorion Team with you. How am I supposed to run my operation without them?"

"We do have an understanding and I'm not taking the Chorion Team anywhere. They're doing this because they know it's the right thing to do. I know you'll do the right thing, too. That's why I'm trusting you with my people's lives. They're good people who have given their best service to Calyx. They'll do the same for you."

"I'll do it for you, Davenport, but I don't have to like it. Just tell your people to come over to me and I'll do the rest."

"Thank you. I'm grateful for all the support you've given me."

Davenport ended the conversation and turned to those around him. Duni stood up from the pilot's station. "Are you sure you don't want me to come with you? You might need me."

"I really wish I could," Davenport replied. "I'm gonna miss you, but I couldn't ask you to go back into custody for this. Stay out here and go with Ekol. He'll make sure you're all right—all of you."

He turned to the rest of the crew. Babcock blinked back tears. "You don't have to do this, Davenport. It doesn't seem right for you to go back to jail."

"I do have to do this. You'll all be all right with Ekol." Davenport shook hands with Kuman, Yogro, Varit, and the rest of the bridge staff. "Stay safe....and try to stay out of trouble. Don't get into another war if you can avoid it."

Chapter 6

D avenport and his crew stepped into the *Tenacious's* cargo hold. The half hour had elapsed long ago, but Pritchard and Treese just leaned against the *Vindicator* talking until the crew came back. Neither sheriff made any attempt to arrest the crew for taking so long or to hurry them on their way.

Davenport hesitated to approach them. He really, really didn't want to go back to jail. He wanted even less for his crew to go back to jail, but they'd all made up their minds.

He strode across the hold and the rest of the crew followed him. None of them brought any weapons.

Pritchard and Treese straightened up as the crew got closer. "We're ready," Davenport told Pritchard.

Pritchard waved toward the ship. "Come on board and we'll get going. We have a long flight back."

He led the way to the rear hatch. Treese went ahead and climbed the stairs to the ship's bridge. He left Pritchard alone with the whole crew of hardened criminal masterminds.

"Follow me," Pritchard ordered and crossed the deck to a row of cabins on the left side. Davenport had been in them once before when he first met Pritchard.

Pritchard went down the line throwing open the doors. "You can space yourselves out—one to a cabin. Make yourselves at home and I'll arrange to send you some dinner on the way."

No one moved except to stare into the cabins. "Aren't you going to take us into custody?" Lyons asked.

"You already are," Pritchard replied. "You're on board my ship. It isn't like you can escape or anything."

He didn't laugh at his own joke. Pritchard didn't laugh.

Fiddler glanced toward the hatch. It still stood open to the *Tenacious's* hold. Any of the crew could have walked off the *Vindicator* whenever they wanted to.

Pritchard crossed the deck to the other side and opened the doors to another row of cabins. "The rest of you can come over here. Sheriff Davenport and Marshall Healey, you can come upstairs. I have a few more cabins up there where you can stay. We'll get underway and then I'll see about...."

Just then, Treese stuck his head out of the *Vindicator's* bridge and yelled down. "Boss! Admiral Joyce is on the horn demanding to talk to you."

"Is that so? Well, what a coincidence. He has timing. I'll give him that much." Pritchard waved to the rest of the crew. "You all make yourselves at home. Marshall—Sheriff—why don't you both come up to the bridge with me? You can listen in on whatever Joyce has to say."

He headed for the stairs. Davenport and Healey exchanged glances and followed him.

The rest of the crew took longer to actually get it through their heads that they would be staying in normal crew cabins for the journey instead of locked up in some moldy cell.

Pritchard held the bridge door open for Healey and Davenport. The three of them walked in to find Admiral Joyce's image already plastered across the big screen.

Joyce's features hardened when he saw Healey and Davenport.

"What can we do for you, Admiral?" Pritchard asked in his most genial tone.

"I just told your deputy that this crew is Reserve Wing prisoners!" Joyce snapped. "These prisoners escaped from my custody once before. I've been trying to apprehend them ever since."

"Interesting," Pritchard countered. "I've been following their progress ever since your last meeting and it seems to me you've been more interested in killing these people—not taking them into custody."

"That's my business," Joyce barked. "You have no jurisdiction to interfere with military matters. I demand that you hand over this crew immediately."

"I'd like to, Admiral," Pritchard replied. "I really would, but you see, my hands are tied. These people have already been charged under Confederate law and I've just taken them into custody under warrants for their arrest. So you see I now have no choice but to return them all to Atlas Arcane to stand trial. Whatever grievance you have against them, I'm sure you'd be very welcome to attend the proceedings and present your evidence then."

He glanced over at Treese and lowered his voice to a murmur. "Where's he transmitting from?"

"He's on board a Reserve Wing Nitrol between Vorax Summa and Macron Calypso."

"Does he still have the Ziprothil on board?" Davenport asked.

Treese nodded. "He's also reading one life sign from a species native to Sacron Enigma. It isn't registered on the Confederate database."

"Beauty!" Davenport whispered.

Treese nodded. "The ship is suffering from some mechanical problems....."

"I intend to lodge a complaint with the Sheriff's Service about this," Joyce snapped. "This is an outrage."

"You do that." Pritchard turned away. "Now, if you don't mind, we have to transport these prisoners back to Atlas Arcane, and as you know, it's a long journey. I wouldn't want to delay justice by keeping them any longer than necessary. If you don't have any other business to discuss....."

"Of course I don't have any other business to discuss!" Joyce snapped.

"You have a pleasant evening, then." Pritchard nodded to Treese, who cut the signal.

Pritchard maintained his blithe attitude until the signal cut out. Then he groaned. "That guy! Someone really needs to put a sock in that yapping hole of his."

"He's setting course for Vorax Summa, Boss," Treese told him.

"Get us underway and send word to the Patrol to keep on their toes on the way back." Pritchard turned to Healey and Davenport. "I wonder if you two gentlemen would like to have dinner with me tonight."

Davenport raised his eyebrows. "Seriously?" He glanced back at the dark screen. "Aren't you at all worried that he'll retaliate and attack again?"

"He won't attack us. It was easy for him to smear you all as criminals. It would be a lot harder to do the same thing to us." Pritchard opened the door and waved out into the corridor. "Follow me. You both probably want to take a shower and change your clothes before you eat. I'll show you where to go."

He led them down the *Vindicator's* upper deck. Treese stayed behind, and in a minute, the engines fired up and the ship got underway.

Pritchard jerked his thumb at the first cabin closest to the bridge. "This is my place. You can come back here when you're ready. You can stay in here, Marshall."

Pritchard showed Healey into the next cabin. It was much larger than the cabins downstairs where Pritchard housed the crew. This one had a big queen-sized bed under a big window where the occupant could see the stars streaming past.

The cabin also had a two-seater couch, a small table and chair in the corner, and a little bathroom opened through the opposite bulkhead.

Healey stopped in the corridor and stared across the threshold in disbelief. He was still standing there when Pritchard showed Davenport to an identical cabin next door.

"The closets have a collection of clothes in them. See what you can find—or you can just put back on what you have. I don't care. I'll see you down the deck there in a little while."

He left them both standing there while he went back to the bridge. He shut the door behind him and didn't watch to see whether they went into those cabins or not.

Healey and Davenport exchanged glances. Davenport found it difficult to believe this was really happening to him. He struggled to remember when anyone had treated him this well.

Ekol would have treated him this well or even much better if Davenport had let him. Davenport didn't let him. Davenport had been on the run all this time. He didn't even get a chance to take a shower at Terminus Anathema.

He and Healey finally stepped across the thresholds of their respective cabins. Even once he got inside, Davenport had to stand there and look around him for at least ten minutes before he could bring himself to accept that this really was his life now.

He was safe. He was on board a friendly ship—and not just a friendly ship. He was on board the *Vindicator*—Sheriff Deacon Pritchard's ship.

Pritchard had always been a legend in the Sheriff's Service—and he believed Davenport. Pritchard wasn't trying to destroy Davenport or end him as a sheriff.

Those words kept coming back to Davenport again and again. *No one deserves justice more than you do and this is the only way you're gonna get it.*

Pritchard understood. He got it in a way no one else besides Healey ever had.

Davenport didn't have to run and fight and struggle and suffer to prove himself here. He wasn't alone anymore.

Was this some kind of trick to get him to accept his incarceration? Was this feeling of relief and safety the bait that lured him into a trap he couldn't get out of?

Davenport couldn't believe that about Pritchard. Davenport had to keep believing in somebody. If he couldn't believe in Pritchard, then Davenport wouldn't be able to believe in anybody.

He went into the bathroom and took the longest, hottest shower of his life. He stood under the spray for what seemed like hours and let the scalding water pound on his skull, but it couldn't wash away the taint of everything he'd been through. None of that would ever wash off—just like the star branded into his chest.

When he got out and dried off, he stood in front of the mirror and stared at the star brand for another eternity. It was still there. It was there on the outside the way it had been branded on the inside.

Larson did Davenport a giant favor by giving him this brand. Larson might have thought he was humiliating and torturing Davenport.

Instead, Larson gave Davenport a priceless gift—a gift more valuable than any other Davenport had ever received. Larson had given Davenport his own soul back. No one could ever take this away from him.

Davenport had to go through another excruciating internal conflict when it came time to get dressed. He found a bunch of clothes in many sizes and styles in the closets. God only knew why Pritchard carried them around with him.

The deputies of the Wide Patrol each flew their own ships. Pritchard usually flew the *Vindicator* alone. No doubt Treese came with him this time just to escort these prisoners to jail.

So Pritchard was the only person who regularly stayed in any cabin on the *Vindicator*. Yet he kept all the rest of these cabins prepared and stocked with anything anyone would need.

Davenport even found some women's dresses, bras, and underwear in the closet and drawers. Pritchard couldn't have prepared these cabins especially for this crew. He really did just fly around with this stuff on his ship all the time.

Davenport found a pair of pants that fit him and buckled his belt, but he found it impossible to put on a shirt. He refused to cover up this star. The decision he'd made at Terminus Anathema stopped him.

This was his star. This was the star he would always wear—the indelible stamp that he was a sheriff to his core no matter what the justice system did to him.

He didn't put on any shoes, either. He was still a prisoner, so why should he pretend to be anything else?

He went out into the corridor and met Healey there. Healey didn't even look at Davenport's chest or his feet.

Healey smiled. "I'm glad I'm not the only one who took a minute to get used to this."

"Don't get used to it because it won't last," Davenport told him.

"Yeah. Let's go have dinner with the man and enjoy ourselves while it lasts."

Chapter 7

Healey and Davenport headed down the corridor to Deacon Pritchard's cabin. Davenport experienced a painful wave of gratitude for Healey. Healey had kept Davenport sane these last several weeks—more than anyone else on his crew.

At least one other lawman was willing to risk everything to cover Davenport's back. Healey had sacrificed his own career and turned fugitive to join Davenport's crew because Healey believed and supported Davenport. That meant a lot.

They found Pritchard alone in his cabin. Treese must still be on the bridge flying the ship.

Prichard had set the table in the middle of his cabin with three places. He was just popping a bottle of Scotch when Healey and Davenport walked in.

Davenport suffered a moment of panic when he saw the bottle. For a split second, he worried that the bottle might be Ezoru Ihi. Davenport would never be able to drink that stuff again without thinking of Calyx.

It wasn't Ezoru Ihi, though. Pritchard poured glasses for all three of them. "Take a seat, you two," he told Healey and Davenport. "I won't ask how long it's been since you had a decent meal, so you might as well have one now."

Healey and Davenport sat down and sipped their drinks in silence while Pritchard kept moving around the cabin and talking the whole time.

"You two might be interested to know that I did some digging into Admiral Joyce's service record while you were all galivanting around the galaxy getting shot at," Pritchard announced over his shoulder. "It turns out that he spent most of his career grooming certain young and upcoming officers for command positions in the Reserve Wing. Come to find out that these same officers are now in command positions in the contingent of the Reserve Wing that Joyce has been using to execute this mission of his. He maneuvered his own people into positions where they could help him turn the Reserve Wing to his own ends."

"You don't say," Healey remarked and took a sip of his Scotch. Davenport passed his back and forth under his nose. He didn't take a sip until Healey did it first.

"Yes, I do say," Pritchard went on. "What Joyce didn't realize, however, is that several of these hand-picked officers of his are related to certain other high-ranking officers in the Confederate Corps and in political positions at Atlas Arcane. These other high-ranking relatives of theirs either don't know what their younger relatives are doing or would be highly shocked if they did know. Once the wider Corps finds out what's going on out here, this thing is gonna blow up like the biggest Aswalt mine in history."

He came over to the table. A succulent smell of roasting meat filled the cabin and made Davenport's mouth water.

Pritchard picked up his glass and held it in front of him. "Here's to two of the finest lawmen I've ever met. You two really make a man remember why he joined the Sheriff's Service in the first place."

"Thank you, Sheriff," Healey replied and both he and Davenport sipped their drinks.

Davenport couldn't speak. He still didn't want to believe that Pritchard was being so nice to them—to him.

Davenport could only tolerate this good treatment because he knew it would end sooner than he wanted it to. This would be one night out of a lifetime—a night to remember when he actually felt human.

Pritchard brought dish after dish to the table and laid everything in front of Healey and Davenport before Pritchard sat down to join them. Davenport had to restrain himself and not touch the food until Healey and Pritchard did it first.

Once they started eating, he had to pace himself and not shovel the food down his neck like a starving man. Healey didn't seem to be having too much trouble eating politely, but he hadn't been locked up at Terminus Anathema until just a few days ago.

Pritchard kept talking about all the different wider aspects of the war that one or both of them hadn't been around for.

"The Sheriff's Service wanted to charge Lyons with Yuki Duetis's murder, but no one can find the evidence that she was the one who capped him. None of Yuki's people will talk. They all clammed up. None of them will even confirm that Lyons was on the planet at the time of his death. Then there's the question of his naked body being found in a ditch miles from town. He was last reported seen leaving a brothel in Acrolith Diastema in the company of two prostitutes, but no one will even tell the local sheriff which prostitutes they were and you can forget about anyone coming forward."

"That's good," Healey interjected. "Yuki had it coming."

"You know what the interesting part is?" Pritchard went on. "All of Yuki's people were very forthcoming when it came to giving all the evidence anyone could ask for that Yuki was the one who hit Rizarth Hudan. Apparently, Rizarth's own people have been sitting on this evidence for years and they're only spilling the details now that Yuki is dead." He shook his head. "The way these people's minds work! It doesn't bear thinking about."

"Did you get any evidence that Joyce shot Flack, Fizzle, Frost, and Friend?" Davenport asked. "Apart from Lyons's testimony, I mean?"

Pritchard shrugged that away. "We have information coming in from all over. It's gonna take some time to put it all together into a coherent defense, but I wouldn't worry about it too much if I was you."

"You'll have to forgive me if I do worry about it," Davenport countered. "I'd rather not rot in jail for the next ten years while someone puts together a coherent defense for me."

"Did you hear that scavengers destroyed the Ultra Meridian jail for the third time?" Pritchard asked. "The Confederate Corps rebuilt it, of course, and you're still listed on the Sheriff's Service roster as the Sheriff of Ultra Meridian. You'll be able to go back there when this is all over."

Davenport stared into his drink. "I'm starting to think it will never be over. Ekol told me that at the beginning. Now I see that he's right."

"Aw, don't get all down in the dumps about it!" Pritchard told him. "I wouldn't have come out to get you if I thought this plan wouldn't work."

"Plan?" Davenport asked. "You have a plan?"

"I told you I did."

"What's the plan, then?" Davenport heard how ungrateful his voice sounded, but he didn't try to keep the bitterness out of his tone. "Your plan is for us to throw ourselves on the mercy of the court and hope for the best? I'm sorry if I can't put my faith in that considering everything that's happened."

Pritchard smacked his lips. "Of course my plan isn't for you to throw yourselves on the mercy of the court and hope for the best! If I thought that, I would have stayed out of the way and let all of you ride off into the criminal sunset. God knows you had enough ships to give the Reserve Wing a pasting they would never forget and then you could all disappear. Throw yourselves on the mercy of the court!" He gasped in exasperation. "What do you take me for?"

Davenport shrugged. "Maybe I've just been dealing with the wrong kind of people for too long."

"I'll say you have." Pritchard stuck a wad of roast napus in his mouth and chewed with the food bulging in the side of his cheek. "Buck up, little camper. Things will get better."

Healey chuckled, but Davenport couldn't enjoy Pritchard's good humor.

"So what is your plan if it isn't throwing ourselves on the mercy of the court?" Healey asked.

Pritchard only shrugged. "Well, you know, we'll see how things go when we get to Atlas Arcane....."

"I think I have a pretty good idea of how things will go when we get to Atlas Arcane," Davenport muttered.

Pritchard turned to face him. "Why did you turn yourself over to me if you think it's so hopeless? You could have stayed out there and stayed free. You didn't have to come over to me, so why did you?"

"I guess I figured that, if anyone could pull off a miracle, you could. Isn't that what you and the Patrol are known for—solving hopeless problems no one else can solve?"

Pritchard slammed his hand on the table and then pointed at Davenport. "Now that's the attitude I want to hear! Anyway, it will take a lot less than a miracle to get you off."

"Off?" Davenport repeated. "You actually think we can get off—as in, off entirely? How is that possible when we really are guilty of the crimes we've been charged with?"

"Will you stop it?!" Pritchard countered. "You're going to get off because you're innocent, man! When are you going to get that through your thick head? Anyway, we aren't here to talk about how things are going to go at Atlas Arcane. We're here to enjoy a nice meal and shoot the breeze until we get there. What happens at Atlas Arcane will take care of itself."

He picked up the bottle and refilled both Davenport's and Healey's glasses. Then Pritchard went on to talk about certain other politics of various crime syndicates around the galaxy and how each one had been touched by the wider war.

Healey got pulled into the conversation and he and Pritchard talked about people, organizations, and syndicates they both knew about. It took a long time for Davenport to put the subject of Atlas Arcane far enough behind him to join the conversation.

"You two must be something pretty special if you got the Chorion Team on your side," Pritchard remarked. "Those boys don't give their loyalty easily."

"They're good boys—some of the best," Healey exclaimed. "I couldn't ask to fly with a better crew."

"I hear you spent some time on their home planet, Marshall," Pritchard began.

Davenport gasped and spun around to stare at Healey. "You did?"

Healey made a face. "I wouldn't choose it as a vacation destination, believe me. I wouldn't be sitting here if I hadn't gone there with the boys."

"Still, it's pretty impressive that you made it off the planet alive," Pritchard remarked. "They say you even went to visit the Kocha tribe."

Davenport gaped at Healey with his mouth open. "No way!"

Healey turned bright red. "Rodeo is the impressive one. He was born in Kocha. It's a miracle any of them survived to get off the planet....but I guess that's kinda the point. They don't survive without their abilities. They told me if a child doesn't develop their abilities early, they die. I understand why now."

"What did you see?" Davenport asked. "What is it like there?"

Healey shrugged. "It's as brutal as they say and the people are the same. That's about the most I can tell you. It's everything you've heard and more. It blows my mind that children actually live in those conditions, but that's how the Chorion Team grew up to be the fine young men that they are. Rodeo actually got nostalgic and wistful about it when he first returned to his home village. The others were all delighted to see their families again, but none of the boys wanted to stay. I guess that tells you everything you need to know."

"What did you think of the people?" Pritchard asked.

Healey shifted in his chair. "They're fine people, too—extremely harsh, brutal, and violent—but exceptionally fine. They're some of the best people I've met anywhere. They're perfectly suited to their home planet. That's all I can say about them." Healey looked up. "Why don't you ask the boys about it?"

"Oh, I have—many times," Pritchard replied.

Davenport spun around the other way, but he stopped himself from asking about that. He already knew that the Chorion Team and the Wide Patrol had crossed paths before.

"And?" Healey prompted. "What did they tell you about Chorion Osiris?"

"Just what you said, but it means something different coming from one of the few humans who has been there and lived to tell the tale."

"How can it mean more if we said the same things?"

"It means more because there's no chance you might be inclined to gloss it over to make it sound better than it is."

"I don't think it's possible to make it sound better than it is," Healey remarked. "All you have to do is look at those boys and see the fires they've been through that forged them into the men they are."

Pritchard nodded, glanced once in Davenport's direction, and went back to his meal. Pritchard talked of other things, but that glance unsettled Davenport more than talking about Atlas Arcane.

Pritchard had wanted to tell Davenport something—or ask him something. Maybe Pritchard was just as curious about what life was like inside Terminus Anathema. Pritchard never would have set foot in the place. He was too noble and upright.

Deacon Pritchard would never do anything to break the law—but that wasn't true. The Wide Patrol routinely crossed the line to help people when they needed to. What was the difference between what they did and what Davenport and his crew had done?

Davenport couldn't define it, but he still put Pritchard and the Wide Patrol in another league than himself. He could never be as good as they were or as noble or upright as they were.

He was their prisoner right now, after all. He was the one going back to Atlas Arcane under arrest, not them.

To his knowledge, none of the Wide Patrol had ever been arrested. Pritchard was right about that. No one ever messed with them—ever. No one would dare.

Chapter 8

D avenport woke up the next morning and stared at the ceiling for a while before he remembered where he was. The steady hum of engine noise vibrating through the bed and the stars whizzing past the window told him he was on board some ship.

Then he remembered. He was on board the *Vindicator*. He was a prisoner, but he'd never been this comfortable in his life.

He still wasn't wearing a shirt. Neither Pritchard nor Healey had mentioned it at dinner last night or even seemed to notice. Was Davenport the only person who cared at all that he'd been going around shirtless all this time?

He sat up and looked around his cabin. He sure didn't feel or look like a prisoner. He felt like an honored guest being escorted home in style. Pritchard sure treated him like one.

He stood up, but this cabin was too small, so he went outside and went downstairs to check on the rest of the crew. They were all hanging out in the galley eating, talking, and laughing.

He left them there and went up to the bridge. Pritchard and Treese were there. Healey wasn't. The door to his cabin was still shut.

Pritchard sat in his chair in the center of the bridge while Treese went back and forth from one station to another.

The faces of Pritchard's other deputies kept popping up on the screen in front of him. "What do you want to do about these cocksuckers, boss?" Jeremy Yarborough asked.

"Don't do anything about them yet," Pritchard replied. "They're just escorting us for now."

"You call this escorting us?" Bill DeRosa demanded. "They might as well take *us* into custody."

Pritchard switched his view to a wider feed of the ships surrounding the *Vindicator*. His deputies surrounded the ship the way they had been last night. They'd flanked the *Vindicator* on both sides.

Davenport stiffened when he saw a contingent of twenty Reserve Wing Daggers surrounding the Wide Patrol. Now he saw what DeRosa meant.

The Daggers closed the Wide Patrol in more than a guarding posture. The Daggers' presence really did give the impression that they were keeping the Wide Patrol under guard for some infraction.

Pritchard turned around and called to Treese over his shoulder. "Track the source of these Daggers. See which Stalwarts they belong to."

"As far as I can tell, they belong to Macron Calypso," Treese replied. "They haven't been involved in any of Joyce's maneuvers."

DeRosa snorted. "Come on, John! You don't really believe that, do you?"

"I'm just telling the boss what's on the records. You asked. I told you. I don't make this shit up."

"Don't do anything about them unless they do something first," Pritchard ordered. "They could have attacked us by now if they were going to."

"Can't you order them to back off a little?" Swygert asked. "They're flying way too close."

"I can't order them to do anything. You all know that, so stop complaining about it. The only thing it would accomplish if I asked them to would be to acknowledge their existence. Pretend they don't exist."

"That's easy for you to say," DeRosa grumbled. "You aren't flying wingtip to wingtip with them."

"Just don't get into any kind of scuffle with them," Pritchard ordered. "We have enough trouble with the Reserve Wing without....."

A glancing burst of gunfire smashed into one of the Daggers and made the ship stagger right into Yarborough's path. The *Conquest* blundered into the *Vindicator's* path and the two ships ricocheted off each other.

"Shots fired! Shots fired!" Yarborough roared. "We got...."

Another blast cut him off. "Who the hell is shooting at us?!" Pritchard demanded.

"Thirty fighter craft coming in from twenty degrees to starboard!" Treese called back. "They're Ekol Thaine's people."

"No! They can't be!" Davenport pounced on a different station and saw right away that they could be and they were.

"They're trying to break you out, Sheriff." Pritchard switched on his communications system again. "Lock and engage! Close behind the *Vindicator!* We'll make a sprint for Atlas Arcane and try to ditch them. Slow them down as much as you can!"

"You got it, boss," Yarborough replied and spun the *Conquest* around. The rest of the Wide Patrol wheeled to confront Ekol Thaine's fighter craft. The Daggers peeled around and fell on the enemy with guns blazing.

Pritchard grabbed the controls attached to his chair and throttled the *Vindicator* into a dead sprint. The engines revved to high speed and the ship launched away from the battle.

The Wide Patrol closed with the enemy craft. Gunfire and explosions erupted behind the *Vindicator's* tail as Ekol's fighters engaged with the Wide Patrol.

Davenport watched in horror as the battle fell farther behind in the *Vindicator's* wake, but a second later, half the fighter craft split away from the battle and came after the *Vindicator* a second time.

They opened fire from behind and deafening booms rocked the ship.

Davenport raced over to Treese. "Put me through to them! I can call them off!"

"Not now, Sheriff!" Pritchard yelled back. "Whatever you were to them, you aren't anymore—not now that Ekol is back in charge."

"We should have known he wouldn't let us take Davenport without a fight," Treese added.

"Get downstairs and man the cannons, Sheriff!" Pritchard ordered. "John will show you where to go."

"I can't fire on *them!*" Davenport countered. "Ekol just saved all our asses against the Reserve Wing!"

It didn't matter in the end. Pritchard fired his cannons from his seat controls, and a second later, the Daggers from the battle caught up and pelted across the *Vindicator's* bow.

The Daggers scattered gunshots through the enemy grouping and two of them exploded right in the *Vindicator's* path.

Pritchard just kept racing ahead without breaking off. He blasted through two burning fireballs. Treese charged for the bridge door and vanished out into the corridor.

Davenport stood rooted to the spot watching enemy ships surround the *Vindicator*. The Daggers traded gunfire with Ekol's people and the Wide Patrol converged from all sides to drive the enemy off. They attacked, feinted, and swooped around each other directly in front of the *Vindicator*.

Pritchard slammed his controls back and forth vaulting over them, skidding around them, and then burning past them to sprint away into the distance.

A second later, the *Vindicator's* cannons opened fire, too. The cannons swiveled into reverse following the combatants as Pritchard left them behind. Then the cannons pivoted forward when Ekol's people got in Pritchard's way and the Daggers and the Wide Patrol rejoined to stop them.

Davenport realized in some fuzzy part of his brain that more than one of the *Vindicator's* cannons was shooting at the assailants. Treese wasn't the only gunner down there bombarding Ekol's people with all those shots. The crew must be firing on Ekol's ships. The crew didn't care that Ekol just saved their asses.

That thought snapped Davenport out of his trance and he sprang over to the controls. He searched the battle for some way to help Pritchard and the Wide Patrol. They were out there defending Davenport and his crew.

Then Davenport remembered. He attacked the controls in a frenzy and sent a transmission to Ekol's ships, but it wasn't a communications signal.

His fingers trembled as he entered his command code—the command code he'd used when he worked as Ekol's enforcer.

Ekol didn't change it—not when Davenport went to Terminus Anathema the first time, not when Davenport became a sheriff working on the other side of the law, and not when Davenport said he would do everything in his power to stop Ekol from getting his hands on the Ithium.

Ekol never stopped believing in Davenport. Ekol always waited for the day when Davenport would return to Ekol's service. Ekol left that code unchanged so Davenport could do what he wanted with Ekol's forces—even this.

Davenport didn't hesitate for a second. Not even that realization could stop him. He had to end this battle before someone else got hurt trying to help him.

He hit the transmission control and sent the message. The engines on three of Ekol's ships blew and the vessels veered out of the battle.

Two more kept racing ahead for a minute and then their engines went haywire. They corkscrewed away while the Daggers, the Wide Patrol, and the *Vindicator* kept gunning it for Atlas Arcane.

The other fighter craft continued to whizz around the Daggers and the Wide Patrol trying to cut their way to the *Vindicator,* but those fighter craft didn't fire anymore.

The Daggers kept shooting, but the fighter craft didn't defend themselves. The Daggers and the Wide Patrol destroyed another ten before the rest realized they'd been disabled. They peeled away, hit their throttles, and ran for it.

Pritchard glanced over his shoulder, saw Davenport standing there, and scowled. "What did you do?"

Davenport shrugged and looked away. "Sorry I hesitated. I shouldn't have done that."

Pritchard had to turn back to his controls. He kept flying at the same speed for a long time. The Wide Patrol and the Daggers took a few minutes to catch up and then they all fell in formation the way they had been before.

Pritchard didn't say anything—not to Davenport. Pritchard hailed the Patrol and got hold of Ace Bolander. "Any sign of them coming back?"

"Nothing," Bolander replied. "They're running home to their mamas."

"Keep an eye on things, but stay in formation," Pritchard ordered. "We don't have time to screw around with these assholes anymore."

A signal on the controls in front of Davenport made him look down. "The captain of the Dagger group is hailing you," Davenport told Pritchard.

"Put him through," Pritchard ordered.

Davenport got to work on the controls. He might have hesitated to man the cannons, but he could at least do something to help Pritchard.

The captain of the Dagger group turned out to be a young guy with black hair and black eyes. "Did you suffer any damage, Sheriff? I don't know what happened there. They just suddenly suffered some catastrophic system failure and the survivors broke off. I've never seen it before."

"We're fine over here, Captain," Pritchard replied. "Thank you for your assistance. We'll be in orbit over Atlas Arcane soon. Once we deliver these prisoners, we shouldn't have any further trouble."

"Yes, Sir. We'll escort you that far and then you and the Patrol can take it from there."

"Thank you again." Pritchard waved at Davenport and he cut the signal.

Pritchard adjusted a few more things and then set the ship on autopilot the way it was before. Treese came back and Davenport saw on his controls that the other gunners were leaving the cannon battery downstairs. The crew was going back to the galley.

"Is there any sign of Joyce?" Pritchard asked.

"He isn't showing up anywhere on the Reserve Wing roster," Treese replied. "I'm running a crawler on communications between this Dagger group and the rest of the Reserve Wing command structure. None of the Daggers has been in communication with Joyce since we left the battle. He's hiding somewhere."

Pritchard humphed under his breath. "He's up to no good. I'm certain of it." He stood up from his chair and turned around. "We'll be in orbit over Atlas Arcane soon, Sheriff. I suggest you go downstairs and start rounding up your crew to disembark."

Chapter 9

"Did you see the way those Daggers blew?" Alla chortled. "That was epic! I am so gonna pull that maneuver again someday."

"How could you?" Laub countered. "You don't have a command code to Ekol's fleet."

"I will someday," Alla told him. "Someday, I'll be Ekol's righthand man."

"You better lose some weight first," Rodeo told him. "You sure as hell won't eat your way to the top."

"Why not?" Alla asked. "I can eat anyone who messes with Ekol."

"Do you think Davenport ate his way to the top?" Bandit interjected. "You're dreaming."

"He didn't eat his way to the top," Alla returned. "He did it by killing Ekol's enemies and that's what I'll do."

"I think there might have been a little more to it than that, pal," Dice interjected.

"Logic doesn't enter the picture here," Healey chimed in. "This is pure, sweet fantasy."

Davenport didn't get involved in the conversation. Pritchard's order to come down here and get the crew ready to disembark at Atlas Arcane gave Davenport a very bad feeling, but he didn't tell his crew that. He didn't want to dampen their enthusiasm.

Spending the night on the *Vindicator* did wonders for their spirits. They responded to the safety, comfort, and protection as never before. He didn't want to rob them of that before he had to.

He knew he was right when Pritchard and Treese came downstairs from the bridge. Pritchard kept his expression neutral, but his very presence sent a chill up Davenport's spine. This was it. The party was over.

He stopped in front of the crew and threw back his shoulders. "I've rarely flown with a finer crew, but we're landing on Atlas Arcane now and I have to start treating you like prisoners. I have to shackle you to deliver you to the jail."

His words cast a pall over the group. "Why do you have to do it *now?*" Emmett asked. "We've cooperated with everything you wanted us to do."

"I have to do it now so I can log your arrest as cooperative," Pritchard replied. "I have to put on my report that you cooperated with everything—and I mean everything. I'll make sure you get a fair trial here. You don't have to worry about that."

"Yeah, right," Bandit muttered.

Pritchard nodded to Treese. He crossed the *Vindicator's* lower deck and took out a bunch of pairs of shackles from the supply locker.

Silence fell over the crew while he laid a pair of shackles in front of each prisoner. Treese shackled Davenport first just to send a message to the rest of the crew.

Davenport saw exactly what Treese was doing. If Davenport cooperated and let Treese shackle him, the rest of the crew would follow Davenport's example.

He had to seriously restrain himself to stop himself from fighting back. He'd always resisted before, but he couldn't do that this time.

Still, his heart sank when Treese locked the shackles around his wrists and ankles. A heavy chain connected them to each other. Davenport was a prisoner again. No prison riot or secret alien accomplice would get him out of this.

Treese went down the line shackling all the rest of the crew. Healey, Dice, Lyons, Fiddler, Emmett, and then all the Chorions stood silently until he finished the job.

"I meant what I said," Pritchard went on once Treese finished. "I'll make sure you get a fair trial and that all the evidence comes to light. Just hold out a little longer. This will be a good thing. Trust me."

No one answered him. Those words bounced right off Davenport. He didn't believe a word Pritchard said.

Nothing could change the fact that Pritchard was taking Davenport by the elbow and leading him out of the Vindicator's *hold.* Treese steered the rest of the crew into line and they left the ship.

They stepped out into a hangar full of Sheriff's Service vessels. A bunch of other sheriffs and deputies stopped what they were doing to watch Pritchard and Treese bring in their prisoners.

Pritchard guided Davenport across the hangar to a door leading into a much larger building. Another uniformed deputy sat inside a reinforced glass cubicle just beyond the outer door.

He had to buzz Pritchard through and then Pritchard stopped Davenport in front of the cubicle to log in the prisoners.

The deputy on duty exchanged some pleasantries with Pritchard. "Good to have you back, Sheriff," the guy began.

"Good to be back," Pritchard replied. "Fifteen prisoners to log in."

The deputy on duty turned to his computer. "First prisoner's name?"

"Mace Davenport," Pritchard replied.

"Location of arrest?"

Pritchard opened his mouth, hesitated, and then glanced at Davenport.

"Pandora's Needle," Davenport answered. "We all were—except for Marshall Healey."

The deputy entered the information. "Prisoner's home address?"

"Ultra Meridian Jail," Davenport replied. Those words gave him just enough fortitude to get through this. Ultra Meridian was still his home. The jail was still out there waiting for him—in his memories and daydreams, at least.

The deputy buzzed Pritchard through another door and Pritchard led Davenport into another much longer room. A different deputy stood behind a caged wall with dozens of shelves behind him.

He bent over to speak to Pritchard and the prisoner. "You'll need to take off everything you're wearing and change into jail-issued attire." He put a stack of clothes on the desk in front of him. "You can change over there."

Pritchard pulled his keys out of his pocket and unshackled Davenport. He took the pants off the stack, but he left the shirt.

"You have to wear all of it," the deputy told him. "That's protocol."

"Leave him shirtless," Pritchard ordered. "You can pass the word up the line that I said so."

The deputy glanced at Davenport, dipped his eyes to Davenport's brand, and snorted. The guy sneered at the star, but he only said, "Yes, Sir," and turned to the next prisoner coming through the door, which was Healey.

Davenport went into a booth at the end of the room and changed into the jail-issued pants. He still wasn't wearing shoes, either. This didn't feel different enough from what he'd been wearing at Terminus Anathema.

He went back out into the main room to find Pritchard gone. A bunch of other deputies had come in with the rest of Davenport's crew.

He would have liked to talk to his people, but they were all too busy getting changed.

Another two deputies flanked Davenport as soon as he came out of the booth. They led him through a different door, down a different corridor, and into a long hallway lined with doors.

The place couldn't have looked more different from Terminus Anathema. None of the prisoners here walked around freely. The walls, doors, and building structure radiated strength and impenetrable solidity.

The deputies opened a heavy door into one of the cells. It didn't have bars or even windows. He couldn't see anything of the cell at all until they opened the door and guided him inside.

The door slammed shut with a finality that drained all the hope from his soul. He was utterly alone in here with no one to talk to. He couldn't see out of this cell, much less see any people or his friends.

A single shelf bunk ran along one wall. A stainless steel toilet occupied the opposite corner. That was the whole cell.

He sat down on the bunk and then, because he had nothing else to do, he stretched out, shut his eyes, and threw his arm over his face. This was a new low. He might be stuck in here for the rest of his life.

He wouldn't be stuck in here for the rest of his life. The absolute worst they could do to him would be to send him back to Terminus Anathema. Was the prison even still standing anymore? What would be the alternative if it wasn't?

One thing he knew for certain. The Sheriff's Service, the Confederate Corps, the Reserve Wing, and the court system couldn't do anything to him that was worse than what he'd already been through. Whatever they did, he would just face it, take the hits, and keep on going. He had no choice.

Chapter 10

Davenport startled out of a doze when the key slammed in the lock of his cell door. He sat up on his bunk and stiffened when two deputies opened the door.

One of them sliced his forefinger toward the corridor outside. "Time for lunch. Let's go."

Davenport frowned. He didn't understand, but he would take any chance to get out of this cell.

The deputies escorted him down the corridor heading in the same direction they used to get here. They passed more doors, but Davenport couldn't see inside those cells to find out where his friends were.

He'd spent a restless first night in jail. His mind kept crashing back and forth between planning how to escape and realizing that he couldn't.

He'd made a commitment to come back here and face justice—for himself, for Joyce, and for the rest of the crew.

Davenport had to cooperate. He had to go along with this even if it didn't work. This was his last chance to make good on the journey that started when he confiscated the Ithium.

The deputies led him through a bunch of other doors, down a bunch of other corridors, and this way and that through the Atlas Arcane Jail.

Davenport found it hard to understand that a jail could be this big and that it could employ this many sheriffs and deputies.

He knew all about that in theory. He'd seen plenty of bigger jails on Macron Calypso, Pandora's Needle, and a few other places, but they were all so different from Ultra Meridian. He sure did miss Ultra Meridian Jail.

The deputies finally pushed him into the jail commissary somewhere buried inside the huge building. The commissary was a big room full of tables surrounded by chairs. Other prisoners gathered at the tables talking.

Another caged area covered one wall with cooks working in a kitchen behind it. They pushed a metal tray across the counter and Davenport took his tray to one of the tables—one of the empty tables.

Everyone in the commissary turned around to stare at him. They all stopped talking and watched him in silence while he got his food and sat down.

The food was Universal Staples. He picked it up to eat it, but he kept an eye on the other prisoners. Which of them would be the first to try something?

He did his best not to look at them too directly, but he would have to be dead not to feel the tension in the room. Did any of them know about his stint at Terminus Anathema? That would be just stellar.

He couldn't decide if he should eat anything, but just then, the door opened again and some more deputies brought Healey, Emmett, Dice, and the Chorions to the commissary, too.

They all got their food and sat down with Davenport. "How long are we going to be stuck here?" Coon asked.

"Who knows?" Healey replied.

"Probably forever," Rodeo grumbled.

"They can't keep us here forever without a trial," Healey pointed out. "They have to charge us and try us eventually."

Davenport snorted. "What have you been sniffing? They sent me up to Terminus Anathema without charging or trying me for anything. They can do it again."

"At least we get to see each other," Emmett remarked. "That cell was driving me insane."

"Have any of you heard what they did with Lyons and Fiddler?" Dice asked.

"I didn't see," Davenport replied. "They took me out of the room before I saw what they did with any of you."

"I gotta find Lyons," Dice exclaimed. "I'm really worried about her."

"Why?" Rodeo asked. "She can take care of herself."

"You don't understand," Dice replied. "She has an explosive temper. She could get into trouble."

Emmett frowned. "She never seemed to have an explosive temper that I saw."

Dice snorted. "You don't know her like I do."

"She did kill Yuki," Laub pointed out. "We saw on the wires the way he got killed. That was cold-blooded."

Emmett glanced around at the other prisoners. "I wonder if any of these guys can tell me what happened to Fiddler."

"What do you want to know that for?" Axel asked. "She's here somewhere the same way we are. They just separated the men from the women."

"The Reserve Wing could have sent her back to Helios Sanctus," Emmett pointed out. "She could be back there now and we would never know it."

"If they did that, they would have come for Jace, too," Jericho pointed out.

"And me," Dice added.

Emmett shrugged and bent over his food. "I guess so."

Alla picked up his Universal Staples, turned it over in his hand, groaned in disgust, and put it back on the tray. "Is this all they're going to give us to eat? This is cruel and unusual punishment."

The other Chorions laughed at him. "Just don't start eating the guards if you get too hungry," Laub told him.

Alla scowled at him and then started grinning. "Fortunately, I have Jace and Jericho around to give me all the copies I need to eat."

More people laughed. "You three are a match made in Heaven," Rodeo told him.

"It's a shame we didn't meet on Chorion Osiris," Jericho added. "We could have lived happily ever after."

The whole crew broke into laughter, but the sound of scraping chairs made them all break off and turn to look behind them.

A group of other prisoners at a different table kicked back their chairs, got to their feet, and squared up to the crew. Three of the prisoners were Hidions. Two were enormous human guys, and the last one was a Zihori.

"Hey!" the Zihori boomed. "You forgot to put your shirt on."

Davenport didn't turn around. He pretended to push his Universal Staples around on his plate. "I didn't forget," he replied over his shoulder.

"I'm talking to you, asshole!" the guy snapped again. "What the hell do you think you're doing coming in here with no shirt on?"

Davenport pushed back his chair, stood up, and turned around very slowly. "I came in here like this so you would be able to concentrate really hard and read *this,* but maybe you missed it. You should be able to see it, now that I'm facing you."

The guy's eyes dipped to the brand and all his friends read it, too. All their expressions changed. "Confederate Sheriff!" the first guy roared. "You're a dead man!"

The six of them surged forward, but just before they got near enough to attack Davenport, Dice stood up and planted himself next to Davenport. "I don't think so, fellas. Take a big step back. You mess with him, you mess with all of us."

Alla stood up, too. "I am getting kinda tired of Universal Staples. Some nice fresh meat would be real nice right about now.'

The rest of the crew stood up, too, but before they could get into position to back up Davenport, Breeze tripped over his chair, fell over his own feet, and the chair landed on top of him.

He grunted and oofed in pain, got tangled up in his own limbs, and then "accidentally" kicked one of the table legs and the whole damn thing buckled on top of him.

The six prisoners furrowed their brows at him floundering on the floor. Coon started laughing and then the rest of the crew burst out laughing, too.

The big Zihori glared at all of them and then at Breeze when he finally threw the table off, kicked two chairs out of the way, and clambered to his feet.

He brushed off his clothes, cast a sheepish glance around the crew, and panted, "I meant to do that."

"What the hell is wrong with him?!" the big Zihori demanded.

"He got dropped on his head as a baby," Davenport explained.

"More than once," Bandit added and the crew split their sides laughing.

"Shut the hell up!" the Zihori roared. "I'm talking to you, porkchop!"

Davenport struggled to straighten his face. "Yeah. I heard you."

"Do you know what we do to lawmen in here?!" one of the Hidions interjected.

"You don't do shit to him or to any of us unless you want me to jam my two fingers so far up your ass that you can't see straight and then rip the rest of you in half," Dice fired back. "Do yourselves a huge favor and go sit down with your Universal Staples before you get hurt."

"Or eaten," Alla added.

"Or trampled," Jericho chimed in.

"Or crushed," Axel finished.

"You think you can mess with us?!" the Hidion bellowed and the six prisoners surged forward one more time.

Dice, Alla, Jace, and Jericho surged forward at the same time, but before any of them could close for the battle of the century, three more prisoners barged between the two groups.

These three were all Zihori, but another five human guys and four Zalvao pushed their way between the two groups at the same time.

The new group turned their backs on Davenport's crew, shoved the first group of prisoners away, and then advanced to put more distance between the would-be combatants.

"You don't touch this crew," one of the newcomers growled in the Zihori's face. "These people are under Ekol Thaine's protection."

The prisoners who had been about to attack Davenport's crew changed their tune instantly. They glanced over the newcomers' shoulders and then shrugged. "We didn't know. This asshole is a sheriff."

"Do you got a problem with that?" the biggest newcomer snapped.

The Zihori shrugged again and tried to turn away. "I guess not. He ought to at least wear a shirt where we don't have to see *that.*"

"Get used to it, pal," Davenport chipped in.

"You heard the man," the big newcomer went on. "You got a problem with them, you can tell us and we'll pass on your complaint to Ekol. Is that clear enough for you to understand?"

The prisoners who had been about to attack Davenport shuffled their feet. All but the first guy backed away. Then the first guy mumbled, "Yeah. It's clear enough," and he left, too.

The new group stood there with their backs to Davenport and the crew until the first prisoners returned to their tables, sat down, and they turned their backs on Davenport, too.

Davenport didn't move. He wouldn't have expected Ekol to keep Davenport under his protection even after everything Davenport had done, but apparently, Ekol's support extended even here.

The big Zihori finally turned around and fixed his hard eyes on Davenport. The two men confronted each other for what seemed like a long time.

Then Rodeo startled Davenport out of his skin by lunging forward, grabbing the Zihori by the shoulder, and shaking him. "Way to put the fear of God into him, man! What are you in for—fighting again? When are you ever gonna learn?"

The Zihori burst into a huge grin and laughed. "You boys have been long overdue to spend some time in jail." He went through the group hugging all the Chorions except for Jace and Jericho.

Rodeo turned to Davenport. "This is our good buddy, Usaga. He's one of Ekol's heavy hitters."

Usaga grabbed Davenport's hand. "It's a pleasure to meet you, Sir. You're a legend in Ekol's service."

Rodeo saved Davenport from answering that by introducing the rest of Usaga's friends. "This is Drego, Chiru, and Todin. They're all good boys when they aren't fighting all the time."

Usaga laughed and his friends joined in. "We don't fight as much as you do."

"We just don't get caught," Axel chimed in. "That's the difference."

Usaga turned to Davenport. "You might want to put on a shirt, though. Walking around with that star is asking for trouble."

"I can't do that," Davenport replied. "I'm a sheriff."

Usaga burst out in laughter. "You're crazy is what you are! Well, we'll let you all get back to your meal." Usaga jerked his thumb over his shoulder. "If you have any problem with them, you let us know. We're under orders from Ekol to keep an eye on you. See you around."

He hugged Rodeo and Bandit and then Usaga and his friends left to go back to their own table.

Davenport and his crew sat back down. Davenport didn't feel like eating, but he forced himself to do it anyway. He was in jail. He needed to eat when someone put food in front of him.

"That was lucky, finding them here," Rodeo remarked.

"Someone is bound to try something sometime," Healey pointed out. "Your friends won't always be here to save our asses, and even if they were, someone might try something even with them around to help us."

"Then we'll deal with it," Coon replied. "We always do."

Chapter 11

Davenport startled upright from his bunk when he heard the lock on his cell door shoot back. He'd just come back from breakfast, so it couldn't be time to go back to the commissary.

He stiffened when the usual deputies came in and told him to go out into the corridor. They escorted him back toward the jail entrance—the entrance he'd used to come in here.

He had no idea where they were taking him. They couldn't be releasing him. He still hadn't been tried or even prosecuted as far as he knew.

He didn't want to ask, but he got his answer a few minutes later. The deputies took him back through the entrance area and showed him into a normal conference room. Lawrence Healey was already in there.

"You okay?" Healey asked.

Davenport nodded. "What are we doing in here? Why did they take us out of our cells in the middle of the morning?"

"I don't know. They wouldn't tell me anything. Maybe this has something to do with the charges against us."

"Do you even know what the charges are?" Davenport asked. "Aren't they supposed to at least inform us of what we're being charged with?"

"They're supposed to, but this whole case is so out of the ordinary that I don't know what to think. It looks like they've thrown the rule book out the window. Anything could happen. Hell, it already has."

"Great," Davenport muttered and looked around, but there was nothing to see. The case might be out of the ordinary, but this room sure wasn't.

Healey asked again, "Are you okay?"

Davenport turned around and discovered Healey studying him too closely. "I'm fine," Davenport replied. "Why?"

"Has the Sheriff's Service given you medical treatment for your injuries?" Healey asked. "They're required under the Confederate Code of Human Rights to give medical treatment to any injured prisoner they take into custody."

"I'm not injured," Davenport replied. "I don't need medical treatment."

Healey made a face. "When was the last time you saw your own reflection?"

Davenport flashed back to that night on the *Vindicator* when he looked at himself in the mirror. He'd still been covered in cuts and bruises with two black eyes and a split lip, but he hadn't been too concerned about that. He'd been more focused on his brand.

He'd gotten used to seeing his reflection beaten up. Only now, when Healey pointed it out to him, did Davenport realize just how awful he looked. No wonder everyone who cared about him kept asking if he was okay.

He definitely would have given a prisoner medical treatment if he took someone into custody who was beaten up as badly as he was. That was just part of the job. That would have been the first thing he did.

He looked away. He didn't want Healey or anyone else looking at him like that. Davenport had been living like this for so long that it just felt normal now. He didn't see how he would ever be able to go back to the way he had been before.

He couldn't even remember a time before. He'd been imprisoned at Terminus Anathema before became a sheriff. He'd been in Ekol's service before that.

Davenport might not have been running, fighting, and getting beaten and tortured to within an inch of his life, but he'd never exactly been at peace. He couldn't remember a time when he had been.

Healey started to say, "I'll be sure to....." when the door burst open.

A guy in a suit bustled in carrying a leather briefcase in one hand and a handheld computer device in the other. "Sorry I'm late!" he gasped. "I got held up in another meeting."

"Who the hell are you?" Healey demanded.

"I'm Jason Burnham." The guy put his briefcase and device on the table, held out his hand, and burst into a giant grin almost too big for his face. "I'm your defense attorney."

Healey's eyebrows flew up. "Defense attorney? Since when?"

"I've been assigned by the court to represent you and your crewmates, but the Sheriff's Service legal fund is paying for my services for both of you. The legal fund exists to defend any members of the Sheriff's Service that need financial assistance in any legal matters that might arise."

Healey glanced down at Burnham's hand and then shook it. Burnham grinned even more broadly if that was even possible and held out his hand to Davenport.

Davenport didn't want to shake Burnham's hand, but Davenport supposed he had to under the circumstances.

Burnham couldn't be more delighted that his two clients could at least handle that simple social ritual. He wouldn't stop grinning when he attacked his briefcase and opened it.

"Okay! Let's get right to it," he exclaimed. "The Reserve Wing is expediting putting your charges through, so I expect to bring all the evidence to a discovery hearing later this week or early next week at the latest. Once we get that out of the way, we'll have a plea hearing and then we can move on to the sentencing....."

"Sentencing!" Davenport countered. "We aren't going from a plea hearing straight to sentencing! We're going to trial! There is no way in hell we're pleading guilty."

Burnham opened his mouth to retort, but Healey interrupted. "Before we get into that, I want to lodge a complaint with the Human Rights Commission. Sheriff Davenport is obviously injured and he hasn't been given the medical treatment he needs."

Burnham opened his mouth again, but Davenport cut him off. "Who gives a shit about medical treatment? We're on trial for our lives and this idiot wants us to plead guilty! We only came back here...."

"You can't plead not guilty," Burnham interrupted. "The evidence against you is overwhelming. You could drag this out for years and still get a guilty verdict. You're *going* to get a guilty verdict. Your only hope is to plead guilty, throw yourselves on the mercy of the court....."

"No, no, no, no!" Healey and Davenport both countered. "Hell no! Forget it! We are not doing that!"

"You have to," Burnham insisted. "As your legal counsel, it's my responsibility to ensure....."

"It's your responsibility to represent us!" Davenport snapped. "And you're going to represent us and get us cleared! That's an order."

Burnham held up his hand and picked up his device. "Just listen, okay? There are over two thousand counts against each of you—that means against each member of your crew. Sheriff Davenport, you've been charged with over three thousand counts of armed assault, insurrection against Confederate law enforcement, destruction of property, conspiracy to mount an assault to overthrow Terminus Anathema, murder of more than twenty guards, wardens, and other prisoners, resisting arrest, trafficking, and open warfare against the Reserve Wing and its accessory branches of the law enforcement establishment."

Davenport fell silent and his heart sank when Burnham put the device down on the table in front of him and turned it around so Davenport could read the charges.

He could also read the dates, locations, and circumstances outlined in each incident. He really did do all that. He didn't have to deny it because it was all true. He was as guilty as Burnham said he was.

Burnham glanced back and forth between him and Healey, but anyone could see the writing on the wall. "Do either of you deny any of these charges?"

Davenport looked away. "No, I guess not."

"Then your best hope is to plead guilty to the charges. You and your crew are considered too dangerous even for Terminus Anathema. You'll be sent somewhere else—somewhere with higher security where you'll be kept isolated from other prisoners....."

Davenport groaned and turned his back to the table. He couldn't listen to this. The silence and isolation he'd been suffering this past week—he could look forward to that for the rest of his life.

No one would ever find out why he did any of this—and even worse, no one would ever find out what Admiral Joyce was up to. Everything Davenport had gone through had been for nothing.

"Sheriff?" Burnham prompted. "Is there any reason you can see why I shouldn't enter a guilty plea for all of you? Your associates are all hardened, notorious criminals and your own record isn't as clean as it could be if you know what I mean. All of that is going to work against you. This is the best way. Trust me."

Davenport couldn't listen to this. "Call the deputies to take me back to my cell."

"We need to make a decision about this...." Burnham insisted.

Davenport cut him off with a wave of his hand, crossed the room, and opened the door himself. Four deputies stood outside.

Davenport stepped out into the corridor. "I'm ready to go back to my cell now."

One of the deputies glanced back into the room. Healey and Burnham were still in there, but Davenport didn't care.

The deputies took him back to his cell without a word. He never thought coming back to this cell would be a relief, but it was.

All those charges—all those times when he broke the law.....

He'd made a commitment when he became a sheriff to uphold the law and he failed to do that.

He'd become more than a fugitive. He'd slipped right back into his old life of crime—the life where he did exactly what he wanted with no regard for the law at all.

He deserved this. He deserved to spend the rest of his life locked up. He wasn't a sheriff. He was nothing. All those years he'd spent at Ultra Meridian were just an act he'd played to cover up the fact that he never really changed.

He collapsed on his bunk and shut his eyes. He actually hoped they would put him away in a maximum-security lockup where he would never see anyone.

That would be the true relief from being himself. Then he wouldn't have to worry about doing anything that might break the law.

Chapter 12

The deputies showed Davenport back into the same conference room. Another week had passed, so the Reserve Wing couldn't be too concerned about hurrying this trial along.

This time, Davenport discovered the whole crew in there, including Lyons and Fiddler. "Are you okay?" he asked them both. "Are they keeping you both isolated, too?"

"We're fine," Lyons replied. "We get to see each other at mealtimes, so it isn't too bad."

"Why are we here?" Rodeo asked. "Does anyone know?"

"We're going in for a discovery hearing," Healey replied. "Davenport and I already had one meeting with our defense attorney...."

"What defense attorney?" Emmett asked. "Who is he?"

"He's been assigned by the court and the Sheriff's Service is paying for part of his fees since Davenport and I are still covered under the Sheriff's Service legal fund. The guy thinks we should plead guilty....."

Howls of protest broke out. "Hell no!" Dice boomed. "We didn't come all the way back here for that....."

They were still arguing about it when Burnham himself showed up grinning as much as ever. "Excellent! You're all here, so we'll just go over a few details before we go into court...."

"We are NOT pleading guilty!" Dice bellowed.

Burnham's usual cheery grin slipped. "Well, fortunately for all of us, we won't be entering any plea today. This hearing is only to determine if there's enough evidence to charge you—but I'm certain the trial will go ahead because—well—" He burst out in nervous laughter. "The evidence against you is overwhelming."

"Fantastic," Emmett muttered.

"I'll just step outside and have a few words with the bailiff and then we can all go into court."

Burnham bustled out the door as quickly as he bustled into it. His bubbly attitude was really starting to get on Davenport's nerves.

"We never should have turned ourselves over to Pritchard," Emmett grumbled as soon as Burnham left. "That was a big mistake."

"What else were we supposed to do?" Bandit asked.

"We should have blown him and the Wide Patrol out of the sky and kept on flying," Emmett replied. "We should have disappeared into Sacron Enigma and left the Confederacy to fend for itself."

"Don't say that," Healey murmured. "None of us would walk away from millions of people potentially getting killed. None of us is that callous."

"What the hell has the Confederacy ever done for us?" Emmett countered. "What's the point of trying to help the Confederacy if it can do this to us? To hell with the Confederacy. I'll never help the Confederacy ever again. I swear it. I hope they all rot in hell."

No one answered. Davenport couldn't argue with anything Emmett said because Davenport had spent the last two weeks thinking the same thing.

Hell, he'd spent the last disastrous couple of months thinking the same thing. He couldn't for the life of him figure out why he was going to so much trouble to help and save people who could treat him so badly.

Was this the thanks he got for turning his life around? Was this the reason he walked away from a life of luxury, influence, and power as Ekol's enforcer—so he could spend the rest of his life in prison as a convicted murderer, insurrectionist, and mass criminal?

The crew was still standing there taking in Emmett's words when the deputies entered to escort the crew to court. Davenport really didn't want to go. He didn't want to hear all the evidence being presented that would cement the crew's fate.

The crew filed out of the conference room. Burnham disappeared somewhere. No one remained but the deputies. Their presence drained the last shred of Davenport's hope. So much for getting justice and clearing his name.

This was justice. He really did commit those crimes. He had to pay for them for justice to be served.

He killed those guards at Terminus Anathema. He destroyed Reserve Wing property and waged open warfare against Confederate law enforcement agencies. He used explosives to destroy the Pandora's Needle Jail so he and hundreds of other prisoners could escape.

Lyons stopped at another door. The deputies patted her down, and when they didn't find anything, they let her pass through the door.

Davenport spotted the courtroom beyond. Burnham was in there hobnobbing with some other guy in a suit near the prosecutor's table. They talked and smiled at each other like old friends. Great.

Emmett entered the courtroom next followed by Fiddler. The deputies had a harder time with Dice. Healey and the Chorions went more smoothly.

Wolf snarled at everyone, but he didn't resist. Davenport had to admire how cooperative Wolf had been since his arrest. He hadn't resisted or attacked anyone.

The Chorions filed through the door one after the other. Davenport stepped forward and raised his arms so the deputies could search him.

One of them waved at him. "You can't go into court like that." The guy called to someone behind him. "Bring over one of the jail-issue shirts from the supply room."

"I'm not wearing a shirt," Davenport countered. "I'll go like this or not at all."

"You have to wear a shirt," the same deputy replied. "You can't go in like that and you have to go in, so you better put it on."

"No," Davenport returned.

The guy ignored him. The deputies all stood around waiting while one of them went to get a shirt.

Davenport's heart turned to granite. He wouldn't put on a shirt. Going to prison was one thing. He wouldn't go as far as this.

He didn't understand himself because he'd just been thinking this past week that he wasn't a sheriff after all. Now the moment came to cover up his star—the only star he had left—and he just couldn't do it.

The deputy came back with a shirt—the same plain white jail-issued prisoner uniform shirt all the rest of Davenport's crew had to wear. Even Healey wore one.

The deputy stopped in front of Davenport and held out the shirt. "Put it on, man."

"No," Davenport replied. "Sheriff Pritchard said I didn't have to and I'm not going to."

"That was just for sitting around in your cell," the first guy who'd initially demanded that Davenport wear a shirt told him. "We can make an exception for you then, but not if you're going into court." He took the shirt from his comrade and held it out. "Put it on. I won't ask again."

"You can ask as many times as you want," Davenport replied. "I'm not putting it on. I won't put it on ever, so go on and do whatever you gotta do."

Someone behind him struck him hard across the back of the thigh and Davenport's knees buckled. He caught a fraction of an instant's glimpse of ten deputies moving in with their batons raised.

Davenport had time to curl into a ball and cover his head before they all attacked at once. They pummeled his body until, inevitably, someone kicked him hard in the head.

His arm protected him from the impact, but the blow threw his arm out of position long enough for someone else to nail their boot into his face.

More blows rained on his head and then a brutal kick to his face made him pass out.

He woke up lying on his bunk in his cell. He winced when he opened his eyes and felt the swelling around the outside bone of his eye socket. His jaw felt three feet thick and one side of his lip had been pulverized even worse than before.

He rolled over and groaned when he felt the bruises on his ribs, back, legs, and stomach. The deputies really did a number on him this time.

He only opened his eyes long enough to see that the cell door was as locked as ever. He wouldn't be able to sneak out to any infirmary this time.

He huddled in a ball of pain, but only for a few minutes before the deputies unlocked his cell. He couldn't even bring himself to open his eyes. He didn't care anymore what they did to him.

"Dinner time," one of the deputies announced. "Let's go, pal."

It was one of the deputies who beat up Davenport. He didn't want to give these cocksuckers the satisfaction of telling him to do anything, but the prospect of seeing his friends proved too strong a temptation.

Davenport dragged his aching body off the bunk and limped out into the corridor. He took a long time to walk down it to the far door. Every step made him wince.

He finally made it to the commissary and got exactly the reception he knew he would get. "Oh, hell no!" Dice growled.

"Did they give you any medical treatment or not?!" Healey demanded. "This is outrageous! It's illegal!"

Davenport looked away. He didn't want to talk about it nor did he want Healey talking about it, but at least someone cared.

"That lawyer was right," Emmett grumbled. "They're going ahead with the trial."

"You didn't really think they wouldn't, did you?" Davenport asked. His voice didn't sound right with his lips and cheek swollen up like a balloon.

"We should just get the hell out of here and go," Dice growled. "I could break us out of here in a few minutes. These dipshits wouldn't be able to stop us."

"We all made Pritchard a promise," Healey countered. "We agreed to come back here and face this. We couldn't go back on that."

"Will you wake up, Marshall?" Bandit fired back. "Pritchard doesn't care about us. He's long gone. He's halfway across the galaxy by now. He doesn't know or care about anything that happens to us. All his promises don't mean squat."

Healey shook his head. "I don't think so. He promised to help us. He wouldn't just say that if he didn't mean it."

"Then where is he?" Coon asked. "He dropped us off here and then bailed. I'm sure he has better things to do than babysit every fugitive he apprehends."

"Jace and I will leave if this trial goes against us," Jericho chimed in, "No way are we spending the rest of our lives in prison."

"No one has to know," Jace pointed out. "We can send one copy each to prison while the rest of us get away."

"Lucky you," Emmett sneered. "Some of us don't have copies of ourselves that we can leave in jail to fool the authorities."

"We would help you, too," Jace told him. "That's what I'm saying. Once our copies get out, we can help the rest of you get free. You don't have to stay here."

Axel turned to Davenport. "What do you say, Sir? We can come up with a plan to blow this joint and hit the highway."

Davenport didn't look up. "You can all go. I'm staying here."

"Are you insane?!" Bandit countered. "You would spend the rest of your life in jail—for what?"

"I'm just sick and tired of running," Davenport murmured. "I can't do it anymore. I bet everything on becoming a sheriff. If I don't get justice here, then I don't want to be free anyway. I'd rather go back to Terminus Anathema as a real prisoner this time—or wherever it is they send me. Nothing is worth this."

Silence answered him. He felt the others losing hope, but he couldn't even look at them, not even to give them some spark of motivation to keep going. What the hell was he doing anyway? Why keep fighting if this was all he got?

More prisoners entered the commissary. The group that threatened him sat down at their usual table and glared at Davenport and his crew. He could just imagine what he looked like to them, but he didn't care about that, either.

Ugasa and his people entered, too. They smiled, nodded, and waved at the Chorion Team, but only a few of the Chorions nodded back. Most didn't acknowledge Ugasa at all.

Davenport didn't even have the energy to go get himself something to eat. Now that he actually got here, he just wanted to go back to his cell, shut his eyes, and forget everything about who he was, where he was, how he got here, and where he was going.

Chapter 13

Davenport stepped into the conference room. Healey was already in there and so was Jason Burnham, their defense attorney.

Healey took one look at Davenport's bruised face and rounded on Burnham. "Do you not see this?! This happened right before he was supposed to go into court for the discovery hearing—and the Sheriff's Service still has not given him any medical treatment! This is a blatant violation of Human Rights law! Aren't you going to do anything about that?"

"There's nothing I can do about it *now.*" Burnham turned back to his device. "We're going in for our first hearing, so you'll need to make up your minds how you plan to plead. Please—be reasonable. There is no way you can get out of these charges. There are too many of them and the evidence against you is overwhelming. You can't win and you've both already admitted that you did commit these crimes. I wouldn't be doing my job if I let you plead anything but guilty."

Healey glanced over at Davenport, but Davenport didn't look up. He was ready to plead guilty. He just didn't want to let Healey down—and the rest of the crew.

They'd all supported him this long. He was the one who got them into this trouble. He should be the one to get them out of it.

He couldn't get them out of it because they were guilty. That was the worst part.

"What do you want to do?" Healey murmured in Davenport's ear.

Davenport only shrugged. "I don't care. You decide."

Healey hesitated and then turned back to Burnham. "Fine. We'll do it."

Burnham breathed a sigh of relief. "Excellent. It's for the best. We can go into court, enter your plea, and then move straight to sentencing. We won't have to drag this out any longer than it already has been. I'll see you gentlemen in court in two hours."

He bustled out of the room. Davenport couldn't figure out how a person could bustle so many places all the time, but Davenport didn't even really care about that.

He couldn't look at Healey, not even after the door closed. "We really need to get you some medical attention," Healey muttered.

"Will you stop it?" Davenport growled. "Just leave it alone."

Healey opened his mouth to argue back and stopped himself. Davenport felt Healey watching him, but Davenport still couldn't raise his eyes, not even to look at the man he considered one of his best friends.

Just then, Healey clamped his hand on Davenport's shoulder. Even that hurt.

"I'm sorry," Healey murmured under his breath. "I tried."

Davenport gulped down the lump in his throat. "It isn't your fault."

Healey's voice trembled when he choked out the words. "Pritchard is right. You're one of the finest lawmen I've ever known. It's been an honor to serve with you....and it's an honor to go down with you. Dedicating myself to your mission—helping you—it's one of the things I'm most proud of in my career. You are....." Healey had to cut himself off and clear his voice before he could go on, but his voice still shook with buried strain. "You are everything I always wanted to be as a lawman."

He barely got the words out before the deputies came back. They took Healey away first and left Davenport standing there by himself.

What was the point of being everything Healey wanted to be as a lawman if this was where it got him? Being proud of what he'd done didn't get Davenport, Healey, or any of their friends anywhere.

He was still standing there feeling glum when the deputies came back for him. They took him back toward the courtroom, and this time, they put him in a holding cell by himself.

What did the deputies plan to do—beat him up again? Maybe that was the best way to avoid having to be in the same room with Burnham when he entered a guilty plea on behalf of the crew. Davenport didn't want to be there for that.

He sat down on the bench that stuck out of one wall. He just wanted all of this to be over.

He didn't plan to get up again until the deputies came back for him, but Davenport shot to his feet when the door opened and Deacon Pritchard entered.

He wore a suit instead of his usual beaten leather pants and vest. His star gleamed on his jacket lapel and a Sheriff's Service tie pin sparkled on his tie.

"You!" Davenport gasped. "What are you doing here? We thought you left to go back out with the Patrol."

"No, I've been here the whole time. I've been monitoring the progress of the case like I told you I would." Pritchard cocked his head and frowned. "Have the deputies given you any medical treatment for that?"

"No, but....."

"We're definitely going to have to change that." Pritchard pounded his fist on the door. One of the deputies stuck his head in. "This man needs medical attention. I'm taking him to the infirmary before the hearing."

"But the hearing is supposed to start in less than an hour," the deputy pointed out.

"Then the court will just have to delay the hearing," Pritchard replied. "He can't go into court like this....and I'll be lodging disciplinary charges against every deputy in this facility for violating his human rights by withholding medical treatment. Now you better go out there and tell all your friends to clear the corridor. If I see any deputy in the halls on our way to the infirmary, I'll be laying more charges for harassment."

The deputy pulled his head back out of the cell. Pritchard caught the door to stop it from locking with him inside it.

Davenport stared at him. "What are you doing?"

"I just told you. I'm taking you to the infirmary."

"No....I mean....what are you really doing?" Davenport asked. "Why are you doing this?'

Pritchard shrugged. "I made you a promise when I took you into custody. I didn't swear an oath to uphold Confederate law to stand by and watch it get trounced by the people who are supposed to be upholding it. Now come on. They won't delay the hearing forever."

He held the door open for Davenport to step outside. They didn't see a single deputy on their way downstairs to the infirmary.

Davenport still had difficulty understanding what was happening to him when he sat down on one of the exam tables. A deputy medic he'd never seen before started running scans on him.

"I'm not picking up any fractures," the medic told Pritchard. "It's mostly just swelling."

"Can you do anything to reduce the swelling in his face? He can't go into court like this."

"I can give him something and I can seal the crack in his lip." The medic came over with a hypodermic injector, injected something into Davenport's neck, and then bent over the burn in his chest. "I won't be able to do anything about this. The tissue damage is permanent."

"You don't have to do anything about that," Pritchard replied. "How long will it take for the swelling to go down?"

"It should start to fade in a few minutes."

He brought over some skin sealant and started applying it to Davenport's lip, but Davenport already felt the swelling-reduction drugs working.

The ache in his muscles faded and his face didn't feel so thick. His lip shrank to something closer to its normal size.

He sat still while the medic finished with his lip. "That's the best we can do for now. If you bring him back here after the hearing, I might be able to do more with the tissue damage to his legs and body."

"That will be good enough." Pritchard pulled Davenport off the exam table and they headed back upstairs.

Davenport kept glancing behind him, but he still didn't see any deputies. "They wanted me to wear a shirt for the discovery hearing."

"I read the deputies' report," Pritchard replied. "They claimed you attacked first, so they had to subdue you."

Davenport snorted. "That's a good one."

Pritchard took Davenport back to the conference room. Davenport stiffened when they walked in and he saw a brand-new suit hanging on the door. "What the hell is this?"

"You can't go into court without a shirt on," Pritchard replied. "You and I both know you're a sheriff on the inside, but the court judge doesn't know that. The whole court needs to see you looking like a sheriff on the outside."

Davenport grimaced and looked away. He didn't want to look at that suit. "It doesn't matter because I'm going back to prison for life. I don't even care anymore."

"That's nonsense and we both know it," Pritchard countered. "You aren't going back to prison and you can forget all that shit about pleading guilty. You're pleading not guilty and you will get off. I told you that once and I meant it."

"How?" Davenport asked. "You should see the list of charges against us—against me—"

"I have seen the list. I've seen it all and read it in detail from start to finish. I wouldn't be here if I hadn't."

"Then you know....."

"I know one thing," Pritchard told him. "I know you've been registered on the Sheriff's Service roster as the Sheriff of Ultra Meridian since this whole thing started. "You're still registered as the Sheriff of Ultra Meridian right now—which means that everything you've done has been in the line of duty. I'm certain you'll get off and I'm certain the rest of your crew will get off, too, because they were acting under your authority as a law enforcement officer. We can claim that you deputized them and that they were following your orders to uphold the law while you tried to retake the Ithium and apprehend the people who stole it."

Davenport stared at him, too stunned to think straight. "But....but our defense counsel already said....He said we had to plead guilty. He said the evidence was overwhelming. He said we couldn't win."

Pritchard smiled, but it was a sad smile. His eye softened in ways Davenport never could have imagined. "I regret to inform you that your defense counsel has been replaced. I found out—and some of your other friends found out—that Jason Burnham wasn't representing your interests the way he should have. He failed to get you the medical treatment you needed in a timely manner. He neglected to hold the Sheriff's Service accountable for their treatment of you and he did not defend your case adequately. This stupid guilty plea idea is a perfect example of that—so he isn't representing you anymore."

"But I can't afford another attorney," Davenport pointed out. "None of us can. Burnham only defended us because the Sheriff's Service legal fund paid for it. If Burnham isn't going to defend us, who is?"

"I am," Pritchard blurted out.

Davenport's jaw dropped. Sheriff Deacon Pritchard—everybody's hero—the man no one dared to question—the man who could break the law and get away with it because no one dared to challenge his commitment to what was right—Pritchard was going to defend this crew?

Pritchard looked away and took the suit hanger off the back of the door. "You might want to get changed. We have a hearing to attend."

Davenport gulped again. This wasn't happening. This was some kind of cruel joke. "You......you....You can do that?"

Pritchard shrugged that away. "It looks like I'm doing it one way or the other. It's like you say. You need some defense counsel and Burnham wasn't doing it, so I am. I guess I can do as good a job or better than he can and I don't charge as much. Now will you please get dressed? We don't have a lot of time."

Davenport turned to the suit, too. His elation at finding out that Pritchard was defending him drained away when he looked at that suit. "I.....I don't think I can. My star is all I've had for so long. I can't cover it up."

"That's why I brought you this." Pritchard pulled a small box out of his inner jacket pocket. He handed it to Davenport.

Davenport stared at the box and then turned it over in his fingers. He recognized it, but he still didn't believe until he opened it and looked down at a brand-new, shining metal star.

The words stared up at him from the imprint around the star's inner circle. *Confederate Sheriff.*

"You're a credit to the star," Pritchard told him. "It's an honor to call you a sheriff."

Chapter 14

Davenport scrambled into his new clothes. Pritchard stood outside the conference room to make sure no one came to bother Davenport while he got dressed.

He straightened the suit as best he could and then pinned the new star onto his jacket. He had to stare down at it for what seemed like a long time. He didn't have to show everyone his brand because he had his star on the outside now where everyone could see it.

Pritchard knocked on the door and called from outside. "You ready?'

"Yeah," Davenport called back. "I'm ready."

Pritchard stepped inside and Davenport stood a little taller, now that he was dressed like this. He tugged his shirt sleeves down inside his jacket sleeves to straighten them. "How do I look?"

Pritchard bit back a smile. "You look good." He straightened the lapels of Davenport's jacket and his lips twitched when he saw the star. He kept brushing his hands down Davenport's jacket front and sleeves. "You look real good. Come on. Let's go."

The two men walked out of the conference room. They did see a few deputies hanging around this time, but none of them interfered with the two sheriffs.

Davenport never would have imagined a suit could make such a difference, but he didn't shrink from these deputies. He walked straight down the corridor.

He didn't have to think about them restraining him or guarding him or escorting him. He walked straight ahead like a real man—like the sheriff he was.

He and Pritchard walked shoulder to shoulder to the courtroom and no one patted Davenport down when he entered the room.

Healey stood behind the defense table. He also wore an immaculate suit with a brand-new Confederate Marshall's star pinned to his chest.

Two men sat behind the prosecutor's table. Davenport couldn't tell anything about them except that they both wore suits and looked like the most boring people he'd ever laid eyes on.

The other defendants sat in the first row of seats behind the table. They all wore brand new clothes and Jericho had combed his hair into some kind of order. He actually looked much more similar to Jace like this. Jericho's old patched clothes from Chorion Osiris made him stand out more.

Fiddler and Lyons both wore business suits with their hair twisted up on top of their heads. Davenport hardly recognized either of them. They might have stepped out of some law firm in the richest financial centers of Atlas Arcane.

The crew's eyes lit up when they saw Davenport fully dressed with his star pinned on.

He would have liked to say something to them—some word of encouragement that Pritchard was going to be defending them now, but their expressions told him they probably already knew.

Healey burst into a huge grin when he saw Davenport, but at that moment, the bailiff called, "All rise! Court is now in session! The Honorable Francis J. Orland presiding."

The judge walked in and sat down behind the bench. He was an old man with greying hair combed over his bald head, glasses perched on his nose, and skeletal hands with spidery fingers.

"Good morning, gentlemen," he began. "This is the case of *The Confederacy v. Davenport, et.al.* The court clerk will now read out the charges for the record."

The court clerk stood up and read out the charges. It took a long time to get through the whole list because she had to read the charges against each of the defendants and the whole crew had been charged for most of the same crimes.

She finally finished and the judge asked, "Are the defendants ready to enter their plea, Sheriff?"

Pritchard stood up. "They are, Your Honor."

"How do the defendants plead?"

"Not guilty to all charges."

A gasp went through the courtroom and the chief prosecutor spun around to stare at Pritchard. "You can't be serious!"

"You're pleading not guilty to *all* the charges?!" the judge fired back. "We've heard overwhelming evidence that these defendants did commit these crimes—and we've also heard these men admit their crimes. What can you possibly hope to gain by pleading not guilty—apart from wasting the court's time?"

"Your Honor, we intend to demonstrate extenuating circumstances to show that both Sheriff Davenport and Marshall Healey were executing their duties as Confederate law enforcement officers during all the events in question and that they were acting within the law at the time they committed these acts. We intend to prove by a preponderance of the evidence that they were in fact attempting to apprehend a much more dangerous criminal at the time. Even Sheriff Davenport's incarceration at Terminus Anathema and now here at the Atlas Arcane Jail—and indeed this proceeding itself—is all an elaborate scheme to stop them from carrying out their duties as dedicated officers of the law."

The judge raised his eyebrows. "Very well. We have no choice but to proceed with opening statements. Go ahead, Mr. Lane."

The prosecutor stood up and basically repeated everything the court clerk just read out. He followed the timeline from Ultra Meridian and the *Echo Omicron's* first battle against the Reserve Wing, the *Artemis Rex's* battle to free the crew from Reserve Wing custody, the crew's assault on the *Trailblazer,* Dice, Fiddler, and Jace essentially destroying Helios Sanctus, Davenport's insurrection at Terminus Anathema, and this latest battle in which multiple criminal syndicates mounted an armed insurgency against the Reserve Wing's attempts to restore order.

The prosecution spun the whole case to make it appear that Davenport was the one who stole the Ithium and that the Reserve Wing had been trying to stop him.

Then Pritchard stood up and told the same sequence of events from a different point of view. "The defense has entered evidence that Sheriff Davenport logged a report with the Sheriff's Service at Macron Calypso that he discovered the Ithium on board the *Echo Omicron.*

"This report was filed mere minutes before the Reserve Wing attacked from orbit and destroyed the Ultra Meridian Jail. Sheriff Davenport has been registered on the Sheriff's Service roster as the Sheriff of Ultra Meridian ever since.

"Everything he has done since then has been designed to track down and apprehend the criminals who stole the Ithium from Helios Sanctus, to retake the Ithium, and to stop these criminals from using the Ithium and two other deadly components to construct a doomsday weapon that would threaten the whole Confederacy and millions of people living in it.

"Sheriff Davenport was still legally in the line of duty when he was imprisoned at Terminus Anathema without a trial. There is no evidence that he killed anyone or that he did anything illegal while he was imprisoned there.

"The defense intends to show evidence that he deputized these other defendants to help him retake the Ithium and bring the perpetrators to justice. These defendants were also within the law when they carried out Davenport's orders and assisted his mission.

"The defense will also present evidence that Marshall Lawrence Healey has also been a full instated Confederate Marshall during all of these events, that he has been supporting and helping Davenport in the same mission, and that Admiral Killian Joyce of the Reserve Wing specifically promoted Healey to the rank of Marshall, removed him from Pandora's Needle, and engaged him to track down Davenport for the purpose of taking the Ithium from him and stopping him from executing his duties to protect the Confederacy from this plot."

The judge stared at him with his mouth open for a minute and then shuddered. "That is one hell of a story, Sheriff. None of this evidence was presented at discovery. If you're right then, I have no choice but to declare a mistrial....."

"No, Your Honor," Pritchard interrupted. "The defendants have already been incarcerated more than once without cause and without being given the proper medical treatment. The defense insists that we go ahead with this trial and that the prosecution show evidence that Davenport and Healey were operating outside the law at any time."

"Your Honor, I really must insist," Lane interjected. "The prosecution must have time to evaluate this evidence that Sheriff Pritchard claims to present."

"The evidence has been presented long ago," Pritchard countered. "Davenport's and Healey's status as fully instated officers of the law has never been called into question. Davenport's incarceration at Terminus Anathema is well-documented as is his report to Macron Calypso. All the Reserve Wing records and evidence are right there for the world to see. This prosecution has cooked up this proceeding to make Davenport and this crew disappear so the real perpetrators can get away with their crimes while no one is looking for them."

"I'll allow the hearing to go ahead," the judge decided. "Mr. Lane, you may call your first witness."

Pritchard sat down and Lane stood up. Lane had to gather himself to overcome the smackdown he just received from Pritchard. Anyone could see that this turn of events rattled Lane. He sure wasn't expecting that.

Davenport's heart threatened to explode out of his chest. It was really happening. Pritchard was presenting all the evidence that would bring the crew's story to light.

Lane called a certain Captain Forest Huette of the Reserve Wing Stalwart *Agamemnon* to the stand. He wore a spotless dress uniform studded with decorations. He sure looked dignified standing up there getting sworn in.

Davenport had to prepare himself to take the stand, too. He couldn't imagine what he would say that Pritchard hadn't already said.

Captain Huette sat down and Lane started questioning him about the *Echo Omicron* attacking Reserve Wing ships over Ultra Meridian.

Huette described taking the *Echo Omicron* on board and then Lane presented log records of Davenport and his crew going through the ship to free Dice and Beauty and steal the Ithium from Reserve Wing custody.

Davenport cringed when Huette described everything Davenport had done. It really sounded terrible when they outlined all his many crimes.

Then it was Pritchard's turn. He stood up behind the defense table. "Thank you for your testimony, Captain. You've described the battle between the *Echo Omicron* and the Reserve Wing. If you don't mind, let's back it up a little bit. I'd like you to recall the time before the battle when you were in orbit over Ultra Meridian."

Captain Huette shifted in his seat. "Yes. Sir."

"You and your fellow Stalwarts fired on the Ultra Meridian Jail, did you not?" Pritchard asked.

Captain Huette glanced toward the prosecutor's table and mumbled, "Yes, Sir."

"You fired on the jail when you could see that there were four people inside it, three of whom were civilians and two were incarcerated prisoners. Is that correct?"

Huette gulped. "Yes, Sir."

"And you could clearly see these people inside the jail on your scans," Pritchard went on. "You scanned the surface before you fired. You had to scan the surface and the jail in order to acquire your target. Am I correct, Captain?"

"Yes, Sir," Huette murmured.

"How long were you in orbit before you fired on the jail?"

Huette squirmed in his seat some more. "Uh....I don't know.....maybe about five hours."

Pritchard's head shot up. "Five hours! You were in orbit over Ultra Meridian for five hours before you fired on the jail?!"

"Yes, Sir."

"And during how much of that time were you scanning the surface?"

"Well.....all of it. We started scanning when we first came into orbit."

"Then you must have seen Sheriff Davenport cross the Ultra Meridian planes, enter the *Echo Omicron* to inspect it, and then return to the jail afterward. Did you see all that?"

"Yes, Sir."

"And since the Ithium cartridge wasn't in any way shielded or concealed, you would have seen that the *Echo Omicron* was carrying it and that he took the Ithium back to the jail with him. Did you see all that on your scans?"

Huette's voice shook. "Yes, Sir."

"And then you fired on the jail knowing there were four people inside it, including Sheriff Davenport, and that the Ithium was inside the jail. Is that your testimony?"

Huette could barely make himself heard. "Yes, Sir."

"Who gave the order for you to fire on the jail?" Pritchard demanded.

Huette glanced around in all directions, but no one could help him. "Well....the order came from the....*Glacier*....."

"I want the name of the officer who gave you the order, Captain," Pritchard demanded. "The order couldn't have come from any other Stalwart captain, could it? The order to fire on a Confederate outpost must have come from a more senior officer. Who gave the order, Captain?"

"Admiral Joyce was in command of the....."

"Did you actually hear Admiral Joyce give the order in his own words?" Pritchard demanded. "Were you actually in direct communication with him when he ordered you to fire on the Ultra Meridian Jail."

Huette sat up a little straighter and hardened his features. "Yes, Sir. I was in direct communication with him and he gave me a direct order in his own words to fire on the jail."

"Thank you, Captain. Now let's roll it forward to the battle itself. You must have been scanning the *Echo Omicron* during the entire battle because your ship was firing on the *Echo Omicron*, too. Is that correct?"

"Yes, Sir."

"So you could see through the entire time that the *Echo Omicron* had the Ithium on board," Pritchard went on.

"Yes, Sir," Huette growled.

"Did Admiral Joyce give the order for you to fire on the *Echo Omicron?*"

"Yes, Sir."

"Would I be correct in assuming, Captain, that Admiral Joyce gave orders for the Reserve Wing to destroy the *Echo Omicron,* not to simply ground it, even though it was already damaged, but to actually destroy it—even when he knew that destroying the ship would cause a catastrophic radiological incident that would have cost millions of Confederate lives? Would that be an accurate construction of Admiral Joyce's orders?"

"Yes, Sir," Huette murmured. "That is what he ordered."

"And were all the Stalwart captains involved aware that, by destroying the *Echo Omicron,* they would also have destroyed the very ships that fired on it?"

Huette looked away, clamped his eyes shut, and croaked, "Yes, Sir. We were aware of it."

"Then Davenport and his crew were doing the only reasonable and honorable thing by returning the Stalwarts' fire, defending the *Echo Omicron,* and taking the Ithium as far out of Reserve Wing reach as possible. Wouldn't you agree, Captain? He was carrying out the duties he was sworn to carry out and it was you, your fellow captains, and Admiral Joyce himself who were in violation of Confederate law by risking millions of lives."

Huette nodded, but he didn't answer.

Excited talk broke out in the galley at this admission and the judge banged his gavel. "This is outrageous! Mr. Lane—Sheriff Pritchard—I'll see you and the defendants in my chambers." He banged his gavel again. "Court dismissed."

Chapter 15

"What the hell is going on here?!" Judge Orland demanded when Lane, Pritchard, Davenport, and Healey got to his chambers.

Pritchard only shrugged. "I already told you. The Reserve Wing has been carrying out a campaign to criminalize my clients and paint them as the ones who stole the Ithium when it was Admiral Joyce who did it. Admiral Joyce stole the Ithium from Helios Sanctus....."

"You have no evidence for that," Lane countered.

"No?" Pritchard asked. "The Reserve Wing records still show the Ithium as being housed in secure containment at Helios Sanctus—yet here it is riding around the countryside in one ship after another with everyone fighting over it. Someone took it from Helios Sanctus and I can prove to you that it wasn't any of my clients. Sheriff Davenport and Marshall Healey have both been recorded at their respective jails right up until this attack on Ultra Meridian, so neither of them could be the thief. Whoever stole the Ithium must have used senior Reserve Wing command security codes not just to take the Ithium but to doctor the Reserve Wing records to make it look like the Ithium was still locked up safely at Helios Sanctus. The Reserve Wing—or one contingent of it, at least—cooked up these charges against my clients to cover up the plot to steal the Ithium and potentially release it on Confederate citizens. This interpretation of the events makes a lot more sense than the suggestion that Davenport or whoever tried to steal the Ithium from the Reserve Wing. That's just nonsense and we all know it."

The judge slumped into his seat, covered his eyes, and groaned. "Jesus, Deacon! You can't be serious!"

"If you're horrified by that, you should be even more horrified by what the Reserve Wing has done to these people—especially Davenport. Sheriff Davenport, Marshall Healey, Deputy John Treese, and I were all in Admiral Joyce's office on board the *Rambler* when he admitted to all four of us that he was after Davenport to get the Ithium. Joyce used his authority to remove Davenport and his crew from Sheriff's Service custody so

Joyce could use truth serum on them to get them to tell him where they'd hidden the Ithium. I can call eyewitness medical personnel who will testify that they were with Joyce and the crew when this happened."

The judge turned to Lane. "Do you have anything to say about this, Horace?"

Now it was Lane's turn to gulp. "Um....no, Your Honor. I don't."

The judge waved them all away. "You're all dismissed. I need to think about this before we move forward."

"Are you still thinking about declaring a mistrial?" Lane asked.

The judge snorted. "You'd like that, wouldn't you? I'm inclined to agree with Sheriff Pritchard on this one. We need to hear this evidence. The Reserve Wing has had its own way for too long. The Reserve Wing is the organization who brought these charges and now we're going to hear them. If it goes against the Reserve Wing, then that's the way the wheels of justice grind. We'll reconvene this afternoon to continue hearing the evidence."

Pritchard led Davenport and Healey outside. "Now what?" Davenport asked.

"Just sit tight," Pritchard told him. "This isn't over yet—and that's a good thing. The longer the trial goes on, the more evidence we can present about what Joyce is doing. Keep your noses clean and I'll see you this afternoon."

He escorted them back to the jail, but the deputies definitely treated both sheriffs differently, now that they were dressed this way.

Davenport paused on the threshold and glanced at Healey. They shared a moment of silent communication before the deputies separated them.

Davenport returned to the supply room where he changed out of his suit. He passed his fingertips over the star when he hung his jacket on the hanger. The star was still there. He was still a sheriff. He always had been.

He left his shirt off when he changed back into his jail-issued pants. He bore that brand with pride now. He really was proud of everything he'd done since he left Ultra Meridian. He'd been doing his duty all along.

He went back to his cell and replayed everything Pritchard said in the courtroom. It all sounded so different coming from him. Not even Davenport himself could have articulated exactly what he'd been doing and why.

Pritchard made it all sound so.....so logical. He made it so obvious what Joyce had been up to and everything he'd put in place to cast blame on the crew to cover up his own crimes.

The deputies came to collect Davenport for lunch. He met up with Healey in the corridor and they both grinned at each other on their way to the commissary.

The crew erupted off their chairs and burst into cheers and whistles when Davenport and Healey walked in. The Chorions stood up and clapped. Dice pounded his hand on the table.

Rodeo clamped Davenport on the shoulder. "You're the man, Sir!"

Davenport had to laugh. "Thanks, boys. I couldn't have done it without you."

Everyone settled down at the table to eat their food. "We never should have doubted Pritchard," Bandit remarked. "He really came through."

"He isn't finished," Davenport replied. "He wants to go ahead and really drive the dagger home."

"He's a total badass," Coon agreed. "We couldn't have asked for a better defense counsel."

"It's hard to imagine us really getting off completely," Dice chimed in. "I don't know what I'd do with myself if a court of law actually declared me innocent."

"You aren't innocent, pal," Healey told him. "The term you're looking for is, 'not guilty'."

"Of these charges," Axel corrected. "We won't get into all the other charges you are guilty of."

Dice laughed. "Yeah, I guess you're right. Still, it brings up the question of what I'll do after I get out of this shithole. We don't have a ship anymore.....and we don't have Beauty anymore. I wonder where he is."

"I know what I'm gonna do," Healey replied. "I'm going straight back to Pandora's Needle where I belong. I hope I never leave it again."

"What about you, Sir?" Laub asked. "What do you think you'll do after this?"

"I'm with Marshall Healey. I'll go back to Ultra Meridian." Davenport smiled to himself and his eyes misted over when he remembered the desert, the smell, and the sand. "I was happy there."

"What about you boys?" Healey looked back and forth between the Chorions. "Don't tell me you're going back to Ekol's service. You could be doing so much more."

"Like what?" Rodeo asked. "And don't say anything about joining the Sheriff's Service."

"I wasn't going to say that," Healey replied. "Something tells me you wouldn't quite fit in."

The boys laughed.

"I'd like to go to Chorion Osiris," Jace announced.

Jericho spun around. "You would?"

Jace nodded. "I'd like to meet my father—and any other family I have there. I've never seen Chorion Osiris. I want to see everything I've missed out on."

Jericho brightened up. "I could take you there. I could show you everything."

"Then everyone would find out about you two," Healey pointed out. "Your secret would be out."

Jericho shrugged. "I guess it's about time we came out of the shadows. It would be nice not to have to keep it hidden all the time."

"Fiddler can come with us," Jace went on. "I'd like her to meet my family."

"Now just hold on a second there, son," Emmett interrupted. "You are NOT taking Fiddler to Chorion Osiris. You aren't taking her anywhere."

Jace turned around. "Why not?"

"Because I don't know you from a hole in the ground.....and because Chorion Osiris is one of the most dangerous planets in the galaxy.....and....."

"I wouldn't let anything happen to her," Jace insisted. "I would protect her."

"Forget it, pal," Emmett snarled. "You aren't going anywhere near my little girl."

Jace's face fell. "But....she said......she said she would go with me and see everything. We promised when we left Helios Sanctus."

Dice slammed his big hand on Emmett's shoulder. "It sounds to me like you might want to check with your daughter about what she wants to do and where she wants to go. She's old enough to make up her own mind."

Emmett looked away. "I don't care what she says. She isn't going there."

"Please...." Jace began and his voice quavered. "She's.....she's all I have.....She's the only one who cared enough to get me out of there."

"Take it easy, son," Healey told him. "Fiddler's a big girl. If she wants to go with you, her old man won't be able to stop her."

"Whose side are you on?!" Emmett countered. "You can't ask me to send my daughter to Chorion Osiris! I'll never see her again!"

"I went there and here I am, alive and well," Healey pointed out. "Jace might not know his way around the planet, but Jericho does. Between the two of them, I'd say Fiddler will be as safe as any human can be on that planet."

"That's easy for you to say! She isn't your daughter!" Emmett turned back to Jace. "You have a father and a brother and who knows how many other relatives waiting for you on Chorion Osiris. Fiddler really is all I have. She's all I have left of the Armageddon Core, too. You are NOT taking her away from me—not after all this. Over my dead body you w ill."

"You could come with us," Jericho suggested.

Jace burst into a huge grin. "Yeah! That would be great!"

Emmett compressed his lips, humphed, and looked away. He didn't answer.

"How about you all leave the negotiations until after the trial?" Davenport told them. "We just had our first hearing. This could go on for a while before we actually get out of here. A lot can happen in that time and things might look different then."

Just then, some of the other prisoners entered. They glared at the crew from another table. Their presence dampened the crew's enthusiasm, but nothing could quash their hopes entirely. Things were finally looking up.

Davenport had to keep his own spirits in check. He didn't want to let himself get carried away with thoughts and plans for a future he didn't even know he had.

It sure was nice to think about, though. He just had to get out of jail and then the world would be his again.

Chapter 16

Davenport, Healey, and Pritchard stood up behind the defense table when Judge Orland resumed his seat behind the bench. He sat down and said, "Call your next witness, Mr. Lane."

"The prosecution calls Captain Lewis Flynn of the Reserve Wing Stalwart *Oriole.*"

Davenport didn't recognize the captain. He was as young as Huette. Davenport was starting to recognize a pattern here. Pritchard must have been right about Joyce grooming these captains and maneuvering them into positions where he'd be able to manipulate and use them later.

Captain Flynn testified about the battle between Davenport's uprising that destroyed Terminus Anathema, Davenport taking over Calyx Elkanon's empire, and then joining forces with Ekol Thaine in a massive assault against the Reserve Wing.

This same captain also testified about Dice, Jace, and Fiddler breaking out of Helios Sanctus and joining Davenport's criminal army. Lane presented log records from the *Oriole* showing that Calyx's and Ekol's troops both took orders from Davenport during the prison uprising and the battle that ensued from it.

Flynn fidgeted visibly when Pritchard stood up. "You were assigned to the *Oriole* during this campaign to put down the unrest at Terminus Anathema, Captain, but you were also present on the Nitrol, *Permian,* when it made an unscheduled side trip to the Pegasus Mine, weren't you?" Pritchard asked.

"Yes, Sir," Flynn replied.

"You went there in company with Admiral Joyce to track down Emmett Duncan, Sabrina Lyons, and four young women identified as Flack, Fizzle, Friend, and Frost. Am I right?"

"Yes, Sir."

Pritchard turned to address the court. "Your Honor, scanner and log records from the *Oriole* show that the four young women in question displayed genetic anomalies characteristic of cloning. In fact, orders from Admiral Joyce to you, Captain Flynn, state unequivocally that these four young women were clones of the defendant Kay Hahn, known as Fiddler, that she was captured illegally from her father's custody when she was a toddler, held at Helios Sanctus against her will, and cloned to produce not just these four young women, but a whole series of identical clones. Isn't that true, Captain? Didn't you receive these records from Admiral Joyce when he commandeered the *Oriole* to go after these defendants?"

Flynn sat up as straight as he could, but he couldn't keep the strain out of his voice when he said, "Yes, Sir. I did."

"And you were present at the Pegasus Mine when Admiral Joyce shot Friend in the head, gave orders to his soldiers to shoot Flack, Frost, and Fizzle, and then Admiral Joyce threatened to shoot Emmett Duncan and Sabrina Lyons, didn't he?"

Flynn mumbled under his breath, "Yes, Sir."

"I'm glad you admit it because scanner records from the Nitrol *Permian* recorded the events of the four clones' deaths. Could you explain to the court why Admiral Joyce did all this? Why did Admiral Joyce want you and the *Oriole* crew to accompany him to the Pegasus Mine to track these people down? We would all really like to know."

Dead silence fell over the court and Davenport's spirits soared again. He couldn't wait to hear this.

"Sheriff Pritchard asked you a question, Captain," Judge Orland snapped. "You're under oath here, Captain. Answer the question."

Captain Flynn cleared his throat with an effort and finally blurted out, "He went there to retrieve a cartridge of Ziprothil that he and Colonel Lillian Casey also stole from Helios Sanctus. Friend stashed the Ziprothil somewhere at Ultra Meridian, and when Joyce found out that she had it, he commandeered the *Oriole* to get the Ziprothil back. He planned to combine it with the Ithium to make it even more destructive. Friend and the others went on the run all over the galaxy trying to keep the Ziprothil out of Joyce's hands.....and we caught up with them at the Pegasus Mine." He glanced once toward the defendants and looked away.

The judge opened his mouth to say something—maybe to interrupt the trial—but Pritchard launched right back in. "You were also present on the *Rambler* when Admiral Joyce used truth serum, first on Wolf and then on Dice, weren't you? You helped to restrain and subdue these prisoners so Joyce could subject them to an illegal medical procedure and then to perform electroshock on Wolf. Weren't you? You witnessed these crimes yourself, didn't you?"

"Yes, Sir," Flynn choked. "I was there."

"The *Oriole* was also among a contingent of Reserve Wing Stalwarts to respond to the destruction at Helios Sanctus," Pritchard went on. "You received orders to track down Fiddler, Dice, and Jace and those orders contained records of their imprisonment at Helios Sanctus. Feel free to stop me or correct me if I'm getting any of this wrong, Captain."

Flynn refused to look up. "You aren't wrong. The records did contain all that information."

"Your Honor, these orders and records have been included in the evidence for the defense. These records indicate that, after administering truth serum to Dice to keep him subdued, Colonel Lilian Casey forcibly abducted Kay Hahn from Ultra Meridian for a second time. Casey took Fiddler and Dice to Helios Sanctus where the Reserve Wing once again attempted to clone Fiddler in violation of Confederate law. The Chorion known as Jace was also abducted from his family as a toddler and held at Helios Sanctus against his will for decades. Wouldn't you agree, Captain, that considering how these three people were captured and held by force, they would have been within their rights as Confederate citizens to leave Helios Sanctus whenever they wished? The Reserve Wing threatened their lives to stop them from leaving, so Jace, Fiddler, and Dice retaliating with deadly force would be considered self-defense according to Confederate law. Wouldn't you agree?"

Flynn nodded down into his lap.

Pritchard prepared to launch into another line of interrogation, but this time, the judge interrupted him instead of the other way around. "I've heard enough of this, gentlemen. Mr. Lane—Sheriff—bring your clients into my chambers—now!"

The courtroom erupted with everyone talking at once—all except the defendants. They sat in a row staring at Pritchard, the judge, and Captain Flynn. He kept his head down when he left the stand and disappeared into the crowd, but he stayed on the prosecution side of the courtroom.

Davenport was having trouble thinking straight, too. All of Pritchard's arguments got mixed up in Davenport's mind.

Pritchard woke Davenport from his trance by touching his elbow. "Come on. Let's go see what the judge has to say."

He led Davenport and Healey back to the judge's chambers. Lane looked pale and kept his hands in his pockets.

"This is just nuts!" the judge kept muttering to himself. "I've never heard anything like this! Do you dispute any of this evidence, Lane? Oh, what the hell am I saying? How can you when it's all right there in the record?"

"We're only getting started, Your Honor," Pritchard cut in.

The judge shot him a deadly look. "You can put a cap on it, Sheriff. You've said enough for one day. I'm going back out there to dismiss all the charges and reinstate Sheriff Davenport and Marshall Healey. If you have anything to say, Lane, you better say it right now."

Before any of them could speak, the door slammed open and Ace Bolander burst in. "Excuse me, Boss—Your Honor—but you have to see this! We just found it!"

"What's going on, Ace?" Pritchard asked.

Bolander held up a computer transponder card. "We found this in Emmett Duncan's personal effects. He had it on him when he booked into the jail."

"What is it?" Judge Orland asked.

"Just look." Bolander went over to the judge's desk and plugged the card into the judge's computer. "It's all the records from Friend's computers on Ultra Meridian. She tracked the Ithium and the Ziprothil from the moment they left Helios Sanctus. She recorded all the ship movements and log records for every ship involved. It's all here. It corroborates everything we know about Davenport's mission and everyone who has been helping him and everyone who has been hunting him down."

The judge stared at his computer screen for a minute and then threw up his hands. "That settles it. Let's go. Get back out to the courtroom. This trial is over."

He shot to his feet and stormed out of the room before anyone could keep up with him. He was already on the bench by the time Pritchard, Davenport, Healey, and Lane returned.

The judge didn't even wait for the bailiff to tell everyone to stand up and sit down. The defendants didn't even get a chance to get out of their seats before the judge banged his gavel.

"In light of the evidence offered thus far and additional evidence that has just been presented, it is the decision of this court that Sheriff Davenport, Marshall Healey, and their co-defendants were acting within the mandate of Confederate law in the execution of law enforcement duties. It is the finding of this court that these defendants were acting in the best interest and for the protection of the entire Confederacy. I am therefore dismissing all charges with prejudice. You are all free to go with the gratitude of the court and the Confederacy. I am also issuing an arrest warrant for Admiral Killian Joyce and all the officers of his contingent who refuse to cooperate with bringing Joyce and his accomplices to justice. Court is adjourned."

The courtroom exploded. Bandit, Laub, and Alla all shot out of their chairs, raised their arms in triumph, and whooped. Dice and Lyons hugged each other.

Davenport turned to Healey. Both of them grinned from ear to ear and then they both burst out laughing when they hugged each other. It was over.

Davenport couldn't contain the exhilaration flooding through him. He had to fight back tears. He never dared to dream this day would come.

He got seriously emotional when he held out his hand to Pritchard. Davenport couldn't even speak to thank Pritchard. Thanking him seemed so pathetic compared to this.

Pritchard shook Davenport's hand and smiled, but he turned away too soon. He had to raise his voice to make himself heard over the noise of all the defendants talking at once. "Come outside, all of you! Come on! Take it out in the hall!"

He steered everyone out of the courtroom. Davenport's blood ran cold when Pritchard guided the crew back toward the Atlas Arcane Jail.

Davenport pulled up short at the doorway leading from the courtroom to the jail. "What are we doing here? We're free to go. The judge said so."

"You are free," Pritchard replied. "Just come in here. I need to talk to you."

"What for?" Dice demanded.

"I would be able to tell you if you come in here. I wouldn't have just stuck my neck out to get you released if it wasn't important. Now come inside."

He clipped off the words in a short, sharp order that left no room for anyone to question. He held the door open, but the crew still held back. No one crossed the threshold until Davenport did it first.

Pritchard led the way back to the conference room and shut the door behind Healey who entered last.

"What's this all about, Sheriff?" Rodeo asked. "Why don't you want us to leave?"

"We just got the word," Pritchard replied. "Joyce is going on the run. He has the Ithium, the Ziprothil, and the chip to detonate them. He's sent out an ultimatum to the Confederacy. He plans to escape into Sacron Enigma, set up his own empire, and if anyone tries to stop him, he'll blow all three components."

"That son of a bitch!" Lyons hissed.

"And you're just gonna let him get away with this?" Davenport fired back. "After everything we've done, the Confederate Corps and the Sheriff's Service are just going to sit back and do nothing?"

"I never said that," Pritchard replied. "That's why I'm here. I'm asking you to finish what you started, go through the processing protocol to get yourselves released from the jail, and then come back on board to help us hunt him down. This is your chance to pay him back for everything he's done to you. Most of the Reserve Wing is still loyal and they all want to put down these rogue elements that have tarnished their reputation. The Sheriff's Service, the Reserve Wing, and the Confederate Corps are all going after Joyce, but we have to be careful. If we corner him too soon or in the wrong place, he'll release his weapon."

"So what are you going to do?" Coon asked. "What do you want *us* to do?"

"That's what I'm telling you. I want you to go back to the Atlas Arcane Jail, go through the whole release protocol, and get yourselves returned to duty. Once you do that, I'll take you all on board the *Vindicator* and fly you out to Vorax Summa to bring in Joyce."

"Vorax Summa!" Fiddler interrupted. "Colonel Casey said they'd diverted to the Achilles Inferno. What is Joyce doing back at Vorax Summa?"

"Who knows why he's doing any of this and who cares?" Pritchard asked. "Just go through the protocols and I'll explain everything once you get released. It shouldn't take more than an hour or two."

Davenport and his crew exchanged glances. He didn't want to wait an hour or two and he saw in the faces around him that his friends didn't want to, either.

Davenport trusted Pritchard, though. Pritchard thought this was the best course and he'd earned the crew's trust.

"We'll do it your way, Sheriff," Davenport replied.

"No one is gonna mess with you people ever again," Pritchard told him. "You can take that to the bank. Go change your clothes and I'll meet you outside. We have work to do."

Chapter 17

Davenport sat in his cell for almost an hour and a half. He didn't think. He just stared at the wall. If he hadn't been wearing his suit and star, he would have doubted whether the last hearing of his trial really happened.

He was going after Admiral Joyce, but this time, he had the whole might of the Confederate Corps backing him up. No one was hunting Davenport and his crew down. Now he was the one doing the hunting.

When the deputies finally came to get him, they didn't give him back the pants he'd been wearing when he booked into the jail. He kept his suit on and met his crew outside.

Fiddler wore the Reserve Wing maintenance jumpsuit she'd been wearing after she escaped from Helios Sanctus. Jace was back in his tan slacks and black T-shirt. Emmett, Lyons, and the Chorions all had on their usual clothes.

Jericho had kept his suit on, too. Dice kept his jail-issued prisoner's uniform. They fit him better than the torn clothes he'd been wearing since he escaped from Helios Sanctus.

The deputies that released the crew left them standing in the hangar where Pritchard had first landed. He wasn't here now. He didn't come to meet the crew the way he said he would.

"Now what do we do?" Axel asked.

"I could steal a ship," Jericho suggested.

"Don't steal anything!" Healey snapped. "We just got out of jail, for Christ's sake! Don't do anything illegal—not when Davenport and I are standing right here."

Some of the others laughed, but just then, two more ships floated into the hangar and touched down in front of the crew. Ace Bolander and Jeremy Yarborough stepped out and approached the crew. "The boss wants us to take you out to the *Vindicator,*" Yarborough informed them.

"He said he would meet us here," Davenport pointed out.

"Something came up." Bolander waved toward his vessel. "Let's go. He wants to see you right away."

Davenport, Healey, Emmett, Dice, Lyons, and Fiddler went with Bolander. The Chorions went with Yarborough.

They bucked into their seats and took off into space. It sure felt strange to Davenport to fly around without anyone shooting at him. He kept waiting for gunfire to strike the ship, but it didn't.

Bolander and Yarborough flew side by side. Healey leaned toward the side window to gaze at Pandora's Needle soaring past. "You'll be back there soon, Marshall," Bolander called over his shoulder.

"I sure hope you're right," Healey murmured.

"Are you kidding me?" Bolander countered. "They can't run the place without you. The Needle has been a mess since you left. They can't wait to get you back."

Healey didn't answer. He kept watching the satellite until Bolander flew past it and Pandora's Needle disappeared behind the ship.

Healey turned back to face front and sighed. Davenport knew how he felt, but they didn't have time to discuss it before both deputies docked with the *Vindicator*. "The boss is upstairs on the bridge," Bolander told the crew. "He said he wants to see you as soon as you get on board."

"You mean.....all of us?" Emmett asked.

"Yes, all of you," Bolander replied. "You're all going, so he wants to see all of you."

"Going where?" Fiddler asked.

"To get Joyce, of course." Bolander walked past them. "You can ask the boss everything. He'll explain what he wants you to do."

Davenport didn't know what to think, but he definitely wanted to get Joyce and Pritchard was the man to help the crew get there.

The two parties met up on the *Vindicator's* deck. The rest of the Wide Patrol was there, too, and everybody went up to the bridge where they found Pritchard and Treese working on the controls as usual.

"Oh, good, you're finally here," Pritchard called over his shoulder.

"What's going on, Sheriff?" Rodeo asked. "Why the big secret about what we're doing?"

"It's only a secret from the enemy and they'll find out soon enough anyway. Come on over and take a look."

He stepped back from his controls and waved at them. The crew gathered around to see what he was showing them.

"The Reserve Wing has Joyce blockaded at Vorax Summa," Pritchard announced.

"Isn't that exactly what we don't want?" Healey asked.

"I don't call the shots when it comes to the Reserve Wing," Pritchard replied. "Someone made the decision to contain Joyce here rather than let him run off to Sacron Enigma where it would be a thousand times harder to send out forces to track and stop him—and I don't say they're wrong. At least we know where he is."

"The Reserve Wing sure is taking this seriously—now that they know about it," Lyons pointed out. "They must have fifty Stalwarts surrounding the planet."

"I think the more accurate term is that they're taking it personally," Treese interjected. "Joyce went to a lot of trouble to make sure he controlled his own contingent of the Reserve Wing with no one in any position with enough authority to question him. He isolated his ships and crews from everyone else so no one found out until now."

"The point is that he's still threatening to unleash this weapon of his," Pritchard went on. "It isn't enough that he can't get away to take it somewhere else. We need to get down on the planet and stop him from releasing it here, but if we do that, he'll see us trying to get down on the planet and he will release it."

"Which is where you badasses come in," Bolander chimed in from the back.

Davenport whipped around to stare at him. Davenport never expected one of the Wide Patrol to call him a badass. Jobs that required badasses hired the Wide Patrol, not Mace Davenport from Ultra Meridian.

The rest of the crew exchanged glances, too, so Davenport wasn't the only one.

None of the Wide Patrol noticed. Pritchard pointed to the display. "The rogue Reserve Wing vessels that are still supporting Joyce have set up a blockade around the planet to stop anyone from getting near the place."

"He shouldn't need that if he has the weapon," Fiddler pointed out. "His threat of wiping us all out should be enough to stop anyone from coming near the place."

"It's enough for him, but it isn't enough for the dopes that have been standing by him all this time—and the dopes that are still so stupid that they continue to stand by him even now that he's been discredited. The blockade isn't there to stop anyone from apprehending Joyce. The blockade is there to stop anyone from apprehending all his idiot toadies from going straight to jail where they belong."

Pritchard traced the line of ships from one side of Vorax Suma to the other.

"Davenport, we need you to call in Ekol's and Calyx's people to engage with these rogues. Lyons will get in touch with Ignus about bringing all her father's people out to join the party. Once they do, the battle should distract everyone while we make a run to the planet to drop you all off. Then you can go after Joyce. He'll be too preoccupied with the battle and his threat to see you sneaking up on him."

Davenport raised his eyebrows. "If we do that....." He trailed off. He didn't want to say it in front of all these dedicated lawmen.

"What he means is," Dice interjected, "if we go down there, the gloves will be off. We won't be going down there to apprehend anybody. We'll be going down there and he won't be coming back to stand trial. It will be curtains for Joyce even if we have to break a few laws to do it."

"The good news is that no one will be able to see what you do or how you do it," Pritchard pointed out. "The planet is a wilderness except for whatever infrastructure Joyce has built there. He sure as hell doesn't have any data feeds showing the rest of the Confederacy what he's up to. Once you go down there, what you do will be between you and Joyce—no one else. No one will ever find out what you do down there—unless you fail and he really does set off this weapon."

"Then we're going," Rodeo replied. "That's all there is to it."

Pritchard smiled at him. "I had a feeling you would say that. Now here's the deal. You all need to load up with Ace here. The trip down to the planet will be kinda cramped because we need to transport all you freaks on a ship that's shielded to conceal your life signs. You take this, Davenport." Pritchard handed Davenport a small metal square. "It's a homing beacon that will allow you to track the Ithium. It will lead you straight to Joyce."

Davenport studied the device in his hand. It had a dial on the top with a magnetic compass needle. The needle swiveled in all directions without pointing at anything.

"The Patrol and I will fly you out to the front line," Pritchard went on. "You can contact your friends on the way. Once we get there, we'll dock with the *Vigilante*. She's carrying the ship that will take you to the surface. Then we'll just wait for the shit to hit the fan and away you go. Any questions?"

"Where can we get some weapons?" Axel asked.

"The *Vigilante* will have all of that on board. You can supply there." Pritchard looked around at the group. "Anybody else?"

No one else said anything. It all looked so straightforward—so legitimate.

Davenport had to keep double-checking himself to make sure he wasn't imagining things. He was about to go on a Reserve Wing mission with the whole Reserve Wing backing him up.

"You can all go kick back in your cabins until we get to the front line," Pritchard went on. "All except you, Sheriff—and you, Lyons. You can get on the horn to your friends and call them in to engage with the rogues."

Chapter 18

Davenport relayed Pritchard's message to Ekol Thaine. It took a while for Davenport to get in touch with Calyx's old forces. They'd gone completely off the map despite Davenport's order for Calyx's people to fall under Ekol's banner.

Davenport finally got hold of the ship he'd left under Kuman's control. Duni answered Davenport's hail.

Davenport frowned when he saw Duni on the screen. "Where's Kuman?"

"We had a reshuffle, so he's on another ship," Duni replied. "I'm in command of this one with another pilot."

Davenport scowled even more deeply. "What the hell is going on out there? Why aren't you under Ekol's authority anymore?"

Duni made a face. "It's complicated."

"So who's in charge of Calyx's people now?" Davenport asked. "I need to talk to someone with some pull with everyone."

"You can talk to me," Duni replied. "If you need something from us, all you have to do is ask."

"You?!" Davenport exclaimed. "You're in charge now?"

Duni laughed. "You know me. I can be a very resourceful guy. What do you need?"

Davenport explained Pritchard's idea.

"So Ekol is gonna be there?" Duni asked. "That's no good."

"What are you talking about?" Davenport demanded. "Why all this hostility between your people and Ekol? You were fighting together to defeat the Reserve Wing when I left."

"That was before," Duni returned a little too shortly. "Him being there will make it harder to convince anyone to come out and help in any campaign he's taking part in."

"Damn," Davenport exclaimed. "That sounds bad."

"Unless you can arrange for us to be on the opposite side of the battle from his forces," Duni went on. "Maybe you could put him on one side of the battle, the Reserve Wing in the middle, and us on the other side of the Reserve Wing. That might work—as long as we aren't anywhere close enough that his forces could attack us."

"What about Rizarth Hudan's people?" Davenport asked. "Are you cool with fighting alongside them?"

"Oh, sure," Duni replied. "They're fine."

"Are you ever gonna tell me what Ekol did to piss you off so badly?"

Duni grimaced again. "Let's just say I don't think he's the same Ekol you think he is. You better watch him, Davenport. He's likely to turn on anyone—even the people he supposedly cares about and respects."

"That's not good at all," Davenport replied.

"No, it isn't. So....do you think you can work it so we aren't near each other?"

"That shouldn't be too much of a problem. I don't know who will be running things once you get here, but maybe no one will be. Maybe, once you show up, you can just go where you want to go and do what you want to do with whoever you do it with."

"Someone better keep the forces separate," Duni insisted. "If they don't, my forces and Ekol's might wind up shooting at each other instead of the Reserve Wing."

Davenport pretended not to notice Duni calling Calyx Elkanon's old force his own. Things must have changed radically while Davenport had been in jail.

Then again, they would have to change radically if Ekol Thaine started turning on his own people. Davenport would have to tell the Chorion Team about that.

"Anyway," Davenport told Duni, "Pritchard just wants to create as much distraction as possible. It doesn't matter if you and Ekol start shooting at each other. It will serve the same purpose in the end."

Duni raised his eyebrows. "Pritchard—from the Wide Patrol? Is he the one organizing all this?"

"I don't know if he's actually organizing it, but he's the one who's handling our end of things. Why?" Davenport asked. "Do you know him?"

"The Patrol gets around, so yeah, I've dealt with him before."

Davenport glanced over his shoulder, but neither Pritchard nor Treese were on the bridge. They'd made themselves scarce so Davenport could talk in private.

Duni read his mind. "They're good people. You can trust them."

"I'm getting that," Davenport replied.

"If Pritchard is the one doing this, then I'm in," Duni went on. "We'll be there, and if Ekol gets in the way, it will be his funeral."

Davenport hung up and went downstairs to see his crew. They were back in the galley and the rest of the Wide Patrol was in there, too—except for Pritchard and Treese. Davenport didn't know where the hell those two were—and he didn't want to know.

Fiddler and Lyons had changed back into their regular clothes. Fiddler had somehow found a pair of leather pants, brown shirt, and a leather vest that fit her. Now Davenport knew for certain the Pritchard did bring these clothes just for her.

Healey had changed out of his suit, too. Now he wore a pair of dark brown jeans, boots, a black shirt, and a sport jacket with his star pinned to the front.

Davenport also spotted Healey's sidearms holstered at his belt. He was back in business.

Someone had dressed up Jericho in some regular clothes, too. They'd found him a pair of tan slacks, polished shoes, and a black T-shirt like Jace's.

They'd also cleaned up his hair. The twins looked much more similar now. Davenport had a hard time telling them apart. They looked more like copies of each other.

Lyons was back in a pair of black pants, black boots, and a tight white T-shirt with a black leather jacket over it. Both women wore their hair down and loose.

"You did look nice in that dress," Jace told her.

"Dress?!" Emmett howled. "She wore a dress?"

Jace nodded. "All the time."

Fiddler grimaced at him. "I hope you'll cherish that memory because you aren't likely to see me like that again—ever."

Jace's face fell. "But.....you looked beautiful like that."

"She.....wore a dress?!" Alla pointed at Fiddler and burst into howls of laughter. "I would so pay to see that."

"I saw it," Dice interjected.

Fiddler narrowed her eyes at him. "And you better take that secret to your grave if you know what's good for you."

He chuckled and pretended to shut her eyes in bliss. "Every time you give me a hard time, I'll just float away into fantasy land and remember you like that."

The Chorions fell over themselves laughing. "What did she look like, Dice?" Laub asked. "Describe her."

"Don't you dare!" Fiddler snapped.

"I can describe her," Jace began. "She was delicate and feminine and swirly and....."

"Stop!" Fiddler roared. "Don't say another word!"

"Swirly?!" Bandit repeated. "She was swirly?!"

"Like a beautiful, delicate flower swaying in the sunshine," Jace replied and everyone burst out laughing.

Fiddler turned bright red. "I only wore it because they made me. I woke up at Helios Sanctus wearing it and they never gave me any other clothes the whole time I was there—except......" She trailed off.

"Except what?" Jace asked. "You were always wearing that dress when I saw you."

"Never mind," she countered. "If any of you teases me about that dress, I can just remind you of the times when I saw you all wearing suits." She cracked a grin that kept getting wider and wider. "I even remember *you* wearing a suit, Dice. Now that is one for the record books."

A hush fell over the group. "Okay, you might have us on that one," Axel replied. "At least no one else saw."

"I liked that suit," Jericho remarked. "I'd like to wear it all the time."

"NO!!" all the Chorions yelled at once.

"Don't start doing that," Laub told him. "We couldn't stand that."

"Why?" Jericho asked. "I liked it."

"What did you wear when you went out doing jobs off the planet?" Rodeo asked. "Don't tell me you wore the same old clothes you wore at home."

Jericho shrugged. "I stole the clothes of whoever happened along—as long as it wasn't a Confederate Corps uniform. I switched around all the time depending on where I was and what job I was doing. I tried to blend in."

"How did that work out for you?" Coon asked.

The others laughed, and just then, Breeze called over from the galley. He'd been rifling the cabinets while the others talked.

"Hey, look what I found!" He held up a package of Asawana Dragonturtle Bombs. "Who wants to bet on the outcome?"

Bolander strode over to him and snatched the package out of Breeze's hands. "Don't touch that, kid. You'll hurt yourself."

"Aw, come on, Ace!" Breeze countered. "Just one!"

Bolander snorted in his face. "Just one? You—just one? You couldn't eat just one. Don't give me that shit—just one."

"Give him one," Yarborough called over from the couch. "What the hell else do we have to do on the way out to the battle?"

"I won't hurt myself," Breeze insisted. "I swear. Come on, Ace! You know you want to play."

"What are they?" Jace asked.

"*You* definitely aren't having one," Rodeo told him. "You'd blow your head off."

Jace's eyes widened. "Really?"

"I'll put five on Breeze," DeRosa called out. "Who'll take odds on Ace?"

"I ain't playing against *him!*" Bolander countered. "Are you insane? I don't have a death wish."

"I'll play him," Jericho interjected.

The table exploded in laughter and excited talk. "Hell, yeah!" Laub cheered and started banging his fists on the table and chanting, "Breeze! Breeze! Breeze! Breeze!"

The rest of the Chorions did, too, until DeRosa bellowed. "SHUT UP!!"

The crew fell silent except for a few snickers.

"You have to promise not to copy yourself," Breeze told Jericho. "It's one on one. No one else."

"I'm in, too," Dice piped up.

"Oh, hell no!" Jericho countered. "We can't play against you! That's no fair! You're too big."

"You think so?" Dice returned. "Are you too scared to go against a real man?"

"I want to play, too," Healey cut in.

"Holy shit!" Yarborough crowed. "This is gonna be crazy."

"I want to play," Wommack added in her soft voice. "I like Dragonturtles."

Everyone spun around to stare at her. "You!" Lyons exclaimed. "They'll flatten you."

"She'll flatten all her competition, you mean," Bolander told her. "None of you stand a chance against her.....except maybe Breeze."

"Breeze! Breeze! Breeze! Breeze!" Laub chanted and the other Chorions joined in.

"What do the Dragonturtles do?" Jace asked again.

"Let's just say they don't call them bombs for nothing," Jericho replied.

Bolander brought the package over to the table. "Clear off, scumbags. Make way."

Everyone stood up and backed off while Breeze, Dice, Jericho, Wommack, and Healey sat down facing each other. Snickers passed back and forth around the room. Yarborough and Swygert both turned around on their couches to watch.

"Kick their asses, Wommack," DeRosa called.

"I'll give you ten on Marshall Healey," Davenport offered.

The Chorions started betting on their favorites and Lyons bet on Dice.

Bolander tore open the package with great ceremony and placed one bomb in front of each person. "No one touches their bomb until I give the word," he ordered. "Understand? Any cheating or false starts will result in instant disqualification."

"That means you, Breeze," Rodeo called. "Don't fall over and accidentally inhale it up your nose."

Davenport couldn't hold back laughter. "You got this, Marshall."

"Lucy is gonna put you all in the ground," Swygert growled.

Bolander got around to the other side of the table and took a step back. Jericho narrowed his eyes at his opponents. Wommack smiled at everyone like this was the best day of her life.

"Okay, go," Bolander told them.

The competitors picked up their bombs, put them in their mouths, and started chewing. The rest of the crew held their breaths watching and waiting for something to happen.

Nothing did happen for a second until Wommack started shaking all over. She convulsed in her seat and her chin fell on her chest. Her hair spilled over her eyes and then growled through gritted teeth.

Just as quickly, the episode passed, she shook it off, and sat up to look around at the group.

The effects had barely worn off before Dice hurtled out of his chair, gave a ground-shaking roar, and exploded to three times his size.

He swelled in a split second, threw out his arms, and his horns erupted out of his skull, but he shrank back to his normal size just as fast.

Before any of them could move, Breeze shot out of his seat. Davenport didn't see what effect the bomb had on him. He just rocketed across the room without seeming to do anything.

He collided with Dice's legs and the impact knocked them both to the ground. Dice's bulk fell across the table and shattered it with them in the middle.

A piece of flying debris hit Healey's chair and toppled him over backward. He somersaulted toward the door, which was lucky. If he'd fallen forward, he could have gotten tangled up with Breeze and Dice.

The Chorion Team erupted in laughter and the rest of the Wide Patrol joined in. Wommack managed to jump out of her chair and back away in time to avoid the mayhem.

Dice tumbled out of the wreckage spitting curses and hauled himself to his feet. Breeze took longer. He floundered among the shattered boards of the table, accidentally kicked one of them, and it flew across the room.

Bolander barely ducked in time to avoid getting the stick impaled through his head before the board's splintered end stabbed into the wall right next to the door—right next to Pritchard who just happened to walk in right at that moment.

Chapter 19

The laughter died when everyone saw Pritchard scowling at the proceedings.

Healey was just dusting himself off. Jericho sat in his chair in exactly the same position he'd been sitting during the game. He hadn't moved even once.

"What the hell is going on?" Pritchard demanded.

No one answered. Breeze kept crashing around in a pile of broken wood on the floor.

Pritchard went over to Bolander, took the package of Dragonturtle Bombs out of his hand, read the label, frowned, and humphed under his breath before he handed them back.

Breeze finally managed to stand up, but he still tripped over his own feet and some of the debris before he straightened himself out. The Chorions stifled laughter at his antics.

"Are you finished, son?" Pritchard asked.

Breeze bit back a grin. "I can be if you want me to be, Sir."

"You deputies get out on patrol," Pritchard ordered. "Playtime is over."

"Until we get to the battle, you mean," Swygert corrected. "Then it will be playtime all over again."

Pritchard raised his eyebrows at the package in Bolander's hand. "You might want to get rid of those. The whole Confederacy is riding on this crew. We don't want them impaired when the shit goes down."

"Who's impaired?" Dice asked. "It looks like we're all working just fine."

Pritchard made a face. "Do me a favor and don't go on a rampage on Vorax Suma. You're supposed to be sneaking up on Joyce. He would see you coming a mile away." He turned back to the Patrol. "Get out there and deploy. We're coming up on the front line."

The Patrol left and Bolander took the DragonTurtle Bombs with him. "Damn it," Breeze muttered. "He never lets us have any fun."

"When the war is over and Joyce is dead, you can eat as many as you want." Rodeo came over and picked up one of the broken sticks from the table. "It's too bad this table wasn't made of metal. Then you could fix it, Coon. I don't like damaging the sheriff's property and leaving a mess."

"I'll fix it." Jace grabbed the boards, started working on them, and then made a dozen of his copies to help him.

Davenport went over to the galley cupboards and found himself a package of Universal Staples. He started eating it when Healey came over to him. "Is something on your mind?" Healey asked.

Davenport raised his eyebrows and then shrugged that away. "I just talked to one of my people in Calyx's fleet. He says Ekol Thaine is doing some weird shit out on the fringes."

"When has Ekol not done weird shit out on the fringes?" Healey asked.

"No, I mean like really weird shit that is totally out of character—like turning on people he once considered loyal. It's not good."

"Maybe everything's in disarray because of all this chaos," Healey suggested.

"Maybe." Davenport took another bite of his food. He would have liked to say more, but then he noticed Rodeo standing across the room.

Rodeo wasn't looking at them. Of course not. He had his head turned with one ear pointed in Davenport's direction.

Davenport took another bite of his food to stop himself from saying anything else. He'd just been thinking he ought to tell the Chorion Team about Duni's warning, but Davenport didn't want to do it here. He didn't want to spoil this one moment of relaxation and camaraderie among the crew.

Healey must have noticed Rodeo listening, too, because Healey didn't say anything else about it. Jace finished fixing the table and the crew sat down again.

They went back to talking and joking. Jericho still didn't show any sign that the Dragonturtle Bomb affected him at all.

Breeze turned to him. "How do you do it? How did you take that bomb so well? Nothing happened."

"Nothing happened to Marshall Healey, either," Laub pointed out.

"Breeze happened to Marshall Healey," Bandit corrected and the others laughed.

Breeze turned back to Jericho. "Really. How did you do it?"

Jericho only shrugged. "I have my ways."

"Tell me," Breeze urged. "I'm dying of curiosity."

"I don't think so," Jericho replied.

"Aw, come on, man!" Breeze pleaded. "I won't be able to stop thinking about it if you don't tell me."

Jericho only muttered, "Be careful what you wish for."

"Please?" Breeze begged. "I'll give you anything you ask for. I'll clean your room for a week. Anything! Please tell me. I'm dying over here."

"Don't tell him," Coon teased. "Make him suffer."

"I'll clean your room for a month," Breeze offered. "I'll be your slave for life. Just tell me. Please."

"How *did* you do it?" Jace asked.

"All right, you win," Jericho replied. "But in exchange, you have to clean up the mess. Understand?"

Breeze nodded fast. "Of course. Anything."

"Fine," Jericho replied. "Here goes."

He produced one copy of himself that stood up and crossed the room. The copy walked back and forth studying the galley until he selected one particular place in the corner. Then the copy turned around and faced the room.

"That's it?!" Breeze exclaimed. "What's so special about that?"

At that moment, the copy exploded. Blood, gore, brain, entrails, and shattered bone splattered the walls and floor.

The copy had chosen a spot in the room where he would be as far from the furniture and the rest of the crew as possible. He chose a spot where he would make the least mess.

"Ugh!" Lyons growled. "I'm glad I don't have to clean that up."

"Are you satisfied now?" Jericho asked. "Now you know."

Breeze gawked at the mess in the corner and then at Jericho. "You better get busy," Rodeo told Breeze. "You need to have this place cleaned up before Sheriff Pritchard comes back."

Breeze shut his mouth with difficulty, stood up, and crossed to the galley cupboards. He opened the broom closet at the far end, took out a mop, and got to work.

"And don't slip in it!" Axel called over.

Breeze bowed his head and started mopping up the blood. "You should have told me ahead of time," Alla said to Jericho. "I could have taken him out for you."

"Breeze wanted to know," Jericho replied. "Besides, I agreed not to use my copies in the game....and Breeze needed something to do. He said he'd be my slave for life....so....."

The other Chorions laughed. Davenport took that opportunity to leave the room, but he had nowhere else to go but up to his cabin.

He wanted to change out of his suit. He didn't expect much from Pritchard's collection, but Davenport should have known better.

He found another set of clothes laid out for him on the bed. Pritchard had brought another pair of leather pants, a brown button-up shirt, a new leather vest, and a pair of steel-toed boots exactly like the ones Davenport always used to wear at Ultra Meridian.

He slipped out of his suit, put on the new clothes, pinned on his new star, and looked at himself in the mirror.

Whatever drug the medic at the Atlas Arcane Jail gave him had reduced the swelling and bruising in Davenport's face. He still had a scab on his lip, but his lip was nowhere near as swollen as it had been.

He looked the same way he remembered from before all of this craziness got started. He looked like the same person on the outside, but he wasn't the same person.

He didn't know who or what he had changed into. Maybe he would just have to get through this and find out on the other side. Maybe he wouldn't find out until he started the next phase of his life.

His life would always be divided into three periods—the time before he found the Ithium, the time when he dealt with Joyce and this plot, and the time after he finished dealing with Joyce and this plot.

If Davenport ever got back to Ultra Meridian—if his life ever went back to normal—then he would be able to think about and explore what this new person was—this person he'd changed into as a result of this experience.

He couldn't define it now. He only knew he wasn't the same person. He looked the same on the outside, but inside, he'd changed forever. He just didn't know how.

Maybe he didn't change. Maybe that was the point. Maybe the change was that he'd only become a purer, truer version of himself. Maybe he'd always been this—this sheriff to the marrow of his bones.

Maybe he had to go through this fire to find that out. Maybe some part of him still doubted. He never had to test his commitment to the law as long as he stayed isolated at Ultra Meridian. He just did his job.

Now he'd been tested and come through it. He'd proven himself, not just to the Confederacy, but to himself. Everyone he knew and respected recognized his commitment to the law.

He'd taken his place with Pritchard, Healey, and the deputies of the Wide Patrol. Davenport was one of them now and they accepted him as one of them. He'd never enjoyed that confidence before.

He passed his fingertips over his star. It was still there on the inside and now everyone knew it. He didn't have to prove himself anymore.

Chapter 20

Davenport sat down at the table in his cabin and went over the log data on Ekol's and Calyx's forces. Davenport tracked what both fleets had been doing after Pritchard had taken Davenport's crew into custody.

Davenport didn't see anything unusual about the two organizations working together. Kuman had taken Calyx's old fleet under Ekol's authority and the two fleets left together to return to Nyx Anonyma.

Davenport was still studying the data when Pritchard stuck his head in. "You might want to come up to the bridge. We're approaching the blockade."

Davenport dropped what he was doing and followed Pritchard to the bridge. Treese was in there communicating with the Wide Patrol. They had all deployed in their own ships.

The blockade had evolved since Davenport last saw it. "Ekol got here in a hurry," Pritchard announced. "It doesn't look like he wanted to wait for the rest of us to launch the battle. He isn't the same old Ekol he used to be."

Davenport stared at the scanner data of Vorax Suma. The Reserve Wing stood off from the planet at a greater distance than it had been before.

It gave plenty of space for Ekol's fleet to attack the rogue vessels that continued to defy the arrest warrant for their capture.

Ekol must have been burning the midnight oil to get here as fast as he did. Davenport didn't understand why Ekol Thaine would be so keen to attack this rogue fleet.

This was definitely not the Ekol that Davenport knew. Ekol never would have pulled a maneuver as rash as this. Why would he? He couldn't possibly stand to gain from it.

He'd brought in an overwhelming number of ships, but the rogue fleet held their own. They probably wouldn't stand up so well once Rizarth's people and Calyx's old force showed up—and that was saying nothing about the regular Reserve Wing.

"What the hell is he doing?" Davenport murmured. "Did he damage his brain when he got shot down?"

"He's forcing our hand," Pritchard told him. "I wouldn't send you down to the planet so soon, but we need to launch this campaign now before he triggers Joyce to release the weapon. Ace will take you over to the *Vigilante* where you can get on board the ship that's gonna take you to the surface. Go get your crew on deck to deploy."

Davenport strode down to the galley. The crew wasn't horsing around or playing any more dangerous games. They just slouched around chilling until the word came down.

They all jumped up and hustled out to the deck when Davenport told them what was going on. The crew armed up, but they had to wait a while for Bolander to come and get them.

The crew stood around shuffling their feet and checking and re-checking their weapons when gunfire struck the *Vindicator*. Everyone looked up. "Should we get on the guns?" Bandit asked. "The sheriff might need us to defend the ship."

"He'll tell us if he does," Laub replied.

That made everyone fall silent, but the noise threatened to snap Davenport's last nerve. He could handle an air battle as long as he was one of the people flying and shooting in it.

Nothing was worse than standing around in the hold of a ship, hearing gunfire striking the hull, and not being able to do a thing about it.

More concussions pounded the *Vindicator's* hull before the hatch yawned open and Bolander flew in. He flew another Phoenix and landed in front of the crew, opened his own hatch, and yelled at them over his shoulder without leaving the cockpit.

"We're flying into a shitstorm!" he hollered. "You better lock and load! It will take all of you to carve your way to the *Vigilante.*"

"What's Ekol doing?" Davenport called back.

"Making a mess of the world!" Bolander replied. "Let's go! Buckle up!"

He didn't even wait for everyone to get into their seats before he shut the hatch and blasted back out into a raging firefight.

The *Vindicator* was in full flight and Bolander dropped the Phoenix out into a hail of gunfire coming from all sides. Davenport grabbed the controls in front of him and opened fire without knowing who the hell he was supposed to be shooting at.

It took a few minutes for him to realize what was going on. Ekol's fleet and Joyce's rogues locked in a death grip shooting at each other.

Their struggle had spilled far enough away from Vorax Summa to pull a bunch of Reserve Wing Stalwarts and Daggers into the confusion.

They started out by just firing on the combatants to drive them back toward the planet. Then Ekol's people returned fire and everything went downhill from there.

The *Vigilante* had also gotten drawn into the confusion, and when the Reserve Wing saw its own ships in danger, more Stalwarts got involved to help their friends.

The Wide Patrol surrounded the *Vindicator* to help Pritchard carve a path to the *Vigilante*. As soon as Bolander launched the Phoenix, the Patrol shifted to surround that ship instead. Even Pritchard broke off to defend the Phoenix.

Davenport wheeled his cannon from one side to the other, but it got progressively more difficult to pick out a decent target. He couldn't tell which Reserve Wing ships belonged to the rogues and which were loyal.

He tried to avoid shooting at Ekol's people, but after a while, he had no choice. They bombarded the Phoenix with gunfire and put the ship in more danger than the rogues did.

Bolander flew rings around them. He had to fly rings around everybody just to keep clear of the enemy gunfire.

"Where the hell are you going, Ace?" Yarborough demanded through the communications system. "The *Vigilante* is in the other direction!"

"I can't even see where the hell the ship is!" Another explosion cut Bolander off as one of the rogue stalwarts detonated right off the Phoenix's flank.

"Ten Daggers coming in fast!" Rodeo called. "Axel—cut 'em off! They're trying to get to the *Vindicator!*"

Axel pulled his cannon around and unloaded on the Daggers as they zoomed past the Phoenix's tail. "Were those rogues or Reserve Wing?" he asked too late.

"They're all Reserve Wing!" Coon hollered. "Who the hell are we supposed to be shooting at?!"

A crushing slam tossed everyone sideways. "Those are definitely Ekol's people!" Bolander told them. "Bring it around to the front! We're going in!"

Davenport didn't see what Bolander wanted to do. Davenport couldn't see anything except a jumbled sea of dozens of ships. Some of them blasted to pieces right in front of him.

"What are you going to.....?" Alla asked.

"Open fire!" Bolander yelled. "All guns to the front!"

Davenport aimed his cannon to the front and opened fire. He didn't see what he was shooting at, but it didn't matter in the end.

Bolander hit the throttle and plowed through the thickest fighting. He smashed the Phoenix into multiple ships, knocked them out of the way, and skimmed clear to the other side of the battle.

Wommack, Swygert, and DeRosa circled the battle at the same time. "Get on board the *Vigilante* while you can, Ace!" Wommack told him. "We'll cover you so no one interferes."

"You got it." Bolander pulled away from the battle.

The Stalwart *Vigilante* loomed over the Phoenix, but the Stalwart was already locked in battle against three other Stalwarts. Davenport couldn't tell if those enemy Stalwarts belonged to the rogues or to Ekol's fleet.

"I can't get near it!" Bolander hollered. "We need something else to draw these assholes away."

"Incoming!" Treese called from somewhere. "Calyx's force is moving in and so is Rizarth's. The cavalry is here!"

Davenport took a split second to see the two fleets moving in. They flew in formation with each other like they were the best friends in the world.

The only problem was that Ekol's fleet was so mixed up with the rogues that Calyx's force flew straight into Ekol's fleet. All thought of keeping the two syndicates separate went right out the window. Davenport didn't even get a chance to tell anyone that they should be separated.

Whether Duni got a chance to tell anyone about that, Calyx's people reacted instantly as soon as they got within weapons range of Ekol's fleet. Calyx's people opened fire and then collided with the battle from the other side.

Calyx's and Rizarth's combined force swept the field and opened fire on absolutely everyone. The hail of gunfire blocked Davenport from seeing or targeting anyone, and a second later, a tide of mayhem overran both the Phoenix and the *Vigilante*.

The fighting broke the *Vigilante* away from its combatants and the Stalwart sailed clear. "Now's your chance!" Bolander called. "Stand by to defend the hatch!"

The Wide Patrol moved in and guarded the area while Bolander flew the Phoenix behind the *Vigilante* to the cargo hold hatch.

Wommack and Swygert backed up in front of him. Pritchard, Treese, DeRosa, and Yarborough maintained their blockade and unloaded their cannons on any ship that came too close.

Plenty of them tried to target the *Vigilante,* but the Wide Patrol kept driving them off. Bolander pulled in closer to the hatch, but nothing happened. It didn't open.

"What's the holdup, Ace?" Pritchard demanded.

"No one on board is responding. I'm hailing them, but no one will open the hatch."

"Stick around," Pritchard growled. "I'll take care of this."

He cut communication so no one would hear what he said to the *Vigilante's* bridge staff. "Someone is going home with a new asshole," Laub murmured.

"Pay attention!" Treese interrupted. "We got some dipshits trying to break our line! Stand fast!"

Davenport swung his cannon to the front. A squadron of Ekol's people was trying to tear away from the battle to get past the Wide Patrol.

Rogue Daggers and random alien vessels from the other two syndicates kept bursting out of the battle, hammering Ekol's people with brutal fire, and driving them back into the battle. That was the only place Ekol's people could hide from the counterassault.

A different group blasted its way through, smashed into the Wide Patrol, and Pritchard's barricade staggered back to overrun Wommack and Swygert.

Bolander spun the Phoenix around to add his fire to theirs, and at the same moment, another flank of enemy fighter craft broke away from the battle.

They swept to the left and came at the Phoenix from that side. Gunfire pummeled the Phoenix's hull before Bolander could correct.

"They're flanking us!" he hollered. "We're pinned down!"

"Hold on, Ace!" Wommack called. "We're falling back to defend you!"

"The hatch is opening!" Rodeo interrupted. "Get on board, Ace!"

"Finally!" He yanked the helm to starboard, gunned the engines, and sprinted on board the Stalwart.

Chapter 21

The Phoenix skidded across the hold floor and Bolander ripped the ship back around to face outward into the battle. "Everybody out!" he called over his shoulder. "I gotta get back out there and help the Patrol! We'll cover you while you load up and launch! Get out there as fast as you can!"

Davenport scrambled out of his seat and the crew crowded to the hatch to deploy. Bolander sprang out of his cockpit and joined them as they all scrambled down to the floor.

Davenport looked around. "Where's the ship we're supposed to take?"

Bolander checked right and left and then smacked his lips. "Son of a bitch! Someone screwed up."

A smash of gunfire made everyone look toward the hatch. It was still open with a galvanic field covering the gap.

Gunfire exploded out there with the Wide Patrol locked in battle against dozens of ships. Some were Reserve Wing vessels. Others belonged to one of the three criminal syndicates.

Stray fire bombarded the hatch opening. The *Vigilante* returned fire and the wreckage of a burning Dagger collided with the hull just beyond the hatch.

Bolander spun around the other way. "Everybody back on board! If you aren't going to the planet, we gotta get back out there!"

He took three steps toward the Phoenix before the door leading to the stairs slammed open. Four uniformed Reserve Wing officers charged out of it.

They ran over to the crew. "Come with us! We'll show you where to go!"

"These people are supposed to be on a ship with shielding to conceal their identities!" Bolander snapped. "The ship was supposed to be here waiting for us! That was the plan!"

"Change of plans!" one of the officers countered. "We need pilots to man our Drifters and Nitrols!"

"That isn't the plan!" Bolander roared. "These people aren't involved in the battle!"

"They are now! Come with me! You aren't getting off the ship any other way!"

Bolander glanced over at Davenport and all the fight went out of Bolander's face. "I'm sorry, Sheriff. This isn't what the boss had in mind at all."

"Don't worry about it," Davenport told him. "Tell him I'm grateful for his help and we'll find a way to get to the planet one way or the other. This might be better than going in one ship anyway." Davenport squeezed his shoulder. "Thank you for bringing us. Get out there and help the Patrol. We'll handle it from here."

Bolander hesitated, mumbled, "Yes, Sir," and went back on board the Phoenix.

Davenport waved his crew to follow him and the officers led them to the stairs. Before they got there, the Phoenix wound up its engines to a screaming pitch and the ship rocketed out into the battle.

Davenport lost sight of the Phoenix among all the other combatants. He couldn't make out any of the Wide Patrol anymore, but that didn't matter. They did their job. They got him and his crew as far as they could go. Now it was his turn.

The officers led the way to the *Vigilante's* hangar bay. Dozens of Drifters, Nitrols, and Daggers sat there unused.

"You take what you want and get out there with the rest of the Reserve Wing!" the same officer told Davenport. "No one will see you. There are too many other pilots out there already."

"We'll stick out a mile," Davenport countered. "The idea was to cover up the fact that an Adik and a bunch of Chorions and humans are trying to make it down to the planet."

"There are plenty of pilots out there from different species. You don't have to worry about it."

"I bet there are no Adiks or Chorion pilots out there," Davenport pointed out. "And none of them is trying to get to the planet."

The officer waved that away. "You won't get down to the planet from this side anyway. Use the battle as cover to skirt to the planet's other side. It's uninhabited. You can land there."

Davenport didn't point out that the other side of the planet was thousands of miles from wherever Joyce would be hiding. It would take the crew weeks or even months to get near him.

His crew wouldn't get to the planet any other way. Davenport saw now that the officer was right about that. The battle was getting too chaotic with too many competing adversaries in the way.

He and his crew needed ships—or a ship. It didn't matter as long as they got to the planet one way or the other.

He turned back to his crew. "Chorion Team—get yourselves a Drifter that looks good to you."

"Yes!" Bandit clapped his hands and rubbed him. "Give me a Drifter any day of the week."

"Dice, Lyons, Fiddler, and Emmett—you can take a Nitrol to yourselves. Marshall Healey and I will take a Dagger with Jace and Jericho as our gunners."

The crew split up. Davenport thanked the officers and the three different crews selected their ships.

Healey and Davenport went to the Dagger's bridge where they both sat down at the conn. "Chorion Team is firing up their engines," Healey pointed out.

Davenport activated the ship's internal intercom to call down to the Dagger's Howitzer cradles. "Are you boys ready to spit some lead?"

"Bring it," Jericho replied.

Davenport checked the ship's internal scanner readings. They showed more than forty people down in the cradles, both as gunners and support staff.

"I'm scanning the surface," Healey reported. "There's no sign of where Joyce is hiding."

"Pull up log records from the rest of the Reserve Wing," Davenport told him. "Find the transmissions for when Joyce threatened the Confederacy. Track the transmission source."

Healey shrugged over his controls. "Good idea."

"We'll need to land close enough to get near him but not close enough for him to see what we're doing. It will be tricky with the battle going on, but maybe we can swing a miracle."

Healey grinned at him. "What's another miracle? Just put it on the list."

Davenport chuckled and fired the engines. The Chorion Team's Drifter was already lifting off and heading for the hatch opening.

Lyons's Nitrol lifted off the floor. She waited for the Chorion Team to launch first and then she and Davenport both raced outside into the battle.

The confusion got worse the farther Davenport flew. He had to dodge everyone to avoid getting plastered.

Jace and Jericho kept up a steady barrage of gunfire on the enemy, but Davenport didn't even know who the enemy was anymore.

He broke through a group of Ekol's fighter craft, only to fly into a different squadron coming from his left. They peppered the Dagger with fire and all the ship's guns swung that way.

"Do you see a pattern here?" Healey yelled.

"You mean how, everywhere we go, Ekol's people always seem to be there waiting for us?"

"You said it, not me."

"Ekol did tell me he wanted the Ithium," Davenport countered. "Maybe this is his way of getting it."

"He must know by now that we don't have it," Healey replied.

"There's one way to get away from Ekol. I'm heading for the surface."

Davenport wheeled the ship away from the battle, but it still took multiple smaller skirmishes to get the Dagger clear of the confusion.

He passed a dozen of Calyx's stolen Reserve Wing vessels tackling a much larger group of Ekol's fighter craft. Davenport tried to avoid getting caught in their conflict, but a second later, another party of Rizarth's people bombed in from the left.

They dove into the dogfight and hammered Ekol's fighters into the ground. Explosions enveloped Davenport's Dagger.

Jace and Jericho swiveled their guns to the right and pounded Ekol's fighter craft with a crushing barrage while Davenport fired the engines to get out of danger.

He zoomed down the line of explosions and nearly collided with a different squadron of unidentified alien craft overrunning him from the right. He didn't see which fleet they belonged to, but they definitely knew who he was.

He veered the Dagger away, but not fast enough before a deafening tempest of gunfire struck the Dagger on the right side. Screams echoed through the intercom from the cradles.

"Jace—Jericho! Are you all right?!" Davenport hollered back.

"They're copies!" Healey yelled. "Get out of the battle and get down onto the planet! We can't stay up here!"

"How?!" Davenport countered. "Find me a route out of the battle and I'll follow it!"

Healey shook his head over the controls. "The whole place is locked up. We gotta....."

He didn't get the words out before a punishing slam struck the Dagger in the port wing.

"We're taking damage!" Healey roared. "If we don't get down onto the planet now, we never will!"

"Where are the other two ships?!" Davenport asked. "Are they clear?"

"I have no idea! I can't see them, either. I can't see shit!"

Davenport took his eyes off the battle for a split second, but one glance at the controls told him the same thing. Rizarth's fleet, Ekol's syndicate, and Calyx's forces had all brought dozens of ships—maybe even hundreds of ships.

Now they all battled over the same patch of sky. Davenport didn't see any of those fleets working together—not anymore. They all pounded each other as fast as they could shoot.

Admiral Joyce's rogue contingent drowned in the mayhem of all those ships shooting at everyone who happened to fly in front of them.

Things disintegrated beyond recognition when the Reserve Wing got involved.

Whatever battle plan anyone might have had in mind degenerated into a brawl of everyone against everyone else. Davenport didn't even see how any of these people avoided firing on their own sister ships and companions.

He punched the throttle to the wall and tried to plow his way out of the battle. If he just kept flying straight ahead, he would eventually make it to the edge of this war zone—theoretically, at least.

Squadrons of attackers cut him off at every turn. He couldn't distinguish them well enough to decide who was trying to stop him from making it to the surface.

They drove him back again and again until, out of nowhere, another smash took out the Dagger's tail. "We got a problem!" Healey hollered.

"I know that!" Davenport yelled. "Just tell me the solution!"

"I don't see one!"

"There has to be!" Davenport gunned the engines one more time, but the ship didn't respond as well.

The copies outdid themselves keeping up with all the enemy gunfire. The Dagger's Howitzers wheeled in all directions and fired incredibly fast, but they still couldn't keep up with all the attackers closing in from all sides.

More shots rained on top of the fuselage. Every barrage smacked the ship from right to left. The engines struggled to keep up. Even when they did, Davenport still couldn't find a route out of this.

"I found it!" Healey bellowed. "I'm sending you a course! Just follow it, Davenport! Don't think!"

Davenport shut his brain off. He didn't let himself think about how risky this was.

He banked the ship around and plunged back into the battle. The crumpled tail didn't steer as well as it should have, but he didn't care. He just had to keep going and follow Healey's course.

Davenport plunged into the heart of the tornado. Exploding ships surrounded him, but none of the attackers pursued him.

He flew away from the planet—back out into space. That was the trick. Whoever had been attacking this Dagger wanted to stop him from getting to Vorax Summa. They wouldn't attack him if he flew in the opposite direction.

He made it halfway to the other side where he would be able to break out into space again. The ships in front of him parted. The stars welcomed him back into the silence where he could go where he wanted.

At that moment, another pelting bolt of lightning severed the port wing from the fuselage. "These assholes are gunning for *us!*" Healey roared. "They're hunting us down!"

"What are you talking about?!" Davenport countered. "They don't know anything about us!"

"They came from across the battlefield just to shoot at us! They're after...."

A crunch of tearing metal interrupted him as a different kind of weapon hit the hull on the starboard side. More life signs blinked out down there, but Davenport didn't have time to ask if Jace and Jericho were okay.

Ten ships soared out of the mayhem and surrounded Davenport's Dagger. These ships didn't belong to any class he recognized. He didn't know their weapons type, either.

He swung around to give the starboard gunners a better shot, but the enemy widened their formation to surround the Dagger. They unleashed another spurt of their mysterious weapons and the port engine exploded.

"We're losing ground!" Healey reported. "We gotta pull away!"

"How can we when they're all over the place?! Who the hell are they, anyway?"

Healey shook his head again. "I can't identify them! I don't know which army they belong to. They might not even belong to any of these groups. They might be using this as a shield to get to us."

Davenport opened his mouth to answer, but at that moment, another ship heaved out of the torrent. It was as big as a Stalwart, but it wasn't a Stalwart. It was one of the alien vessels belonging to one of the criminal syndicates.

The ship hurtled at his Dagger so fast he didn't have time to correct or get away from it. He couldn't have gotten away even if his ship hadn't been irretrievably damaged.

The ship opened a hatch on its front. It levered down from the ship's nose like some kind of gaping mouth. It rushed the Dagger.

Davenport had been hearing and seeing too many signs that Ekol had gone off the reservation. Neither Rizarth's people nor Calyx's army wouldn't have come after Davenport like this.

He could only think of one of the five armies involved that would use this battle as a staging ground to capture Davenport and his crew.

He instinctively pulled the helm away, but the Dagger didn't respond. It just sat there while the ship swallowed the Dagger whole and plunged the ship into darkness.

Chapter 22

Lyons rocketed her Nitrol through the battle trying to find a way to rejoin Davenport and the Chorion Team.

Her four gunners slammed their guns in all directions. Dice, Fiddler, and Emmett were too busy clearing a path for the Nitrol to think about or even see where Davenport and the Chorion Team were.

Lyons spotted a bunch of Ekol Thaine's fighter craft ganging up on a rogue Dagger. Ekol's people hammered the Dagger into a corner only to fall to another posse of Nitrols moving in to defend their sister ship.

Lyons fought the controls to work her way to the side of the battlefield closest to the planet. She needed to get through this chaos somehow and land on the surface.

She broke out of one skirmish and nearly flew straight into another one. A dozen Reserve Wing Stalwarts, three rogue Stalwarts, and ten alien ships revolved around each other and peppered each other with shots before whizzing away to target another adversary.

Lyons decided to use their conflict to distract everyone around here while she raced away to freedom.

The instant she got near them, a blinding explosion distracted her from her right. She barely glanced that way. There were too many ships fighting over there. She couldn't tell one from another....and then she saw a Drifter in trouble.

"Chorion Team!" she yelled. "Hold on, boys! I'm coming to get you!"

"We're blocked in!" Bandit called back. "These assholes came after us!"

"I'm on my way! Dice—target those ships!"

"Which ships?!" he countered. "There are ships all over the place!"

"I don't know who or what they are. They're unknown, but they're blocking the Drifter from getting near the surface. Bring your cradle around, Emmett! You, too, Fiddler! We gotta help the Chorions!"

Lyons peeled the Nitrol in that direction. The three gunners targeted the ships in question, but before Lyons could get near them, another group of Ekol's fighter craft streaked out of nowhere and darted between Lyons and her target.

The fighter craft whizzed into position to block the Nitrol from getting near the Chorions' Drifter. All the gunfire in the world couldn't break through.

"We're hit!" Bandit hollered. "We can't make it to the planet! You go ahead, Lyons! We'll keep these cocksuckers tied up here while you break away!"

"No chance, pal!" She punched the throttle, swerved sideways to give Dice and Emmett a clearer shot at the enemy fighters, and then sprinted behind the unknown attackers.

She skidded into position near the Drifter's flank and swiveled back to the front. Fiddler and Emmett bombarded the enemy with dozens of shots.

Three alien vessels exploded around the Drifter and the rest of the attackers turned on the Nitrol, but the Drifter had already taken too much damage. It couldn't get away.

Bandit fired the one remaining engine and inched the ship out into the main battlefield. The enemy let the Drifter go and all the fighter craft closed to block in Lyons's Nitrol.

"Now you really pissed them off," Dice growled.

"Then it's time we pissed them off even worse. Keep it going, folks! Don't let off the gas."

"What are you gonna do?" Emmett asked.

"I'm gonna teach these fools not to mess with my friends." Lyons throttled forward and dove into the thickest weeds. Gunfire surrounded her ship on all sides, but she didn't try to get away.

She took her hands off the throttle and grabbed her own cannons to lay into the enemy. They surrounded her in droves, but she didn't care.

"Aren't we supposed to be getting to the surface?" Emmett asked. "Admiral Joyce is down there."

Lyons was so busy shooting that she had to concentrate to pull herself out of her battle frenzy. She checked the readings. The Chorion Team had made it only a third of the way across the battlefield. They were nowhere near getting clear.

She pulled away one more time and followed them to give them any protection she could. Before she could catch up with them, another flock of Ekol's fighter craft hurtled out of nowhere.

They cut across the Drifter's port side and the fighters pounded the Drifter one after another. They carved a deep breach in the hull and then smashed off the tail.

"We're venting life support gas!" Bandit called. "We're stricken!"

"Not so fast!" Lyons countered. "We'll get you out of this!"

"How?!" Bandit fired back. "We're suffering an electrical systems overload! We'll self-destruct in thirty seconds!"

Lyons opened her mouth to answer, but she already saw that it was hopeless. The loyal Reserve Wing Stalwarts were the only vessels big enough to save the Chorion Team and none of the Stalwarts were close enough. They were all too engaged in battles of their own.

Lyons gulped. Her mind raced in all kinds of crazy directions trying to figure out a way to get over there and get the Chorions off the Drifter before it exploded.

She couldn't do that when they were both out in space. This Nitrol wasn't big enough to take the Drifter on board.

How many seconds had already passed? How many did she still have left to come up with a solution? Ten? Five?

She sensed Dice, Fiddler, and Emmett all listening and watching to see what she would do, but she couldn't do anything.

She cast a hopeless glance around the battlefield. She needed to call out to someone for help, but she didn't even have time for that.

She shut her mouth to swallow again. She couldn't just sit here and watch the Chorion Team die, but right at that moment, a giant ship barreled out of the confusion.

She didn't recognize what ship type it was or even which fleet it belonged to. It delivered one more punishing gunshot that ruptured the Drifter's hull and then a hatch opened under the ship's nose.

It widened into a mouth that swooped down on the Drifter and engulfed it. The giant ship kept going a short distance and then it turned to confront the Nitrol.

Lyons stared up at it in stupid horror. It towered over her and that same hatch yawned open to swallow her ship, too.

An explosion somewhere brought her back to her senses. She wasn't dead yet nor was her ship damaged. She tore the helm hard to port and plummeted into the battle. The Chorion Team might be gone, but she wasn't.

She barely glanced at the scanners. She couldn't see Davenport's Dagger anywhere. She had to assume he fell in the battle, too.

That left her, Fiddler, Dice, and Emmett to finish this thing with Joyce once and for all. She had to get down to the planet.

She didn't have Davenport's device to show her where the Ithium was. She would just have to improvise. She could do that. She'd been doing it for years.

She gritted her teeth and nailed the throttle all the way down. The battle threw too many obstacles in her path, but she dodged them, traded gunfire with a few different adversaries from every fleet, and kept on going.

She lost sight of the huge ship in the storm. She put it out of her mind and concentrated on avoiding skirmishes that might slow her down. Only the planet mattered.

She spotted a grouping of Rizarth's ships not far ahead and she pushed the Nitrol faster to catch up with them. They were engaged with a squadron of Ekol Thaine's fighter craft.

Lyons whizzed into line with her own people and joined their fire with theirs. The lead ship opened communications with her. "Identify yourself, Nitrol," a gruff voice barked. "Which fleet do you belong to?"

"Ignus—it's me, Lyons," she called.

He frowned at her. "What are you doing in that Nitrol? Do you need help? We can take you on board if you need it."

"I need to get to the surface. Can you help me?"

"The surface of what?" he asked.

"The surface of the planet, Ignus—of Vorax Suma."

He furrowed his brow. "Why do you want to go there? There's nothing there."

"I don't have time to explain. I need you to block me in so I can get out of the battle on the planet side."

He shrugged. "That's easy. Just give the word."

"I'm giving it. Pull into formation now."

She hauled the Nitrol into reverse and banked toward the planet. Ignus's ship and the others with him eased off their assault on Ekol's fighters.

Rizarth's forces backed away and formed a gauntlet to protect the Nitrol while Lyons gunned her engines toward the planet.

More of Rizarth's ships broke out of the battle to join the two sides of her funnel. They blocked any other ship from getting near her.

The planet glowed bluish-green in the distance. She was going to make it. The gunfire and explosions faded behind her along with the battle and all its combatants.

She couldn't fly any faster than she already was. "Yeah!" Dice hollered. "We're through! We're on our way!"

She laughed in relief. "Yeah, we...."

She broke off when a huge shape materialized on her right. The big mouth ship appeared out of nowhere. It was coming straight for her.

She reacted on pure instinct, jerked the helm to port to get away from the attacker, and then pulled up hard on her controls to zoom over the larger ship.

The three gunners opened fire and pounded the enemy's hull, but the Nitrol's guns didn't damage the alien vessel.

"Keep going!" Fiddler yelled. "Just keep away from that mouth!"

Lyons took a turn around the ship's tail. The gunners hammered the enemy vessel with everything the Nitrol could throw at it, but nothing worked.

"I'm going for the bridge!" she called to the gunners. "We have to damage it some way."

"Does this thing have any guns?" Dice asked. "I don't see it shooting at anybody."

"I don't care as long as it doesn't shoot at us." Lyons went into a swan dive heading for the ship's bridge. "Here we go. We'll destroy these bastards."

She forgot for a minute that this was the vessel that took the Chorions on board. She just wanted to destroy the ship and get to the planet.

She swooped over the ship's roof and angled down at the bridge from above. The three gunners opened fire and Lyons added her fire to theirs.

She couldn't see any window or any other vulnerability, but she had to try it. She had to try anything to stop this ship from capturing her the way it captured the Chorions. She didn't even know if they were still alive.

The Nitrol's guns bombarded the ship's front end, but that course brought her dangerously close to falling into the ship's mouth—or whatever it was.

She ripped the Nitrol away to make another break for freedom. The rest of Rizarth's fleet showed up a second later to assault the strange vessel.

She swiveled toward Vorax Suma. She was going to make it this time, but before she could even hit the throttle to flee from this enemy, twenty of Ekol's fighter craft sprinted out of nowhere, opened fire, and smashed the Nitrol straight back into the strange vessel's mouth.

Chapter 23

"What the hell was that thing?" Rodeo asked.

"I barely got a look at it before it was on top of us," Bandit replied.

"What did you see?" Axel asked.

"Not a lot. It was big....and black.....and it had a hatch in front that opened like a mouth...."

"We all saw that, dumbass!" Alla countered. "Tell us something we don't know."

"Breeze—get your foot out of my armpit!" Laub snapped and thumping noises struck the floor under the Chorion Team.

Coon lay under a pile of bodies on the floor of some very dark, very cramped compartment. His friends' weight prevented him from moving more than a pathetic wriggle.

"Coon.....are you there?" Rodeo whispered.

"I'm here," Coon replied. "Where else would I be?"

"Can you tell where we are?"

"Give me a second." Coon groaned when he struggled to pull his arm out from under Alla's weight. "You really need to stop eating so much, pal."

"Tell Rodeo that," Alla countered. "He's the one that keeps throwing me in front of huge creatures and telling me to fight them. What am I supposed to do?"

"Stay away from Jace and Jericho from now on, too," Axel added and the others laughed.

"Find out what ship we're on, Coon," Rodeo repeated, "but do it quickly. Don't exhaust yourself."

Coon stretched his hand toward the floor. He had to extend it past Wolf who lay smashed at the bottom of the stack.

He kept yowling in fury and hissing and spitting in Coon's face, but only because Coon was the closest. None of the Chorions could do anything, much less get off each other.

Coon's fingertips grazed the metal floor and he twined his filaments into it. His mind went blurry and he became one with the ship that captured the Chorion Team's Drifter.

He traveled through the ship's hull, through its engine room and all its other departments, and finally made it to the bridge.

Most of the bridge staff were human with a few different aliens in different roles. He didn't see anything to tell him whose ship the Chorion Team was on or why they captured the crew.

He was just about to withdraw and tell Rodeo that he couldn't find out who captured them. Coon started to retract his filaments and then, for no particular reason, he happened to cast his awareness toward the ship's supply room and weapons armory.

Coon froze when he saw a short man with pudgy legs and a white beard. "Oh, no!" Coon whispered.

The whole group stiffened. "What's wrong?" Rodeo asked.

Coon swallowed hard and pulled his filaments the rest of the way out of the ship. He didn't need to see any more, but before he could tell anyone what he'd seen, someone dropped onto the pile from above.

A body landed on top of Bandit, who lay on the top of the stack. Whoever it was grunted in pain and Bandit howled. "Aarrgh!"

Wolf gave a hideous shriek as the weight fell on him and Coon rolled his eyes in agony.

"Bandit?!" Davenport countered and tried to turn over to see who was lying underneath him. "Wolf—is that you?"

"Don't move, Sir!" Laub hollered from farther down the pile. "For the love of God, don't move!"

"What are you boys doing in here?" Davenport asked, but right then, Healey slammed down on top of Davenport and they both roared in pain.

A second later, another dozen bodies dropped out of the darkness one after the other. The whole stack seethed trying to free themselves, but no one could move.

"Jace—for God's sake, collapse your copies!" Rodeo ordered. "You, too, Jericho! You're crushing all of us."

Coon couldn't feel any difference. He couldn't be sure if Jace and Jericho did collapse their copies, but at least the people lying on top of him stopped squirming.

"How did you boys get here?" Healey asked.

"The same way you did," Axel grumbled. "That ship captured us."

"So what are we doing here?" Davenport asked.

"That's what we were just trying to figure out," Rodeo replied. "Coon....."

At that moment, another colossal weight slammed down on top of everybody. The whole crew groaned as one when Dice crashed onto the very top of the stack.

Coon barely felt Fiddler, Emmett, and Lyons land on top of Dice. He roared in fury and every move he made squashed those under him.

The whole crew yelled at him at the same time. "Keep still, Dice!" Rodeo snapped.

"I can't!" Dice thundered. "These idiots are lying on top of me!"

"How do you think we feel?!" Axel countered. "You're lying on top of us, so you better keep still!"

Dice roared again and Lyons squealed. "Ow!"

"Does anyone know where we are?" Fiddler asked.

"We're on a ship," Coon told her.

Silence fell over the group and he cringed. They were all listening to him.

"Which syndicate does it belong to?" Lyons asked. "It isn't Rizarth's."

"It's Ekol's," Coon replied. "This is Ekol's ship. He's the one who captured us—which means he turned against us."

"Bastard!" Rodeo snarled. "He better not be doing what I think he's doing."

"Duni tried to warn me about this," Davenport muttered.

"Who's Duni?" Bandit asked.

"He's a friend of mine from Terminus Anathema. He's running Calyx's operation now and they had some conflict with Ekol. Duni said Ekol isn't the way he used to be. He'll turn on anyone—even one of his loyal people."

"That's not good," Lyons remarked. "A syndicate can't run without loyalty."

"You would know," Emmett mumbled.

"We always knew this would happen someday," Rodeo added. "This isn't a surprise. The only surprise is that it didn't happen before now."

"Why did you always know this would happen?" Davenport asked. "Ekol never did anything like this when I worked for him. He was solid—always."

"He got worse these last few years," Bandit chimed in. "Whatever happened to him didn't happen when the Reserve Wing shot down Ekol's ship. At least, it didn't all happen then. It started a while ago."

"That's no good at all," Davenport murmured. "He really must have changed."

"Anyway, we're here now and we can't keep lying in this pile forever," Fiddler pointed out.

"Oh, we can lie in this pile forever," Axel countered. "We can lie in this pile for as long as Ekol leaves us down here."

"Why would he throw us in here?" Healey asked. "What's the point?"

"He wants to humiliate us," Rodeo replied.

"He wants to contain us so we don't go anywhere," Alla added.

"We're contained, you dope," Laub snapped. "We're about as contained as it's possible for anyone to be."

"Maybe there's something about this ship....." Emmett suggested.

"There isn't," Coon interrupted. "The ship has a containment level attached to that mouth thing. This ship was designed to capture other ships."

"Where did it come from?" Lyons asked. "I didn't recognize it."

"The ship's computer systems say it was designed by a species called the Zairia. That's all I can tell you."

"I've never heard of that," Davenport exclaimed.

"No one has—not even Ekol," Coon replied. "He stole it from a group of traveling aliens from another galaxy. They stole it from another group who stole it from another group who stole it from another group. Whoever the Zairia are, they're a long way from here. I doubt they're even in Sacron Enigma. They're even farther away than that."

Jericho sighed and settled down on the pile of bodies. "I guess we just hurry up and wait, then......unless you want me to make a bunch of copies to climb out of here."

"NO!!" everyone yelled.

Silence fell over the group except for Wolf growling at everyone every few minutes. He growled even if Coon breathed too deeply.

"How long is Ekol gonna leave us down here?" Dice growled.

"I have to go to the bathroom," Breeze announced.

A few people snickered. "You better hold it," Axel told him. "You'll be sorry if you don't."

"I'm already sorry," Breeze muttered. "I'm sorry I came on this trip."

Lyons sighed. "There must be some way to pass the time."

"Try keeping quiet," Emmett fired back.

"Watch it, old man!" Dice snapped. "Don't talk to her like that."

"How about we all just lie still and try to stay calm?" Davenport interrupted. "Moving around and arguing will only make us more uncomfortable. We can all be grateful we're not in Coon's and Wolf's positions right now."

"You can say that again," Coon choked and Wolf growled in agreement.

No one said anything for a few minutes. Coon started to feel like he needed to go to the bathroom, too, but he didn't say so. He did his best not to squirm. Wolf was the worst off and he complained the least.

Coon shut his eyes and resisted the urge to interface with the ship again. His curiosity got the better of him. He really wanted to find out if Ekol Thaine was on this ship, what Ekol was doing, and what the ship was doing.

If Coon could just interface with the ship's computers, he could find out what the crew's objective was and why they captured Coon and his friends. It would be so easy for Coon to stretch out his arm and touch the floor again.

He couldn't do that. He couldn't exhaust himself in case he needed to interface with the ship later.

He turned his attention back to the one subject that could always take his mind off of anything else—food. He was just about to bring it up with those around him when the bottom dropped out of the room they were in.

One minute, they all lay there in a pile. The next minute, the floor levered out of position and dumped everyone out onto a slanting metal ramp. Light shone all around Coon so he could see exactly where he was going.

Coon and Wolf landed first and somersaulted downward. Coon didn't have time to see where he was before he tumbled across another section of flat floor and landed on his stomach.

The rest of the crew rolled down after him, but at least they didn't land on top of him.

He pulled Wolf out of the way in time to make room for Axel, Laub, Breeze, Alla, Bandit, Rodeo, Davenport, Healey, Jace, Jericho, Dice, Lyons, Fiddler, and finally Emmett to sprawl on the same section of floor.

This one had carpet on it, but that didn't soften the blow. Coon got to his feet and helped Wolf stand up....and then Coon's blood ran cold when he saw Ekol Thaine standing in the same room.

Coon froze....and then Wolf froze. The other Chorions turned to see what they were staring at and then the whole crew froze.

Ekol stood off to one side. The pinchers around his mouth waved a little faster—a sure sign that he was in a deadly mood.

The others picked themselves up and dusted themselves off in as dignified a way as they could, but Ekol didn't make it easier by glaring at them all.

Davenport finally stepped forward to confront him. "Why did you capture us like that?" Davenport asked. "If you wanted to talk to us, all you had to do was ask."

"I didn't want to talk to you, my friend," Ekol breathed. "That is what I did NOT want to do."

"Then what did you want to do?"

"I'll be the one to ask the questions here, Davenport," Ekol murmured in a dangerous undertone. "I see you escaped from Reserve Wing custody after all."

"We didn't escape," Healey interjected. "They put us on trial and we were acquitted of any wrongdoing. Now it's our turn to go after Joyce and stop him from detonating the Ithium the way he plans to."

Ekol turned to Healey. "You were on your way to Vorax Suma....which means Joyce is on Vorax Suma.....which means the Ithium is on Vorax Suma."

Davenport grimaced. "You aren't getting it, Ekol. You don't deserve the Ithium any more than Joyce does."

"How will you stop me from getting it, Davenport?" Ekol breezed. "You're all my prisoners here. You have no ship. You have no weapons. You don't even have this."

Ekol held up a small metal box. It was the device Pritchard had given Davenport—the homing beacon that would lead Davenport to the Ithium.

Davenport's hand flew to his vest pocket, but the device wasn't there anymore.

His eyes flew back to Ekol and then Davenport's features hardened. "Give that back, Ekol. I won't ask again."

"You needn't have asked the first time." Ekol turned away. "You can all stay here until I retrieve the Ithium. Then I'll decide what to do with you."

His many jointed legs carried him across the room toward the only door apart from the one over the crew's heads.

"Ekol!" Davenport called after him. "Why are you doing this? You used to be reasonable. You used to value your people and treat them well. Now you're making enemies all over the galaxy. You're making enemies of the people you once valued the most."

"Everything changes, Davenport," Ekol growled over his shoulder. "Valuing people only made my organization weak. Now that's about to change. As soon as I get the Ithium, everyone will know that my syndicate is the strongest. Then no one will question how or why I do things ever again....starting right now."

He crawled out the door and it swung shut behind him. It clicked into place with cold finality.

"Great!" Lyons muttered. "This is just great."

"How do we stop him?" Fiddler asked. "If he goes after the Ithium, he could trigger Joyce to release his weapon."

"Unless Ekol is really after the weapon," Bandit pointed out. "The Ithium is only good as a weapon. Ekol might not know that Joyce has already processed the Ithium into a weapon."

"He probably doesn't know about Joyce's threat, either," Healey replied. "Or if Ekol does know about it, he probably doesn't care. He probably thinks he can overcome Joyce before he releases it."

"You wouldn't think Joyce would want to kill himself along with everyone else in the Confederacy," Jericho pointed out. "You would think a sane man would at least want to survive to enjoy the benefits of all his hard work."

"I think we can remove the word, 'sane' from any discussion about Admiral Joyce," Healey countered.

"It doesn't matter because we're on the side of the law now," Davenport interjected. "I'm a sheriff with the authority to apprehend Joyce and stop this plot and that's what I'm gonna do."

"We're going down to the planet to get revenge for Flack, Frost, Fizzle, and Friend," Emmett added.

"I'm going to the planet to get revenge for myself," Dice rumbled.

Davenport turned to Coon. "You can interface with this ship, can't you?"

"Of course. I already did."

"Then you can do it again—quickly, I mean," Davenport explained. "You can open that door...."

"We can overrun the ship once we get out of this room," Jace suggested.

"While Coon is opening that door, he can send a message to the other combatants to turn on Ekol," Rodeo added.

"They already have turned on him," Lyons pointed out.

"But they probably don't know that he's actually on this ship," Rodeo went on. "We can send out word for them all to attack this ship at the same time. If nothing else, it will distract the crew while we get to some other vessel and get out of here."

"Okay, here's what we'll do," Davenport finished. "Coon, you'll open the door and send the message to the other combatants. Alla, you'll go first and eat anyone you can find."

"Just don't ever complain about my weight again," Alla grumbled.

"Jace and Jericho, you go next and take control of this ship," Davenport continued. "The rest of us will go downstairs and find another vessel to take us to the planet."

"Then what?" Laub asked.

Davenport blinked at him. "Then we go get Joyce. Simple."

"How will we find him without the device?" Fiddler asked.

Davenport thought about it. Before he could answer, Jace interrupted. "I'll get the device back. I'll make sure we have it on board our escape vessel before we leave."

"Make sure at least one of your copies makes it to the vessel before we leave. You getting out of here is more important than the device."

Jace grinned at him. "Don't worry. I'll be there."

"All right. Here we go. Coon, do your thing."

Coon went over to the door. The rest of the crew crowded behind him so they'd be ready to rush outside the minute the door opened.

"You'll need to work fast once you interface with the ship," Rodeo told him. "You'll still need the strength to get out of here once you finish."

Coon nodded. He mentally rehearsed what he was going to do and then raised his hand. He held it inches away from the metal wall. "Get ready."

"Do it," Davenport ordered.

Coon let his hand fall on the cold steel. His filaments twisted into it and his vision blurred. He found himself gliding through the ship. He soared down bundles of fiber optic cable, through the engines, and found the compartment where Ekol imprisoned the crew.

Coon popped the lock. He became distantly aware of his friends rushing past him and vanishing into the rest of the ship. Everyone ran off and left Coon where he was with his filaments threaded inside the ship.

Only Jericho stayed behind. He left one copy standing there next to Coon while the other copies charged out into the corridor.

Coon immediately switched to the ship's communications system. He sent a message to every ship in the whole battle, including Joyce's rogue fighters.

Coon alerted everyone that Ekol Thaine was on board this ship right now and that he was on his way to Vorax Suma to take the Ithium for himself.

Coon stayed inside the ship's systems just long enough to make sure all those vessels turned on Ekol and attacked in force. Punishing gunfire hammered the outer hull and one of those shots punctured the hull near the engine room.

Coon withdrew his filaments and slumped against the wall cradling his head. "Are you all right?" Jericho asked.

Coon drew a shuddering breath and sighed. "I'm okay," he gasped. "I'm just....just a little light-headed."

"Let's go downstairs and find the rest of the crew. I'll help you if you need me to."

Coon looked up and smiled. "Thanks. Thanks for staying."

Jericho only nodded. "Of course. We can't let anything happen to you." He took Coon's elbow. "Come on. You can let me know if you get too tired. Now we gotta get out of here."

Chapter 24

Healey ran out of the room into the corridor. He considered staying behind to make sure Coon got out all right, but when Healey looked back, he saw one of Jericho's copies keeping an eye on Coon.

Healey glanced left and right. Davenport, Lyons, Dice, Fiddler, Emmett, and the Chorions took off heading left toward a stairwell at the end of the corridor.

Alla turned right just as a squad of armed gunmen charged around the corner. Some of them were human, but most belonged to a mixture of species.

Dozens of Jace's and Jericho's copies streamed past Alla, rushed the attackers, and overwhelmed them in seconds. The copies closed with the enemy too fast for Ekol's defenders to even raise their weapons.

The twins fought the enemy hand to hand, stole their weapons, and then tossed their defenseless assailants back to Alla, who gobbled them one after the other without chewing.

The twins worked their way through thirty of Ekol's men, took all their weapons, and armed their copies. Alla and the copies kept moving down the corridor and would have passed out of sight.

Healey should have gone with Davenport and the others. Healey wouldn't be able to do anything against Ekol's people that Alla and the twins couldn't do, but he decided to go with them anyway.

Alla kept advancing with a steady, unwavering tread. The twins produced hundreds of copies that poured into every room and compartment on the ship. The copies held the crew at gunpoint, threatened them not to try anything, and then stood guard while Alla and the others went on.

"You should go back, Marshall," one of Jericho's copies told him.

"We need to get control of the ship and find Ekol," Healey told him. "We need to get that device."

Jace cocked his head and flicked his hair out of his eyes. "Davenport and the others are meeting resistance. Marshall Healey is right. We need to take control of the ship so we can secure a vessel to take us to the surface. How do we get to the bridge?"

"I don't know," Healey replied. "I don't know anything about this ship."

"Let's go up the stairwell," Jericho suggested. "We can send our copies ahead to search the ship and they can tell us where to go."

Jace nodded. "Good plan."

The four of them entered the stairwell—or at least Healey, Alla, and the two copies he'd been talking to did. More and more copies split away. They exited at every deck and kept multiplying out of control.

A squad of twenty armed copies surrounded Healey and his companions. Healey had seen enough not to delude himself into thinking that these were the original Jace and Jericho. He would probably never meet them if they were even still alive.

The twins paused at each level and shook their heads. "This isn't it," Jericho decided at the tenth level up from the room where they started.

"We need to keep going," Jace reported at the twentieth level.

"It sure would be nice if Coon could stay connected to the ship for longer," Healey remarked.

"He's on his way downstairs," Jericho replied. "He's already tired out. He won't be able to help us with anything else."

"We'll just have to do this the hard way." Healey stopped at another landing while Jace and Jericho waited for their copies to check that level.

"This is it," Jace announced. "The bridge is at the end of this deck."

Jericho pulled the door open and the copies walked out into a massive gunfight raging across the deck. Forty armed copies fought against at least fifty of Ekol's men. They blockaded the bridge and everything behind them.

"Have your copies been deeper into this level?!" Healey yelled to Jericho.

Jericho shook his head and replied, but Healey couldn't hear him above the noise.

"We have to find Ekol!" Healey repeated.

Jericho nodded and divided. He stayed where he was while four of his copies spread out to search the deck behind the copies that were fighting Ekol's men. Alla hung back behind the copies' protection. He couldn't get anywhere near the gunmen.

Healey tried to see anything beyond the gunmen. A heavy, reinforced door blocked the way to the bridge. A few side rooms and staterooms led off the main corridor.

"Ekol isn't on the bridge!" Jericho yelled in Healey's ear. "He's in a stateroom somewhere back there!"

He pointed back toward the stairwell. Healey didn't see anything back there, but at that moment, one of the gunmen lobbed an explosive projectile into the mass of copies. They all ducked, but the explosion still took out almost half of them.

"This is stupid!" Jace yelled. "This is taking too long!"

"Davenport can't get to the ship!" Jericho added. "There are too many men guarding the deck! Come on! Let's go!"

Healey didn't see what he meant until Jace and Jericho both produced another devastating tide of copies. The twins flooded the corridor with so many copies that they flattened the gunmen in seconds.

The copies brought the gunmen to the ground, stripped away their weapons, and Alla moved in to clean up the mess. Now nothing but the reinforced door stopped the friends from entering the bridge.

As soon as the noise of gunfire died, Healey heard more punishing booms rocking the vessel from the outside. Deep, shuddering concussions quaked the ship.

The bombardment from outside must be escalating faster than anyone realized. Those people out there sure did hate Ekol.

Jericho tried the bridge door, but it was locked. He turned to Jace. Jace stepped forward, took hold of the knob, and yanked the door up hard enough to break the lock.

"How did you do that?" Healey asked.

Jace cracked a grin over his shoulder. "That's another two hundred points for me."

"But who's counting, right?" Jericho pushed past him.

Healey stopped Alla before he entered. "Don't eat the bridge crew, okay?"

"Who me?" Alla's hand flew to his heart. "I only eat the best people."

Healey snorted. "I'm glad I'm not one of the best people."

They entered the bridge, but no one offered any resistance. As soon as Healey crossed the threshold, he realized that Ekol's crew had much bigger problems than Healey and his friends.

"Another fourteen Daggers coming in from behind!" one of the bridge officers called. "They're Calyx Elkanon's people from Terminus Anathema! They're targeting our exhaust pipes!"

"We can't take much more from Rizarth Hudan's people, either!" another officer yelled over the noise of gunfire. "They've already destroyed the starboard hull! Another barrage like that and they'll hit the plasma reactor!"

"Return fire!" the captain barked.

"Our weapons systems are down!" a third officer countered. "We can't defend ourselves! We have to abandon ship before they destroy us completely!"

No one answered for a second. Jace, Jericho, Healey, and Alla stood at the back of the bridge listening. The twins didn't attack anyone. They didn't need to.

The bridge controls showed hundreds of ships all surrounding this one vessel. The crime syndicates that had been fighting each other just a few minutes ago all joined forces to bring down Ekol.

Healey even saw some of Ekol's own ships moving in to join the killing frenzy. How could one man turn so many people against him so fast?

Another splintering crash struck the ship's starboard side. "They got the engine room! We have to abandon ship, Sir!" the third officer repeated.

"Abandon ship!" the captain ordered. "Withdraw everyone to the flight deck immediately!"

The bridge staff sprang out of their seats and rushed the door. Some of them bumped into Healey and Alla.

None of the bridge staff tried to make the four friends leave. None of the bridge staff even asked what Healey and his friends were doing here. The crew just bolted.

Healey glanced behind him, but the crew was already vanishing into the stairs. Jace pounced on the controls. "We need to shut down at least one ship so the crew doesn't take it. I'm going with something big enough to carry us all to the surface."

Jericho joined him to look at the controls over his brother's shoulder. "Let the rest of the crew go. We got everyone who could cause us trouble."

"Can you locate Ekol?" Healey asked. "We need that device to find Joyce."

"Ekol is in his stateroom." Jericho pointed behind the stairwell where he'd been pointing earlier. "He doesn't hear orders from the crew. He probably doesn't realize how bad the situation is."

"Is there any way to salvage the ship?" Healey asked.

Jericho shook his head. "We'll be pushing it by going after Ekol. We'll be lucky to get the device and then get off this wreck before it blows."

"We better hurry, then. Come on." Healey headed back to the corridor, but he had to wait for the twins to show him where to go.

The corridor ended at the stairwell. The twins reentered it, climbed a few steps to another landing, and then descended another few steps to a different corridor. It crossed the ship heading in the other direction with the stairwell at the center next to the elevator shaft.

The second stairwell was lined with cabins, staterooms, and other residences. No one performed any command functions here.

Dozens of the twins' armed copies guarded the corridor. The copies stood guard over the door to one particular stateroom.

Jace and Jericho led the way and stopped outside the door. "Do you want to do this, Marshall?" Jericho asked. "Or we could do it our way."

"Let's see what he does first." Healey tried the door. It was unlocked. "Just be ready if he does try something."

He pushed the door open. It swung inward on a luxurious apartment lined with plush furnishings and a giant bed in a separate bedroom. The living area would have been spectacular if Ekol Thaine hadn't been in it.

He clicked his pinchers at Healey. "Are you here to arrest me, Marshall?" Ekol hissed.

"Those people out there are the ones who are here to arrest you," Healey replied. "I'm only here for the device you stole from Davenport."

"He has no right to the Ithium," Ekol snarled.

"You're in luck because he doesn't want it." Healey nodded to the twins. "Search the apartment. If Ekol wants to act like a common criminal, we'll treat him as one."

"Stop!" Ekol barked. "If I give you the device, will you leave me alone?"

Healey's eyes dropped out of their sockets. Ekol really didn't know that his precious ship was about to blow up with him on board.

"What do you say, Marshall?" Ekol murmured. "The device in exchange for my freedom and immunity from prosecution. You can't ask for a better trade than that."

Healey thought it over for a split second. Jace and Jericho both glanced at Healey waiting for his answer. Neither of them said anything about the ship's engines going critical or the dozens of ships outside all gunning for Ekol's blood.

"I shouldn't," Healey mused. "I should hand you over to Alla here….."

"Are you joking?" Alla interrupted and curled his lip at Ekol. "You couldn't pay me to eat *that.*"

Healey chuckled. "You see, Ekol? You've made yourself so hated that not even Alla will touch you. All right. You win. You give me the device and we'll vacate your ship and leave you free and immune from prosecution."

"Do you swear it?" Ekol hissed.

Healey raised his right hand. "On my honor as a marshall. No one will molest, arrest, or prosecute you for any crime. You'll be free for the rest of your life."

Ekol crawled across the room, pulled a cushion off the couch, picked up the device from behind the cushion, and tossed it into Healey's hands. "There. Now you can leave."

"There's an ambush waiting for us outside this room, Marshall," Jericho interrupted. "Ekol has kept us in here talking just long enough for his men to surround this room."

"Is it anything you can't handle?" Healey asked.

"We should be able to handle it," Jace replied. "It will take a lot of copies...."

"Excellent," Alla exclaimed. "All the more for me."

"We need to take their weapons first, so don't eat their weapons," Jace told him.

Alla stuck out his tongue. "Yuck! I don't eat weapons!"

"Just people, right?" Healey replied. "Let's go."

"We had a bargain, Marshall," Ekol called after him.

"We certainly did," Healey replied over his shoulder. "I wish you health, prosperity, and long life, Ekol. It's been a pleasure doing business with you."

Healey stuffed the device into his vest pocket and returned to the door. Jace and Jericho positioned themselves at the front. The four friends nodded to each other and Jace pulled the door open.

The twins charged outside and unleashed an avalanche of copies. They ran into another deafening storm of explosions going off all around them.

Healey spotted a dozen of Ekol's men crouched behind corners and doorways, but they'd rigged up the whole corridor with explosives instead of relying on gunfire.

"Get to the stairs, Marshall!" Jace bellowed. "Take Alla and get to the ship!"

"What about you two?!"

"We'll catch up!" Jericho called. "Go now!"

Healey ran through clouds of pelting debris as the walls around him disintegrated in explosions. Fire erupted from his left and he ducked under his arms to protect his face.

He and Alla charged for the stairwell. The copies completely blockaded the corridor behind and in front of them. The explosions tore hundreds of copies to pieces and left their dismembered bodies all over the floor.

The copies couldn't protect Healey and Alla from everything. Splinters stung Healey's cheeks and bit through his clothes. Alla screamed. He couldn't run very fast. Healey wound up pushing him the rest of the way to the stairwell.

Four copies made it—three from Jericho and one from Jace. The party thundered down the stairs putting the explosions farther behind them, but Healey didn't trust that to last.

The party made it five floors before another four of Jace's copies burst into the stairwell from the side corridor. All the copies carried numerous weapons stolen from Ekol's men.

One copy shoved a rifle into Healey's hands and another into Alla's hands. "We got trouble ahead, Marshall," the copy panted and tried to throw his hair out of his eyes, but it stuck in the sweat on his forehead.

"What's the trouble—besides everything?" Healey asked.

The copy grinned. "That's it. Just everything."

"Where is it?" Healey checked the weapon. "How far down is the trouble?"

"It starts another five floors down," Jericho replied. "After that, it's all the way down to the flight deck."

"Spectacular," Alla groaned. "Why oh why did I have to get born with the ability to eat everything? Why couldn't I have been born with a nice boring ability like the ability to fly everything like Bandit does?"

Healey chuckled. "Hey, be grateful you were born a Chorion. You could have been born a nice boring human being like me with no ability at all. How would you like that?"

Alla frowned. "You're right. I would hate that." He shrugged and his expression cleared. "Oh, well. At least I won't go hungry."

The copies laughed and the party started making their way down the stairs again, but Healey didn't let himself relax. He kept his weapon at his shoulder so he'd be ready to meet this trouble when the group found it.

He didn't have to wait long. They only descended one floor when they heard gunfire. "Are those yours?" he asked Jace and Jericho.

"Mine," Jace replied. "They're tying up Ekol's men so they don't go any farther down toward the flight deck."

"Where are Davenport and the others?"

"They're already down there waiting for us, but they're pinned down. They can't get to the ship."

"The ship is deactivated anyway," Jericho pointed out. "No one will be able to leave until we get there."

"All right," Healey replied. "Let's move."

The party climbed down faster. The twins produced more copies the farther they went. By the time the group came to the firefight, dozens of copies blocked Healey and Alla from getting near it.

Plenty of gunshots pinged up the stairs and the friends had to crouch behind the copies for cover. "How do we get through?!" Healey yelled.

"Follow me, Marshall!" Jericho replied. "You, too, Alla! Just be ready."

The twins exchanged a knowing glance and Jace nodded. He stayed where he was with his copies while Jericho led the way to another corridor. It circled the firefight on the left.

The three of them crouched behind a wall. Then, when they turned a corner and left the firefight behind, the three friends ran for it.

They only made it a dozen yards before gunfire blasted in Healey's ears. He ducked again, but Jericho grabbed Healey's sleeve and towed him forward.

Alla started to fall behind, but three of Jericho's copies hustled up behind Alla and forced him to keep going.

They broke out in a different section of corridor behind Ekol's men. They kept shooting at Jace's copies while Healey and his party sprinted for the stairs.

Another catastrophic detonation exploded the wall right in front of Healey. Rubble pelted him in the face, but he just had to keep on running.

Jericho ran into a withering blast as another wall evaporated right on top of him. He screamed once and his dead body hurtled into Healey. He only had time to throw the body aside and keep on going.

He ran alone for a minute with only his own fist clenched in Alla's shirt. Healey floundered through a solid wall of debris and then blundered into the stairwell.

Gunshots ricocheted up and down from all directions. He shrank back only for five of Jace's copies to push Healey and Alla forward.

"Keep going!" Jace ordered. "Don't stop for anything! Get ready to shoot your way through, Marshall! You, too, Alla! Get your weapon up! It's time to kick some ass!"

Another burst of gunfire ruptured behind them and the copy that just spoke went down. That noise triggered Healey's adrenaline and he leapt down the stairs.

He opened fire even before he saw who he was shooting at. He sprinted down the stairs and ran into another crowd of Ekol's gunmen, but they all had their backs to Healey's party.

They were all in open warfare against more of Jace's copies. Healey opened fire, cut down fifteen gunmen, and stormed through to join up with the copies.

They all wheeled backward and descended another five levels before three of them turned off. "This way! We can get to the flight deck from here! Follow me!"

Healey didn't argue. So many of these copies crowded the ship on every level that they must know where they were going.

Jace pushed into another corridor, ran down it to a different stairwell, and finally descended to the flight deck. A single vessel sat there waiting for them, but there was no one else around. Davenport and the others were long gone.

Chapter 25

Davenport, Lyons, Fiddler, Emmett, Dice, and the rest of the Chorions made it to the stairwell and started running down the stairs headed for the flight deck to find a ship. Davenport had no idea where to go, but a second later, one of Jace's copies caught up with their group.

The copy ran in front of Davenport. "Follow me, Sheriff!"

Davenport didn't argue. Fiddler ran over to Jace. "Where's Marshall Healey? He should have come with us."

"He went with Alla," Jace replied. "They're looking for Ekol to get the device that will let us track the Ithium."

"Can you tell if Coon is okay?" Bandit asked. "We can't leave him behind."

"I'll ask Jericho," Jace replied, but he didn't move. He just kept leaping down the stairs three at a time.

"How can you ask him when he isn't here?" Axel asked.

"My copy will ask his copy," Jace replied.

"You know what all your copies are doing...and even what conversations they're having?" Davenport asked.

"Of course." Jace grinned at him. "They're me, aren't they?"

Davenport didn't ask any more questions, but a second later, the party ran into a posse of armed men coming up the stairs from below.

Ekol's men would have gunned the friends down in seconds. The gunmen raised their weapons to fire, but Jace charged them and splintered into dozens of copies.

The copies ran straight into the path of the gunfire. "Come on!" one of them yelled over his shoulder. "Keep moving! Don't stop!"

Davenport and the others hesitated, but Fiddler ran ahead. She shadowed Jace all the way and the others followed her example.

The copies spread out taking hits and dropping like flies. Their bodies protected the crew in the middle and then the copies swarmed the gunmen's position.

The copies attacked Ekol's men, fought them hand to hand, took their weapons, and turned them on the gunmen. By the time Davenport got near them, the gunmen lay bleeding on the floor while the crew ran past them.

"The bombardment is getting hotter!" one of the copies called over his shoulder. "The other fleets are trying to blow the ship! We need to get off it as soon as we can."

"What about the others?" Davenport countered. "We can't leave without them."

"They're coming! They'll be here!" Jace burst out into another corridor. Davenport didn't have a clue where Jace was going. "This way! We're almost to the flight deck!"

The crew swerved one corner after another. The Chorions kept turning back as more Ekol's people charged out to stop the crew from escaping, but Jace always defended them.

His copies kept multiplying, splitting off to different parts of the ship, and dripping back to confront anyone who came out to attack the crew.

The copies vanished or died, but more copies always came back to rejoin the crew. Somehow, these copies always managed to arm themselves with Ekol's weapons while the copies were out there fighting everybody. Davenport didn't see how they did it.

One of the copies drew level with him and handed him a rifle. "Take this." More copies passed out weapons to the rest of the crew. "We're going to need them."

"What do you mean?" Davenport asked.

"We got trouble ahead. Another group of Ekol's men is blocking the flight deck. We're going to have to fight our way through."

Davenport gritted his teeth. "Whatever it takes."

Jace paused outside another doorway. "Here we go. Ekol's men are beyond here and the flight deck is behind them. Get ready."

The crew crowded close behind him and Davenport raised his gun to his shoulder. He didn't hear any noise coming from beyond that door—which could have been good or bad.

Jace paused there, and while the crew waited for him to make his move, Coon showed up with one of Jericho's copies. Babcock was with them.

Coon and Babcock joined the crew. Jericho pushed his way to the front and took his place next to Jace.

They exchanged a knowing glance, Jace pulled the door open, and the twins sprang across the threshold. Hundreds of copies poured through the doorway and gunfire exploded out there, but all the copies blocked Davenport from seeing anything.

More and more copies reproduced themselves.....and then the gunfire stopped. The last copies went through the doorway and the crew could finally follow.

They made it into the flight deck. Dozens of vessels stood in rows just waiting to launch, but none of them belonged to the Reserve Wing. All these ships followed some alien make that Davenport had never seen before.

Jace tossed his hair out of his eyes. "That was easy!" he chirped. "Which ship should we take?"

"We can't take anything until the rest of the crew catches up," Lyons pointed out.

Jace cocked his head to one side. "Come over here." He waved everyone toward one particular ship. "We'll take this one."

"Why this one?" Emmett asked.

"The crew is on their way down here," Jericho replied. "The ship is overloading. It will blow up soon."

"We have to go now!" Fiddler exclaimed. "We have to get off the ship before it blows."

"Not without Alla and Marshall Healey," Bandit countered. "We aren't leaving anyone behind."

"The crew is abandoning ship," Jace replied. "They're on their way down here right now. They'll take every other ship except this one." He waved everyone toward the back wall. "Come over here. Our copies deactivated this ship so the crew won't take it. We have to wait for them to leave."

He pushed everyone back and then the copies stepped forward to guard the crew. Within seconds, Ekol's people charged out of the stairwell and fanned out across the floor heading for all their ships.

A dozen people ran for the ship Jace and Jericho set aside for the crew to take. Ekol's people went on board, but when they couldn't get the ship running, they ran off somewhere else.

One ship after another launched. They sprinted away into space and vanished leaving only the one vessel behind.

"How do we get it going once we're ready to leave?" Lyons asked.

"How much time do we have left?" Emmett asked.

"Alla and Marshall Healey are on their way downstairs," Jericho replied. "Marshall Healey got the device from Ekol."

"So.....what are we doing about Ekol?" Davenport asked.

"Nothing." Jericho tossed his hair out of his eyes exactly the same way Jace did. "Marshall Healey made a deal with Ekol that we would leave Ekol on board the ship unmolested and that he would be immune to prosecution for the rest of his life."

Davenport's eyes widened when he realized what Jericho meant. Then Davenport burst out laughing. "That's perfect. I gotta hand it to Healey. He really....."

He broke off when another group of Ekol's men charged onto the flight deck, but they didn't run for any ship. There were no ships left.

The gunmen wheeled toward the crew and opened fire. Davenport raised his weapon and so did the rest of the crew.

The two sides exchanged fire and the copies rushed forward to take the brunt of the assault. Ekol's men used guns to assault the crew at first. Then the attackers lobbed some kind of explosive projectiles into the crowd of copies.

"Back away!" one of Jace's copies yelled over his shoulder. "We need to draw the fight away from the ship so they don't damage it!"

He steered the crew toward another passage leading deeper into the ship. Davenport didn't see where the passage went, but he did see all the copies dying out there.

The battle escalated with more explosions wiping out copies as fast as the twins could produce them. So many explosions flashed on the flight deck that he couldn't see much, but he didn't see Jace and Jericho making any progress toward defeating Ekol's men.

The crew hustled down the passage and wound up in a different compartment behind the launch bay. "Stay here," Jace panted. "This place is more defensible than the flight deck."

"There are more enemy gunmen coming down the stairs," Jericho added. "They're in battle against Healey and Alla."

"Please tell me some of your copies are there, too," Rodeo chimed in.

"Of course," Jace replied. "I wouldn't leave them unprotected. Healey and Alla are fine. They'll be here in a few minutes."

"Here?" Lyons looked around. "Where are we?"

"This is the pilots' briefing room," Jericho replied. "This is where...."

"Does it matter where it is?" Axel interrupted. "How can we get on board the ship with so many of Ekol's men out there?"

Jace shrugged that away. "I'll take care of them."

"How?" Emmett asked. "It looked to me like they were handing all your copies just fine."

"They're running out of ammo now." Jericho inclined his head the other way. "It's safe now. We can go. Hurry. The ship is about to go up."

He led the way back down the passage back to the flight deck. They found Healey, Alla, and a bunch of copies standing around waiting for them. "Quick! Everyone on board!" Jace ordered.

The crew loaded up. The ship's bridge occupied a position all the way at the top of the vessel. Passenger compartments lined to two sides on the lower level with gun turrets in the ship's hold.

"Get inside those turrets!" Jericho ordered. "Get ready to defend the ship as soon as...."

A catastrophic blast threw the vessel sideways. "The ship is exploding!" Jace yelled. "Get in position! Come on, Sheriff! Come to the bridge!"

The crew split up. Davenport followed Jace and Jericho to the bridge where the twins divided themselves between every station. One of Jace's copies took the helm and Davenport jumped on a station next to him.

One glance at the controls showed Davenport all he needed to know. The flight deck's front wall dissolved in flame and hurled debris at the ship. The shockwave smashed the ship back against the opposite wall.

"Activate the ship's engines, Jericho!" Jace called over his shoulder.

"That's what I am doing!" Jericho countered. "The bridge is exploding! It's playing hell with the controls."

"You better hurry up before we all go down in flames!" Davenport scrambled to get the controls working.

The ship's power system worked just fine. The lock Jericho had put on the controls returned an error message every time Davenport tried to do anything.

Another shuddering boom rocked the vessel and a punishing blast took out the wall on the ship's port side.

"What's the holdup?!" Jace bellowed over the noise.

"Got it!" Jericho called. "Go, go, go!"

Davenport fired the engines, but Jace was already ripping the ship away. A bone-crushing explosion punched through the forward wall that was already on fire.

The impact smacked the ship backward again and it soared out into space. Jace punched the throttle just as Ekol's vessel detonated with him on board.

The erupting fireball caught the crew's escape vessel from behind and hurled it clear. Davenport read the battle still in progress.

"I'm setting course for Vorax Suma," he called over to Jace. "Get us as far away from the battle as possible."

Jace nodded, but Ekol's exploding ship blocked anyone from coming after the crew. So many other ships escaped from Ekol's vessel that the other fleets in battle had their work cut out for them to break away from the enemy to go after everyone.

Jace fired the engines to their full speed and the ship plunged for the planet's surface. "I'm going around the planet to the other side," he told Davenport. "We can figure out where the Ithium is from there."

Davenport didn't argue. He got busy checking the scanners and trying to find someone in the mayhem that he recognized.

He finally located the *Vindicator* and hailed Pritchard. Pritchard had a hard time talking with all the explosions going off around his ship. He had to steer the *Vindicator*, fire his cannons, and talk at the same time.

"What the hell are you people doing?!" he roared. "You should have been on the planet by now."

"It's complicated," Davenport replied. "We're going there now."

Pritchard furrowed his brow at his controls. "What the hell is that thing you're flying? It isn't shielded like we planned."

"Like I said, it's complicated. We're on our way to......"

Jericho interrupted. "Three more of Ekol's warships are moving in to block our path. They're hailing us."

"Get Babcock up here," Davenport replied and turned back to Pritchard. "I'll be in touch, Sheriff. Hold the fort."

Pritchard snorted. "There is no fort to hold in case you hadn't noticed."

Davenport chuckled, but at that moment, the communications system switched on by itself. "They're forcing a connection," Jericho reported. "I guess they really want to talk to us."

Davenport looked down at the hideous face of a huge Zihori. "You destroyed Ekol Thaine's ship! Hand over the man responsible or we'll...."

"I'm responsible, Valli," Davenport snapped. "I'm taking command of Ekol's force."

The Zihori frowned back at him. "You! You have no authority over Ekol's force. You're nothing."

"Ekol didn't have time to escape. He left me in charge. I can prove it."

Babcock scrambled onto the bridge in time to hear this and Davenport waved him forward. Babcock stepped in front of the screen to show Valli his face.

"Withdraw all of Ekol's forces from the battle, Valli," Babcock told him. "Davenport is taking command of Ekol's empire."

Valli scowled. "I don't like this. We should confirm it first."

"You wouldn't be able to confirm it with anyone but Ekol and he's dead," Babcock countered. "We all saw what happened when we thought he was dead and there was no one to take charge. It's better this way."

"Fine," Valli humphed and turned to someone off the screen. "Pull all our vessels out of the battle."

"Withdraw to the following coordinates." Davenport got to work on the controls. "I'm sending a message to Calyx Elkanon's people to withdraw to the other side of the battlefield. Keep out of each other's way and don't antagonize each other again. I'll be sending my own people over to your ships to take command."

"Who are these people?" Valli demanded. "It better not be anyone from the Sheriff's Service."

"It isn't. Don't worry. It's someone you know. Now withdraw. I'll be there in a minute."

Davenport cut the signal. "Are you sure you know what you're doing?" Babcock squeaked.

"It beats all these people fighting each other over nothing." Davenport stood up and turned to Jace and Jericho. "Identify the command vessels from Ekol's fleet and send word to each of them that I'm putting my own people in command of each one. Tell them they've made a royal mess of this battle and I don't trust them not to do it again. Tell them anyone who steps out of line will suffer the consequences.....and tell the Chorion Team to meet me downstairs ready to deploy on the other ships."

Chapter 26

"**W**hy do we have to go?" Bandit asked.

"Because no one is better at flying a ship than you are," Davenport replied. "I need you all up here. I need to be able to call on Ekol's force to help me and I can't trust anyone but you boys to do the job. I need you to take control of this force and make sure no one tries to land on the planet. That might trigger the disaster we're all trying to prevent."

"I guess so," Bandit grumbled.

"Take Breeze with you. I don't want him flying anything and he can make sure everyone follows your orders." Davenport surveyed the rest of the crew. "Wolf, you can go with Rodeo. I would put you in charge of your own ship, but we need someone who speaks English."

"Let me come with, Sir," Axel urged. "I can help you on the planet."

"Me, too," Alla added. "I don't want to sit this one out."

"All right. You two can come. Babcock can go with Coon and you can take a ship, too, Laub. Jace and Jericho will take the rest."

"You got it, Sir," Laub replied.

Just then, the ship slammed into something and the hatch slid open behind Davenport. "Go on," he told the boys. "I need you up here more than I need you down there."

"Whatever you need, Sir." Rodeo waved to his friends. "Let's go."

He, Bandit. Breeze, Wolf, Laub, and Coon walked through the hatch into the vestibule of another ship. The escape craft the crew took from Ekol Thaine's exploding warship had docked with one of his stolen Reserve Wing Stalwarts.

One copy each from Jace and Jericho went with them. The Chorions halted in the vestibule and turned around to face the rest of the crew.

Babcock paused and pressed Davenport's hands between both of his. "I wish I could convince you to take over for good, but I know you won't do that."

"Let's make sure we're all still alive after this before we have that conversation," Davenport replied. "Go on, Babcock. These boys will need your support to keep control of the fleet."

Babcock nodded, compressed his lips to hold back emotion, and crossed to the vestibule. Coon and Breeze both raised their hands to wave and then the doors shut between them. Davenport lost sight of them.

"Let's kick this sucker into next week," Dice rumbled and turned away. "We should have landed on the planet hours ago."

The crew broke up. The ship didn't feel right without the Chorions on board, but Davenport had a job to do.

He, Jace, and Jericho returned to the bridge where Jace disengaged from the Stalwart. Davenport cast one backward glance at the ship as it drifted out of position.

It glided toward another nearby Stalwart. The Chorions would divide up between these ships. With luck, Davenport would be able to contact one of his friends when this was all over—whenever that happened to be.

He turned his attention to Vorax Suma. "Is there any sign of the Ithium?" he asked Jericho.

"Nothing," Jericho replied. "There's no sign of any human life or any structures on the planet, either. Whatever Joyce has been doing here, he's covered his tracks."

"Just get us onto the planet," Davenport ordered. "We'll take it from.....hold up. I see something." He zeroed in on one section jungle.

"What is that?" Jace asked.

"It looks like vehicle tracks," Davenport replied. "Whatever infrastructure Joyce built here, he must have used some kind of machinery to build. Then he vacated the planet and the vegetation grew back."

"Do you want to land there?"

"Not too close." Davenport sent him another set of coordinates. "We don't want him to feel threatened by us. We have to make it look like our landing was an accident. Set us down in those rocks over there. That's far enough away."

Jace turned the ship in that direction, but at that moment, the communications system came on by itself again. "We got a problem, Sheriff!" Bolander hollered. "We've all been so locked up with the battle that we didn't check the long-range scans."

"What's wrong?" Davenport asked and glanced at his scanners. A shiver went up his spine when he saw hundreds of Cannibal ships moving in.

"Shit!" Jericho murmured.

"They're moving in on Vorax Suma!" Jace added. "Do you still want to land there?"

"We have to," Davenport decided. "We'll just have to deal with it. Take us down."

Jace dove for the planet's atmosphere, but the Cannibals moved in way too fast. How did they get the jump on....well, everybody?

Countless ships landed on the planet and Cannibals swarmed the surface. Even more ships swooped around the planet and opened fire on the fleets that had only just been shooting at each other a few minutes ago.

Gunfire scattered in all directions. Ekol's people, Calyx's forces, Rizarth Hudan's syndicate, the regular Reserve Wing, and the rogues all plunged into the attack. All their hostilities against each other evaporated, now that they faced an overwhelming common enemy.

"Break away!" Davenport ordered. "Get out of the line of fire and get to the planet!"

"We'll be flying straight *into* the line of fire if we go there!" Jericho countered.

"We'll be in the line of fire either way and we only have one chance to get Joyce! Take us in, Jace!"

Jace fired the engines, but the crew couldn't escape so many Cannibals. The Cannibal horde surrounded Vorax Suma in a curtain of gunfire. Jace flew right into it.

The gun turrets down below returned fire, but one ship couldn't break that line. Davenport tried to hail some of his friends for help, but they were all too busy fighting their own war.

Cannibal ships surrounded the crew and hammered the vessel away from the planet. Davenport feared the worst when ten Stalwarts plunged out of the chaos and surrounded the little craft.

"Fall in with us, Sir!" Rodeo ordered through the communications system. "We'll get you down there. Then it's up to you."

"Thanks, man," Davenport choked. He would have liked to say more, but the constant smash of gunfire on his hull stopped him.

The Stalwarts flew more slowly, but they surrounded the little ship in so much fire-power that the crew made better progress this way.

Jace dropped into the pocket with the Stalwarts all around him. The Stalwarts' big sides took the Cannibals' gunfire and protected the little ship.

The Cannibals responded by turning their attention on the Stalwarts and another battle broke out. Jace skimmed between the Stalwarts and made his last headlong dive for the surface.

"The jungle you wanted to land in is full of Cannibals!" Jericho reported. "Are you sure you want to land there?"

"Is anywhere else on the planet safer?" Davenport asked.

"Nope."

"Then it's up to you two and Alla to get us to Joyce's hidden bunker—or whatever the hell it is. Do you think you can handle all those Cannibals?"

"We'll have to," Jericho replied. "Set us down, Jace."

Jace lowered the ship between the trees, broke the branches, and descended closer to the ground. The Cannibals had all been swarming in one direction before. Davenport didn't see where they wanted to go or why. They didn't usually need a reason.

They all spun around and attacked the ship with their bare hands as soon as it got low enough for them to get their dirty little hands on it. They tried to pull it down even though it was already down.

"Get downstairs and get ready to deploy," Davenport ordered. "Take Alla with you."

Jace and Jericho both left the bridge and Davenport took the controls. He landed the ship, powered down the engines, and went downstairs to the hatch.

Jace, Jericho, and Alla stood at the front waiting. Healey, Axel, Emmett, Fiddler, Dice, and Lyons stayed behind those three.

The crew looked awfully small like this. Davenport sure wished the others were here, but it was too late to regret that.

Dozens of pounding hands beat the ship's hull and rocked the vessel on its landing gear. That noise got louder and the jostling became more violent. The Cannibals would upend the ship any second now.

The friends exchanged one glance and Jericho made eye contact with Davenport. "Take the crew, break away, and get to the weapon," Jericho told him. "Leave the Cannibals to us. Understand?"

Davenport nodded. He would have to put any desire to defend his friends out of his mind and concentrate on the mission.

Jericho popped the hatch, and in seconds, hundreds of copies stampeded outside. An overwhelming tide forced the Cannibals back and left enough space for the rest of the crew to get outside.

Alla rushed between the copies swallowing Cannibals as fast as he could. Davenport tore himself away with an effort. The copies swept the Cannibals forward so Davenport and the crew could skim alongside the ship and get behind the Cannibals' line.

The Cannibals centered their attack on the highest concentration of copies. The Cannibals either didn't notice or didn't care about a handful of people darting behind the ship and sprinting away into the forest.

Davenport made it a hundred yards before he dared to stop and listen. Screams, roars, and gunshots echoed through the trees behind him. He turned around to look just as Alla charged him along with four copies, two from each twin.

The noise and commotion drifting through the trees from the ship kept getting louder and more nerve-racking. "What's happening over there?" Axel asked.

Alla shook his head fast. "You don't want to know! Let's get out of here!"

Davenport turned in the direction where he'd seen the tire tracks. He didn't know if he would find Joyce there, but those tracks were the only sign that humans had ever been on this planet.

He hiked another half a mile and stopped. "Get out your device, Marshall," he told Healey. "See if we're going in the right direction."

Healey took out the device and switched it on. Its dial swiveled in all directions. "This isn't showing any Ithium on the planet."

Lyons pulled a card out of her pocket. It showed scanner readings of the nearby rocks. "These rocks are probably shielding the readings.....Oh, hold on a second. There are more human life signs ahead.......and one reading native to Sacron Enigma."

"Beauty!" Dice growled. "He better not be working for Joyce."

"Joyce could only have gotten the Ziprothil from Beauty," Lyons pointed out. "Beauty may be a captive."

Davenport looked at the readings over her shoulder. "They're near the tire tracks. Let's go."

Chapter 27

The crew snuck through the undergrowth and halted in view of another stand of tall rocks. The jungle surrounded the spot and concealed it from view.

Lyons scanned the surroundings and Davenport looked at the readings over her shoulder. "There's a cave system up ahead with a human and alien life sign underground," she remarked. "Joyce has ground troops stationed around here. We better be careful."

"There's still no sign of the Ithium or the Ziprothil." Davenport frowned. "Why are the scans turning up so many life signs and not the weapon?"

"The question is why we can read these scans down here but the Reserve Wing can't pick up all these life signs from orbit," she replied. "These rocks must give off some electromagnetic interference—or else block electromagnetic waves from escaping into the atmosphere. I can't think of any other explanation."

"We can't tell which life signs are Joyce's, either," Healey pointed out.

"We'll just have to assume that Joyce is the one human life sign that's actually inside the caves. He wouldn't be out here while someone else was inside with Beauty."

"Unless Beauty is a captive and someone is down there guarding him," Fiddler suggested.

"That makes no sense," Lyons countered. "Joyce will be wherever the weapon is. He won't let it out of his sight. If the weapon was on the surface, everyone would be able to see it. We can't see it because it's underground—under those rocks. Come on. We have to get down there."

She started to stand up, but at that moment, a squadron of Reserve Wing Nitrols screamed out of the distance. They shrieked across the landscape, wheeled over the jungle where the friends were hiding, and hovered directly above the hidden crew.

"What is the Reserve Wing doing down here?" Emmett snapped.

"This isn't the Reserve Wing," Fiddler replied. "These are rogues. They're Admiral Joyce's followers."

Dice spun around, raised his weapon, and took aim at those ships. "Stop!" Davenport pulled Dice's gun down. "Don't shoot! It will give away our location."

"They already know our location," Axel pointed out. "They can see human, Chorion, and Adik life signs, now that we're in the open."

Davenport pulled Dice deeper under the canopy, but just then, thirty Cannibal ships plummeted over the horizon, took aim, and bombarded the rogue vessels.

One of them exploded and the others staggered away from the crew's location. The Cannibal vessels advanced driving the rogue Nitrols farther from the rocks.

Another two erupted right above the crew's heads. "Go!" Davenport hollered. "Get to the caves!"

"What about the soldiers?!" Lyons asked, but before anyone could answer, a wave of ground troops swept out of the jungle making for the crew's position.

All those troops wore Reserve Wing uniforms and carried Reserve Wing guns. These had to be Joyce's rogues, too.

Davenport raised his weapon to gun them down. Jace and Jericho divided into a swarm of copies, but just as fast, a matching wave of Cannibals charged out of the undergrowth and overran the rogue ground troops.

Davenport staggered back to get away from the Cannibals and tripped over Emmett and Axel. The friends grabbed each other and blundered deeper into the jungle to get away from all these combatants.

The Cannibal ships kept pounding rogue vessels overhead and a burning fuselage plunged down on top of the Cannibals on the ground. Screams, roars, and tearing sounds filled the jungle behind the fleeing party.

Davenport pushed his friends ahead of him, but the Cannibals gained on them. Alla and the twins dropped back to cover the crew's retreat.

Davenport glanced behind him in time to see dozens of copies guarding the crew's rear. The rogue ground troops and the Cannibals rushed after the crew, but in that split second, Davenport saw that the troops, the copies, and the Cannibals weren't fighting or attacking each other.

A cloud of some unknown creature darkened the jungle and enveloped everything in its path. These weren't the burrowing armored creatures that devoured the *Echo Omicron.* These looked more like flying insects with gossamer wings, spindly legs, and thin, segmented bodies.

The crew's flight disturbed these creatures that must have been lying dormant in the jungle. Thousands of them burst out of nowhere, gathered into a solid black mass, and launched at the combined mob of copies, Cannibals, and rogue ground troops.

The creatures hit the ground troops first and consumed them entirely, including the bones. The Cannibals nearest sprinted away and drew closer to the crew.

Alla darted between the crew and the Cannibals, stretched his mouth, and engulfed a dozen Cannibals in each swallow. He kept gulping as fast as he could go and his body kept swelling bigger and bigger and bigger.

The copies surrounded him. "We gotta move, Alla!" Jericho yelled in Alla's face. "Stop eating!"

"Can't....." Alla stammered between gulps. "Gotta.....!"

Jace rushed him, multiplied into another fifty copies, and they all picked up Alla. He'd swollen to whale sized and his stomach encompassed his thighs all the way down to his knees. His arms from the elbow down stuck out of a body so round that he couldn't even move.

The copies hoisted him off the ground and took off running through the trees. Axel dropped back to follow the crew, but the copies were already there.

The copies didn't need to do anything with the insects mowing down first the ground troops and then starting on the Cannibals. Cannibals bumped into Davenport in their haste to save themselves, only for the Cannibals to get pulled down by the bloodthirsty swarm.

Something hit Davenport in the back, and out of nowhere, Axel leapt behind him, pulled one of the creatures off Davenport's shoulder, and tore it apart.

Axel spun backward to face the cloud of insects and they surrounded him all attacking at once.

"AXEL!!" Alla screamed, but the copies didn't put him down.

Davenport and the rest of the crew kept on running until they came to a river. A waterfall fell over some high cliffs and misty spray filled the air with rainbows.

Fiddler and Emmett raced ahead, leapt over stepping stones to the other side, and the cloud of insects stopped when it got as far as the spray. The insects wouldn't fly through it.

The copies put Alla down on the ground. "Axel!!" he kept wailing. "AXEL!!"

"He'll be all right," Jace panted.

"We have to go back for him!" Alla moaned. "The ground troops might take him."

"The ground troops have more important things to worry about right now," Lyons pointed out.

"*You* aren't going anywhere," Healey pointed out. "You won't need to eat again for a month at least."

Alla rolled onto his side. He couldn't stand on his own. "You'll go back for him, won't you, Marshall? You won't leave him to die on this planet, will you?"

"Axel can take care of himself," Healey replied. "You, on the other hand, will have to stay here."

Alla tried to twist the other way, but his enormous body wouldn't let him. "I'll stay with him," Jericho offered. "We should be all right as long as we stay inside the spray."

"Just don't go anywhere," Davenport told him. "Make sure we can find you when it's time to get out of here."

Jericho turned to gaze down at Alla. "It's like you say. He won't be going anywhere."

"I mean don't carry him anywhere. Just stay put. We don't want to have to search the whole planet for you."

"Unless it's dangerous," Jace added. "Then you can move."

Jericho cracked a grin at him, but just then, footsteps crashing through the jungle made everyone look up.

Axel stumbled out of the trees. Blood soaked his hair and deep gashes marked his face and arms. "What happened?" Healey exclaimed. "They.....they cut you!"

Axel pressed his wrist to his forehead and collapsed on the moss next to Alla. "They.....I don't know what they are. Their teeth—" He shook his head and ran his bloody forehead across his shoulder.

"You better stay here with Alla and Jericho," Davenport decided. "We'll go on to the cave."

Axel pointed to the north. "The swarm is moving off. You should have a straight shot to get inside. I think those things ate all the guards."

"I could have done that," Alla grumbled.

"Is there any limit to how much you can eat?" Fiddler asked.

"Can we talk about that later?" Davenport interrupted. "Come on. Let's get underground and get this done."

Axel stood up. "I'm going with you. I might not be able to stand up to those creatures, but Joyce and the Reserve Wing haven't developed a weapon yet that can scratch me."

Davenport hesitated. Axel looked terrible, but the determined light in his eye left no room to doubt. "All right," Davenport replied. "You can come."

Chapter 28

Davenport snuck back to the same spot where Lyons could scan the caves ahead. "Axel is right. The guards are all gone."

"Did you think I lied about it?" Axel fired back.

"Come on," Davenport whispered. "Let's get in there before any of the ground troops come back."

He crept out of hiding and darted up to the cave opening. It was deserted, but he heard people moving around in the undergrowth.

"Joyce and Beauty haven't been separated since we got here," Lyons murmured. "They must be working on the weapon."

"Beauty couldn't be working on the weapon," Dice countered. "He hates Joyce."

"Either way, they're together."

"Show us where they are," Davenport told her.

She went ahead. Jace and Jericho followed with one copy each and the crew worked their way deeper into the cave system.

Lyons followed her scanners to a large cavern deep inside the rock. She waved the crew against a wall somewhere and they peered around a corner at piles of crates, equipment, machinery, and everything anyone would need to stay hidden on this planet for a long time.

Davenport stiffened when he recognized two voices coming from behind all the supplies. One was Admiral Joyce's and the other belonged to Beauty.

They talked to each other in what sounded like a friendly, conversational tone. It didn't sound like Beauty was a captive at all.

Lyons tiptoed into the cavern, ducked behind some big crates labeled, *Aswalt Mines,* and the crew followed her around some excavating machinery getting closer to those voices.

She flattened herself against another enormous container and the crew peeked out at Joyce and Beauty working together.

Joyce stood by a metal cylinder with wires and tubes running out of it. Steam billowed from cracks in the cylinder's housing and the wires ran to a computer console.

Beauty squatted on top of the console working on the controls. "It's almost ready," he rasped.

Joyce bent over the cylinder and frowned at it while he punched the buttons on a different control pad built into the housing. "The Ithium and the Ziprothil aren't interacting the way they should. Something must be wrong with the chip. It must have gotten damaged in all the fighting."

"The chip is working fine," Beauty growled. "It has some unique programming. It isn't as compatible with your systems as it could be, but I can reconfigure it to make it work."

Joyce smacked his lips and turned around to glare at Beauty. "How long with that take?"

"How long is a piece of string?" Beauty bent over the controls. "I'll get started on it now."

"Well, hurry up," Joyce snapped. "I'm threatening the Confederacy with a weapon that doesn't work. If anyone finds out, I'm history."

"It will work," Beauty replied. "I'll make sure it's ready when you need it."

"That little shit!" Lyons hissed. "He's actually helping Joyce! I'm going out there to wring his sorry little neck!"

Davenport held her back. "Wait. Not yet."

He didn't know what made him stop her. The crew would never get better odds than them against just Joyce and Beauty, especially when the crew had Jace and Jericho on their side.

The words barely left Davenport's mouth before a dozen uniformed soldiers strode into the cavern. "Sir....." one of them panted. "The air battle is turning against us! The Cannibals....."

"I don't want to hear about the air battle right now!" Joyce fired back. "This is much more important. The Reserve Wing won't dare to land on the planet as long as I have this weapon."

"It isn't the Reserve Wing, Sir," the soldier blurted out. "The Cannibals are on the planet and overrunning our positions. We won't be able to hold them back......and then these creatures came out and attacked us......"

Joyce spun around to confront Beauty and snapped, "Hurry up! This is important!"

"There's another army on the surface, too, Sir," the soldier went on.

Joyce barely looked at him. "Who is it this time—one of the syndicates?"

"We can't identify them, Sir—unless they're clones. They all have identical DNA patterns."

Joyce's head shot up. "Clones! They can't be clones. Cloning is illegal in the Confederacy. The only clones are at Helios Sanctus."

"There must be a thousand of them out there, Sir," the soldier insisted. "They keep coming out of nowhere to attack us when we least expect it."

Jace and Jericho gave each other a fist bump, but Joyce was already losing interest. "It doesn't matter, because as soon as I get this baby up and running, we'll level them along with the Cannibals."

The soldier glanced at the weapon and gulped. "Um.....Sir.....You won't detonate the weapon while we're on the planet, will you? How will you detonate it with enough time for us to escape?"

"You leave that to me, Sergeant." Joyce waved him away. "Go back outside and make sure none of these clones gets near enough to the caves to interfere with this."

Joyce waited for the soldiers to leave and then rounded on Beauty. "What the hell is taking so long? Can't you make it work yet?"

"I'm working as fast as I can," Beauty growled. "These things take time. You wouldn't want me to make a mistake that could be catastrophic, would you?"

Joyce humphed and crossed the room to a different computer console. Neither of them had been working on it before.

"The Cannibals are getting closer," Joyce barked. "We need to move the device deeper underground. I can't run the risk of them finding it."

"I can work on it on the way." Beauty pulled another card out of the console. "It's nearly ready."

"It better be." Joyce crossed to the device, unhooked a bunch of the wires, and picked up the cylinder in his arms.

He cradled it and headed to another side tunnel leading deeper underground. Beauty hopped off his console and padded after Joyce. Just before he left the cavern, Davenport spotted Beauty grinning at Joyce behind his back.

This wasn't Beauty's friendly, sheepish grin. It was a grin of pure murderous hatred.

Lyons turned around to face the rest of the crew. "We have to stop them before they get that weapon active."

"I have a plan," Davenport replied. "We can create a diversion to lure Joyce away from the weapon. Then we'll pounce and grab him."

"Who's doing the pouncing?" Fiddler asked.

"I have to be the one to pounce," Davenport replied. "I'm the sheriff here. I'm the one empowered to arrest Joyce."

"What about Marshall Healey?" Axel asked. "He can arrest Joyce as well as you can."

"Don't worry," Healey interjected. "I'll create the diversion, but it would work better if you helped me, Dice."

Dice rolled his eyes and groaned. "Always with the diversions. Fine. What do you want me to do?"

"I'll show you. Come on."

Healey led the way back to the entrance to this large cavern. He waved Davenport and the others into a hidden corner while Healey pulled Dice into the open. There were no other soldiers around—not that anyone could see. They had to be lurking around here somewhere.

Davenport, Fiddler, Lyons, Axel, and Emmett spread themselves behind the supplies on both sides of the cavern entrance.

Davenport held his breath waiting to see what Dice and Healey would do. Healey waited until everyone got into position and then he grabbed Dice's arm. "You're under arrest for disturbing the peace and reckless endangerment! Put your hands behind your head and get down on the floor!"

Dice reared back with a deafening roar. "You son of a bitch!" he thundered and wheeled around. He raised his other hand in a fist to club Healey to the ground.

"Confederate Marshall!" Healey bellowed. "Surrender immediately or suffer the consequences."

Dice roared again and lunged for Healey. Davenport couldn't imagine Dice playing an act as well as this. He really must have thought Healey was trying to arrest him and Dice reacted that way.

He grabbed Healey by the front of his vest, but when Dice clenched his fists in Healey's clothes to pile-drive him into the floor, Dice's hand closed on Healey's star.

The metal pierced Dice's hand and he yanked it away with another earth-shaking bellow. "Aarrgh!"

Healey charged again and elbowed Dice in the face. Dice roared even louder, staggered backward, and nearly trampled Davenport and the others before Dice smashed into the crate the crew had been using as a hiding place.

Healey followed up his advantage, punched Dice in the nose, and then hooked his elbow around Dice's neck to slam him face down on the floor.

Healey wrenched Dice's arm behind his back. "Don't move! You're under arrest!"

"You cocksucking piece of shit!" Dice thundered. "I swear I'll kill you for this!"

The noise brought the same twelve soldiers rushing back. They charged in from outside and slowed to a walk when they saw Healey wrestling Dice under control.

"What the hell?!" the first soldier snapped. "What are you doing here?"

"I'm Confederate Marshall Lawrence Healey," Healey announced. "I'm arresting this Adik for disorderly conduct, resisting arrest, reckless endangerment, and destruction of property. Don't worry. I'll make sure he doesn't hurt you."

"I'll hurt you!!" Dice roared. "Get your stinking hands off me, you bastard!"

Dice reared off the floor a few times and almost bucked Healey off. Another soldier asked, "Do you need any help there, Marshall?" but none of the other soldiers stepped forward either to interfere or to help out.

Healey smiled up at them. "I got it. You just have to know how to handle these creatures. They're really pussycats when you get the hang of it."

"You filthy, rotten, traitorous son of a bitch!" Dice roared and gave one more heave off the floor.

He didn't have too much trouble leaping back to his feet and throwing Healey off. Healey weighed half as much as Dice and Healey wasn't trying too hard to restrain him.

Dice flung out his arm, sent Healey flying, and Healey smashed into one of the excavators standing nearby.

Dice spun around to bare his fangs at the soldiers. He was already starting to swell.

"Come on!" Healey ordered. "We all have to attack him at the same time! All together!"

He rushed Dice. The soldiers hesitated, but when they saw Healey about to attack Dice all alone, the soldiers joined in. They surrounded him, tried to grab his arms to hold him down, and another two went sailing off to slam into the walls.

Davenport got so fascinated with the scene that he didn't see Joyce coming until the Admiral barged right up to the fight. "What the hell is going on? I told you not to let anyone in here!"

No one answered him. Healey and the soldiers were too busy trying to keep their grip on Dice's enormous arms.

He dislodged the soldiers just by flailing his arms and smashing them aside. He didn't do the same thing to Healey.

Davenport didn't wait around to see anything else. He launched himself out of his hiding place, tackled Joyce around the middle, and flattened the guy to the floor right in front of the spot where Axel and Emmett were both hiding.

The rest of the crew jumped out of hiding and dove in to help Davenport. Joyce fought back, and a second later, another six soldiers materialized out of thin air.

They pounced on top of Davenport and his friends and an unholy brawl broke out on the floor. Fists and elbows landed all over Davenport.

He had to let go of Joyce to defend himself against the soldiers. Davenport twisted around trying to get some purchase on his enemies. The minute he got hold of one of the soldiers, an almighty force ripped the man away.

Dice towered above Davenport and Dice snarled in fury at everyone. He snatched soldiers off the pile and sent them cartwheeling into the walls. They slammed against the rock and fell unconscious to the floor.

Chapter 29

Davenport picked himself up, dusted himself off, and peered up at Dice's gruesome face. "Are you okay?"

Dice snarled under his breath. "That son of a bitch tried to arrest me! What the hell was I supposed to do?"

Davenport glanced around. Healey lay in a heap across the cavern where Dice had thrown him, too, but Healey was already getting to his feet and shrugging his clothes back into place.

Davenport cracked a grin at Dice. "You did great. That was one hell of a diversion."

"It didn't work, though, did it? Joyce is gone."

Davenport looked over his shoulder. It was true. Joyce was nowhere in sight and now Beauty and the weapon weren't here, either.

Lyons and Fiddler came over from somewhere. Neither of them appeared to have sustained any damage. Axel looked the same as he did outside.

Emmett sat up from where he'd fallen on the floor. Fiddler helped him stand and Lyons pulled out her card again. "The rocks are hiding the Ithium again. We might have to search before we find Joyce."

"Then let's go," Davenport replied. "We don't have much time left."

"I'm gonna kill that little shit Beauty," Dice growled. "Like we haven't gone through enough already and now he's actually helping Joyce."

"I don't think so," Davenport told them. "I think he might be sabotaging Joyce somehow."

"How could he?" Axel asked. "Joyce already has all three components assembled into one device."

"I don't know how, but I think we're about to find out."

The crew followed the tunnel where they'd seen Joyce take the device. They only made it a hundred yards before yelling voices told them exactly where to go.

The voices got louder as the crew inched forward. Davenport recognized Joyce's voice, but not the others.

When the crew made it to the next corner, they all peered around the wall at five soldiers in open confrontation with Joyce.

One of them was a captain. "If you detonate the device here, we all die!" the guy snapped. "That isn't what we agreed. You said we'd be safe and you also said you'd make arrangements for our families."

"We sacrificed everything for this plan," a lieutenant commander added. "Now we're fugitives from Confederate law with warrants out for our arrest and you don't even care!"

"You all signed up for the chain of command," Joyce countered. "You agreed to follow my orders. If you don't like it, you can go back to the Reserve Wing and take your chances."

"You aren't going anywhere without us," the captain returned. "You only made it this far thanks to our help."

Joyce's lips split in an evil grin. "That's what you think."

"If you don't change this plan to include us getting out of here with our lives, then you're done," the lieutenant commander finished. "There are a lot more of us than there are of you. You'll deactivate the device and use whatever means of transportation you have to take us to Sacron Enigma. We aren't detonating the device. That is not going to happen."

"You don't think so?" Before any of the others could do anything, Joyce pulled a handgun from his pocket and blew the guy's brains out right there.

The body buckled and Joyce spun around to turn the weapon on the captain. The captain reacted just as fast, lunged for Joyce, and the other three soldiers standing there attacked at the same time.

The captain grabbed Joyce's wrist and knocked the gun upward just as it went off. The shot smashed into the ceiling and rock shards rained on the combatants, but none of the soldiers noticed.

One of them tried to wrestle the captain's hands away to free Joyce from the guy's grip. Another attacked his friend to give the captain free access to Joyce.

Davenport didn't see what the third guy was doing. In a split second, the captain wrenched the gun out of Joyce's hands and turned it on the admiral.

Joyce broke away, but instead of running for it, he grabbed the man who'd just been helping him. The captain fired at Joyce. Joyce ducked behind the man and yanked the man into the path of the gunshot.

The soldier's chest exploded and the captain hesitated just long enough for Joyce to back away using the body as a shield.

He pulled another gun from somewhere and fired past the dead soldier's shoulder. The captain and the last soldier had to dive into another side tunnel to take cover.

The two soldiers took off heading somewhere else. Davenport and his crew stayed hidden until all the noise died down.

By the time Davenport inched out of his hiding place to go after Joyce, the crew found nothing but the dead soldier lying in another passageway farther along. Joyce, Beauty, and the device were nowhere in sight.

Lyons tugged Davenport's sleeve to get his attention. "The device is showing up on the scans now. We must be getting close."

The crew followed the scans down dozens of winding passages, through multiple caverns, and deeper underground.

Lyons eventually led the way to an even bigger cavern with piles of supplies and even a Dagger resting on its landing gear.

An opening in the ceiling let daylight into the cavern, but it wasn't a straight shaft. It curved in different directions. That must be how the rock continued to conceal this place from any scans of the surface.

Joyce strode across the cavern to where Beauty squatted next to the device. "You shouldn't have brought the device down here," Joyce growled. "There are intruders in the upper caverns. They could have followed you here."

Beauty tilted his head back and gave Joyce a full, beaming smile. "I couldn't let it fall into the wrong hands, could I? Anyway, I got the chip working while you were busy. The device is primed and ready to go. You can detonate it anytime you want. Just push this button."

Beauty handed Joyce another small controller. Joyce looked back and forth between it and Beauty. "Did you really? It's all fixed?"

"It's in perfect working order." Beauty waggled his ears. "Just like you asked."

"I guess I can take it on board the ship now. I'll just have to contact the Reserve Wing to let them know not to mess with my ship."

"We'll have to wait until you get airborne," Beauty told him. "These rocks block communications transmissions."

Joyce frowned. "Damn! That's no good. How can I find out how many ships are in orbit and who they're working for?"

Beauty shrugged. "We'll be able to see all of that as soon as we launch."

Joyce turned away. "I will be, you mean. You're staying here."

Beauty's cheery grin evaporated. "I'm going with you. You said you'd take me with you."

Joyce snorted. "I don't think so. I'm going alone."

He bent over to pick up the device. Beauty lunged for him and knocked him away from it. "You can't leave me behind! I did everything you asked. The device is working now because of me! If you leave me here, the Reserve Wing will arrest me as one of your accomplices."

Joyce only sniffed at him. "That's the breaks. I'm not taking you anywhere."

He walked back over to the device, and when Beauty made another dive to intervene, Joyce kicked him away. Beauty bowled across the floor. That left Joyce alone with his device.

Davenport didn't wait to see anymore. He strode out into the cavern, pulled his XQ into position, and walked right up to Joyce. "Back away from the device, Admiral. Keep your hands where I can see them. You're under arrest."

Joyce stared at Davenport in dumb shock for a minute. Davenport realized in that moment that Joyce didn't even recognize him. Joyce had put Davenport so far out of his mind that Davenport was the last thing Joyce would have thought of.

Without warning, Joyce lunged for the device, snatched the cylinder off the floor, hugged it to his chest, and backed toward the Dagger. Joyce held out the controller in front of him, laughed in crazed glee, and his eyes flashed with insane triumph.

"You're too late, Sheriff!" Joyce crowed. "Nice try, though. Take another step and I'll detonate this weapon and wipe out the whole Confederacy!"

Davenport froze, but he didn't lower his XQ. Healey and the others angled around Davenport with their weapons raised and pointed at Joyce, but none of them could get near him when he held the device and the controller in his hands.

Joyce backed closer to the Dagger. He had to stop by the hull to open the hatch and Davenport saw his chance.

He charged Joyce and aimed his attack to grab Joyce around the torso. Davenport clamped Joyce's arms to his sides to keep the cylinder pinned between his own body and Joyce's.

Davenport reacted on pure instinct, seized Joyce's wrist, and slammed it hard against the ship's hull. Joyce's knuckles banged on the metal and the controller hit the floor. That left just the device itself.

Healey and the others advanced to surround Joyce in guns, but he fought back just as hard here as he did in the upper cavern.

He wrenched himself in Davenport's grip. Healey took another step forward to help Davenport subdue Joyce, but before Healey could get near them, Joyce jerked sideways and yanked Davenport off his feet.

Davenport landed on top of him, but Joyce's body cushioned the device. The others swarmed the pair. Jace produced five copies to hold down Joyce's legs. The rest of the crew tackled Joyce as soon as Davenport got out of the way.

Jericho, Axel, and Dice pried Joyce's arms away from the cylinder while Healey lifted it out of Joyce's grip. Healey set it down on the floor where it would be safe.

Davenport and the others flipped Joyce onto his stomach. Fiddler found some rope among Joyce's supplies and the crew tied his hands behind his back.

He floundered to sit up and backed against the ship, but he couldn't go any further. Davenport and his friends stood over him glaring down at Joyce.

"You're under arrest for conspiracy, treason, armed insurrection, murder.....and a bunch of other stuff," Davenport informed him. "You have the right to remain silent. Do yourself and the rest of us a big favor by exercising that right until we take you to Atlas Arcane to stand trial."

Joyce grinned up at him. "You would know all about that, wouldn't you, Davenport?"

Davenport bent over and punched him across the jaw. "I told you to keep quiet." He turned to his friends. "See if you can find a way to communicate with someone in orbit to come and collect this pile of shit. Better yet, see if you can contact the *Vindicator.*"

Joyce's smile drained off his face, but he didn't say anything else.

The crew spread out to search the cavern. Healey and Davenport stayed where they were standing guard over Joyce. Davenport didn't trust Joyce not to try some other dirty trick.

Lyons crossed the cavern to another console of electronic equipment, but when she checked it, she shook her head. "Beauty is right. We can't communicate with anyone from inside these rocks."

"We'll have to take Joyce on board the Dagger," Healey suggested. "As soon as we get airborne, we can contact the Wide Patrol and the Reserve Wing. We can tell them we have Joyce in custody and transport him to Atlas Arcane."

Davenport nodded, but before he could say anything, Joyce flipped over. He flung himself across the floor, swung his legs sideways, and slammed his foot down on the floor.

Davenport didn't see what Joyce was trying to do until his heel smashed down onto the weapon's controller that had fallen on the floor a few feet away.

Joyce's heel compressed the button and the control panel on the cylinder's house blinked on. It immediately started counting down from thirty.

"Ha ha!" Joyce howled. "You thought you could beat me! Did you really think I would make a hollow threat about setting off this weapon? I'll see you all in Hell where you belong!"

He broke into cruel laughter. Davenport stared at the device. The numbers had already counted down to twenty. Twenty seconds. He had twenty seconds to save the Confederacy.

Joyce grinned up at him with a sickening leer. Davenport couldn't stand to look at him.

Axel and Emmett rushed the device and started pushing every button on the control panel. Lyons and Fiddler raced over there and stood behind them. "You have to stop it!" they both yelled. "You have to find a way to stop it."

"I'm trying!" Axel hollered back and he pushed a few more buttons.

"There's no way to stop it," Beauty growled.

The timer counted down to ten seconds.

Healey charged over to the control console. "We have to contact the Reserve Wing! There has to be a way to get them to evacuate the area before the whole thing blows."

Davenport froze as the numbers finished counting down. 5.....4......3......2.....

He couldn't do anything. It was too late. Joyce had won.

The time hit one and then it switched to double zeroes. Nothing happened. It beeped a few more times.

Axel froze with his fingers still poised over the control pad. Emmett, Lyons, and Fiddler stood behind him blinking at the double zeroes still glowing on the panel.

Healey stared at the device from behind the console. Davenport, Dice, and Joyce all stared at the device from their own places. It didn't blow up. The cylinder just sat there doing nothing.

Joyce broke the silence by scrambling onto his knees. He gaped at the cylinder in disbelief. "That's impossible! It has to! It was working just fine a second ago!"

Davenport couldn't move, not even to stop Joyce from getting to his feet. The device—the doomsday weapon—it was a dud.

Joyce had nothing left to threaten the Confederacy. Every shred of his power was gone.

No one tried to stop him from stumbling toward the cylinder and staring down at it in flabbergasted shock. "It has to....." he kept stammering. "It has to....." He spun around. "Beauty! You said the chip wasn't damaged! How could you make a mistake like this?"

Beauty beamed up at him, and this time, it really was his brightest, most delighted smile of unvarnished happiness. "Oh, the chip is working just fine. It worked exactly the way you wanted it to. It detonated exactly the way it was supposed to. There just isn't any Ithium or Ziprothil inside the device. See?"

He grinned at Joyce in obvious pleasure. Joyce blinked at him and then frowned. "There isn't? Where is it, then?"

"I hid them......" Beauty's eyes ranged around the ceiling. "I hid them somewhere in these caves, and since the rocks conceal everything from scanners, you'll never find them." Beauty's eyes rested on Joyce again and Beauty smiled in heavenly ecstasy. "That's the breaks, Admiral."

Beauty burst out in childish giggles.

"You're a hero, Beauty," Healey murmured. "You deserve a medal for this."

Beauty glanced over at him and blushed. "Shucks, Marshall."

Joyce blinked a few more times. He couldn't tear his eyes away from Beauty.

Healey stepped forward and took hold of Joyce's elbow. "Let's go, Admiral. It's time you went home to Atlas Arcane Jail where you belong. I hope they treat you better than they treated us."

Joyce didn't move for a second and then, without warning, he swung around and shouldered Healey out of the way. Somehow, Joyce got the ropes off his wrists, followed up his attack by seizing Healey's sidearm, and then lunged for Beauty.

Joyce hooked his elbow around Beauty's neck and crammed Healey's weapon into the side of Beauty's head. "No one will be pinning any medals on this little freak!" Joyce hissed. "Back off—all of you—or I blow his brains out! You know I'll do it! Get your hands off your weapons!"

Joyce dragged Beauty toward the ship. Davenport searched everywhere for an opening to save Beauty, but before Joyce could get near the ship, he bumped into something very big and very solid.

Joyce glanced behind him and froze when he came face to face with Dice. "Remember me, asshole?" Dice boomed. "I'm the guy who's gonna kill you."

Joyce opened his mouth to say something, but Dice attacked too fast. He seized Joyce's arms and ripped them away from Beauty. Beauty scampered and Davenport pushed him toward Jace and Jericho. "Get him out of here!"

Four copies surrounded Beauty and hustled him out of the cavern while Dice went to town on Joyce.

Dice slammed him against the ship and crushed Joyce's gun hand in an iron fist. Dice twisted the gun out of Joyce's fingers and tossed the weapon across the floor.

Dice hauled back his other hand, clenched it into a fist, and punched with all his strength at Joyce's head.

Joyce ducked at the last second and Dice's fist crumpled the metal hull. Just as fast, Joyce pulled some other device from his pocket, stabbed it into Dice's neck, and Dice buckled to the floor while Joyce dove for the Dagger's hatch.

He hit the hatch release on his way there and dove on board. Davenport realized a second too late that Joyce was going to get away.

Davenport whipped his weapon to his shoulder and opened fire. All the others did, too, but their shots hit some kind of protective field surrounding the Dagger.

The engines flared to life. Davenport charged the hatch, hit the field, and bounced off. He couldn't figure out how Joyce got inside it, but Davenport couldn't. Axel, Healey, and Lyons all rushed it, too, but the same thing happened.

The ship lifted off the floor. Davenport fired at it dozens of times, but his shots bounced off the field and did no damage.

The ship pivoted its nose upward and then rocketed upward into the curved opening leading into the atmosphere. Admiral Joyce was getting away—again.

Chapter 30

One of Jericho's copies rushed down the tunnel and met Davenport and the others on their way up to the surface. "The Wide Patrol is coming down to meet us. They're tracking Joyce. He's on his way to Sacron Enigma."

"We gotta go after him," Davenport exclaimed.

"You tell Pritchard that," Jericho replied. "He says for all of you to stay here until he takes custody of the Ithium, the Ziprothil, and the chip. He says none of us is going anywhere until he gets them."

Davenport and Healey exchanged glances. Davenport had always wondered who in the whole Confederate law enforcement system he could trust to take the Ithium and the Ziprothil off his hands. Now he found out.

He didn't want to stick around to wait for Pritchard or anyone else. Davenport wanted to leave right away and track down Joyce, but some things were more important.

The crew climbed all the way up to the surface where they discovered their stolen escape craft parked outside the cave entrance. That explained how Jericho had been able to contact the Wide Patrol.

The crew also found Jace's copies standing guard over Beauty. "Do you hear that, Beauty?" Lyons asked him. "Sheriff Pritchard wants you to turn over the Ithium and the Ziprothil. You better go get them before he shows up."

Beauty only nodded and vanished back inside the tunnels. He was still gone when a squad of rogue soldiers marched out of the jungle and approached the crew.

One of their lieutenants drew himself up in front of Healey and Davenport. "Sir!" the lieutenant snapped. "We'd like to turn ourselves over to Confederate justice. Please....take us into custody. We're prepared to cooperate."

"You can turn yourselves over to the Wide Patrol," Healey told him. "You can wait here until they come. Leave all your weapons on the ground right here and then you can all go stand over there."

He pointed to the rocks surrounding the cave. The soldiers did exactly as he said, deposited their weapons on the ground, and retreated.

Davenport shuffled his feet. "This is taking too long. We should be out there hunting down Joyce instead of waiting around."

"I'm just glad someone else is taking charge of this thing," Healey replied. "In a few minutes, someone we all know and trust will have the Ithium and the Ziprothil. We won't have to worry about them anymore. We can just concentrate on Joyce and nothing else."

Davenport sighed. "We almost had him, man! We had him tied up on the floor. We should have been more careful."

"He's a crafty son of a bitch. I'll give him that," Healey replied. "He won't get away, though. We'll find him—and the Reserve Wing is tracking him for us. He isn't gone."

Davenport didn't answer. Joyce had gotten away from Davenport too many times before. Would this nightmare ever be over?

The ships belonging to the Wide Patrol landed beyond the fringe of jungle. They couldn't land any closer, so it took a while for Pritchard, Treese, and the other deputies to get to the cave opening.

They showed up just as Beauty returned from the caverns. Pritchard frowned at him. "Do you have something you want to say to me, Beauty?"

Beauty turned bright red and lowered his eyes to the ground. "No, Sheriff. I don't have anything I want to say to you."

He held out his hand, and when Pritchard extended his, Beauty deposited three small objects in Pritchard's palm. Two were tiny cartridges barely two inches long. The other was a computer chip no bigger than Davenport's fingernail.

Pritchard stared down at them and then stuffed them into the pocket of his vest. "Thank you, Beauty. I doubt all the millions of people you saved today will ever find out what you did for them." Pritchard turned to Davenport and the others. "We have to search the compound, but you folks should all get out of here. You have a fugitive to apprehend."

"Dice is down there and he needs medical treatment," Lyons interrupted.

"We'll make sure he gets it," Pritchard replied. "You can stay with him if you want to or you can go with your crew to bring in Joyce."

Lyons glanced around and her dark eyes found Davenport. "Davenport.....I just....."

"Stay," he told her. "Stay. You don't need to come. None of you does."

"Are you insane?" Emmett snapped. "That asshole's head is mine."

"All right," Davenport replied. "Let's go."

The crew loaded back onto the ship they stole from Ekol. Jace and Jericho joined Davenport on the bridge again, but when the crew got into orbit, they rendezvoused with Rodeo, Bandit, Breeze, Coon, and Wolf on board a Reserve Wing Stalwart. None of them were flying Ekol's ships anymore.

"Ekol's people went back to his territory," Bandit told Davenport. "So did Calyx's people and Rizarth's fleet. Everyone is back where they belong."

"None of them wants to cross into Sacron Enigma," Rodeo explained.

"So who's going after Joyce?" Davenport asked.

"Just us and the Wide Patrol."

"The Reserve Wing is giving us another Drifter." Bandit had to bite the inside of his cheek to conceal his exhilaration. "It's the only thing fast enough to catch up with him."

Davenport had to laugh. "All right, man. I guess you earned the right to fly as fast as you want. So what are we waiting for?"

"We're just waiting for the Patrol to come back from the surface," Rodeo replied.

"But we can check out the ship while we wait," Davenport suggested. "Right?"

The Chorions couldn't fall over themselves fast enough to go down to the Stalwart's cargo hold and scramble onto their new Drifter. Its name was *Aries Royal*.

Bandit lowered himself into the pilot's cradle with an ecstatic groan. "Ah! Home at last! I'm gonna buy me one of these just as soon as I get rich enough."

Rodeo climbed into the tactical cradle and his fingers explored the controls. "It isn't the *Artemis Rex*, but it will do the job."

"The Patrol is launching from the surface," Bandit reported. "The *Vindicator* is splitting off to Atlas Arcane to deliver the goods to....wherever Sheriff Pritchard is going to deliver the goods."

"Contact him and find out when he'll be ready for us to leave," Davenport ordered from the command cradle.

"He's contacting you." Bandit patched the message through to Davenport's controls.

"Treese and the rest of the Patrol will go with you," Pritchard told Davenport. "I'll catch up if I can, but I'll probably get stuck down there filling out all the paperwork you boys are missing out on."

Davenport laughed again. He was feeling much better, now that he didn't have to worry about Joyce blowing up the whole Confederacy. "I never thought I'd look forward to that part of being a sheriff, but I actually do look forward to it. I can't wait to get back to my jail and fill out some nice boring paperwork."

Pritchard only grinned. "Enjoy your freedom while it lasts."

"Here come the *Conquest* and the *Fortitude,*" Rodeo announced. "Hit it, boy."

Bandit launched off the Stalwart and joined up with the rest of the Wide Patrol. The *Vindicator* soared past them on its way to Atlas Arcane.

Bandit put the hammer down and the whole crew shot away toward Sacron Enigma.

A line of Reserve Wing vessels marked the trail that Joyce used to escape from Vorax Suma. None of those Reserve Wing vessels interfered with the crew or the Wide Patrol except to report how recently Joyce had passed.

The Reserve Wing blocked any of the wider battle from getting in the Drifter's way. The Reserve Wing still fought skirmishes with what was left of Joyce's rogue fleet. He'd abandoned them to their fate. Now they just fought to avoid getting caught themselves.

Joyce had extended a sizable lead on Davenport's crew, but Davenport's pulse quickened when he saw the Drifter creeping up on Joyce's Dagger. Davenport couldn't let Joyce get away this time—not again.

Joyce penetrated deep into Sacron Enigma by the time the Drifter caught up with him. The Wide Patrol drew into formation with the Drifter, but before the party could intercept Joyce, a platoon of fast-moving alien fighter craft rocketed from a nearby planet and surrounded the Patrol.

The Drifter's communications system went haywire. "Aargh!" Bandit winced and grabbed his ears. "What the hell is that noise?!"

"They're trying to communicate with us," Rodeo replied. "The computers can't translate it."

"Make it stop!" Bandit countered, but right then, the fighters bombarded the Drifter with gunshots.

Actually, the fighters bombarded the whole Patrol with gunfire. "Floor it!" Treese ordered. "We have to get out of their territory. Put the pedal down, boy!"

"Yes, Sir!" Bandit replied and he dropped the throttle to the wall.

The whole Patrol gunned their engines. Bolander and Yarborough fired to the rear to pepper the attackers on the way.

"Did I say shoot at them?!" Treese snapped. "What the hell are you doing?"

Bolander laughed. "You didn't say NOT to shoot at them. You said floor it and I am."

"You wouldn't do that around the boss," Treese countered.

"Of course I would," Bolander replied. "I'll get away with anything he lets me get away with."

"I'm gonna tell him you said that," Treese returned.

"I'll tell him myself if you want me to."

The attackers hounded the Patrol for another five minutes, but pretty soon, the aliens dropped back and returned to the same planet.

"Cowards!" DeRosa yelled after them. "Don't come out if you can't play with the big boys."

"Joyce's Dagger is coming within range," Bandit called.

"Circle him and bring him to a stop," Treese ordered and opened hailing channels to the Dagger. "Admiral Joyce, this is Deputy John Treese of the Confederate Sheriff's Service. You are under arrest for crimes against the Confederacy. Bring your vessel to a stop and prepare to be taken into custody. If you resist, we will open fire and destroy your vessel. This is your final warning. Bring your vessel to a stop and prepare to be taken into custody."

No one answered and then the Dagger opened fire on DeRosa's ship, the *Celestis*. "You cocksucker!" DeRosa roared. "You asked for it, you son of a bitch!"

DeRosa fired back and the rest of the Patrol did, too, but Joyce didn't stop or even slow down. He kept streaking away deeper into Sacron Enigma where law and order didn't exist.

The Patrol's shots didn't damage the Dagger, either. Whatever protective field stopped Davenport from boarding the ship on Vorax Suma still protected the ship from battle damage here, too.

Bandit gunned the engines even harder to keep pace with Joyce. The Drifter's guns hammered the Dagger from one port side and smacked the ship toward the deputies to starboard.

They returned fire and batted the ship back to port, but no matter what the Patrol did, batting it back and forth was all they could do. They couldn't make a dent in it.

"He isn't giving up!" Davenport pointed out.

"We'll end him, then," Yarborough growled.

"We can't with that field surrounding the Dagger," Rodeo pointed out. "We need another plan."

"Get me into contact with his ship," Coon called up from his cradle. "I'll bring the field down for you."

Rodeo cocked his head to one side. "Yeah? You could do that?"

"Sure, but I would have to be in contact with his ship. Make contact between our hull and his. That's all I need."

"You heard him, Bandit," Rodeo ordered. "Make contact with that ship. Don't do anything until I tell you, Coon. Don't interface too soon. Understand?"

"I know what to do," Coon replied. "You don't have to tell me."

"Wide Patrol, stand by to fire on my signal," Rodeo called. "Take us in, Bandit."

Bandit burned up alongside Joyce's Dagger, darted in from the side, and bounced off. The field still held and the Dagger jostled back onto its old course.

"That ain't gonna do it, boy!" Rodeo snapped. "Quit playing with your food."

"I just wanted to soften him up first," Bandit replied, and without waiting for another word, he yanked back the controls, vaulted up and over the Dagger, and dove back down.

The Drifter's belly slammed into the Dagger's roof. Both ships' engines shrieked to the breaking point, but they didn't break apart. "Now, Coon!" Rodeo ordered. "Wide Patrol—fire at will!"

The Wide Patrol pounded the Dagger from all sides. The field wavered, but it still offered too much protection. A second later, the two ships broke apart and the Drifter peeled away.

"I can't get through!" Coon panted. "It's too strong."

Davenport sprang out of his cradle. "Do it again, but this time, open the rear hatch. I'm boarding him."

Bandit tried to spin around in his cradle, which didn't work out too well. "Are you stupid?! You can't board a moving ship....from another moving ship!"

"Pull the hatches together, Coon!" Davenport ordered. "I don't care how you do it. Just get me onto that ship. I don't care about anything else."

He didn't stick around long enough to hear Bandit talking shit about Davenport's mental state. Davenport didn't come this far to let Joyce get away.

If he got away from the Patrol now, they would never catch him. He would disappear into Sacron Enigma and no one would ever see him again.

Davenport sprinted into the back. The Drifter shuddered a few more times and gunfire scattered across the hull. He couldn't see what was happening outside and he didn't need to

He braced himself near the hatch. Coon would get Davenport onto that Dagger. Davenport didn't have to worry about that. Davenport would have to handle whatever happened after that.

More gunshots tossed the Drifter from side to side. Davenport had to brace himself against the bulkhead and then the hatch cracked with a bang.

It slammed open and howling wind tore at Davenport's skin, hair, and clothes as the Drifter started to depressurize.

The Drifter rocketed in reverse with the hatch facing the Dagger's hatch, but the Dagger's hatch remained firmly closed.

An invisible force dragged the Drifter closer to the Dagger's rear end. Davenport gripped the bulkhead tighter to stop himself from getting dragged out into space.

He couldn't breathe. Crushing force smashed him all over his body.....and then the Drifter slammed into the Dagger with their tail ends stuck together by some invisible magnetic power.

The Dagger's hatch slammed open and Davenport launched himself against the depressurizing rush of air coming out of the Dagger. He hurled himself across the gap and landed hard on the floor in the back of the Dagger.

The hatch slammed shut behind him and the Drifter, the Chorion Team, and the Wide Patrol all vanished out of Davenport's life. He was on Joyce's ship. They were alone together and one of them wouldn't be going home today.

Chapter 31

D avenport climbed the stairs to the Dagger's bridge. Admiral Joyce stood at the controls yanking the ship back and forth to drive the Wide Patrol and the Chorion Team away.

Joyce fired gunshots at everyone, but their return fire barely touched the Dagger. That protective field shielded the ship from everything.

Davenport stepped off the stairs and approached Joyce from behind. How should Davenport handle this? Should he knock Joyce out from behind—or confront him—or offer Joyce the chance to surrender?

Davenport decided to tackle Joyce from behind, knock him away from the controls, and then take the helm to bring the ship to a halt. Then the Wide Patrol could come on board and take Joyce into custody. That would be the best way.

Davenport took a few more steps. Joyce didn't see or hear Davenport. The noise and concussion of battle drowned out all noise. Joyce had to concentrate on the controls to stay ahead of the Wide Patrol.

He chuckled under his breath. That sound set Davenport off and he surged forward to bring Joyce down.

Before Davenport could move, Joyce spun around, aimed a gun at Davenport, and fired. Davenport had a split second to duck out of the way before the shot hit the wall behind his head.

Joyce whipped back to the front, chuckled under his breath, and went back to what he was doing. "You're a persistent bastard. I'll give you that, Sheriff."

Davenport took one more step. He considered giving Joyce an ultimatum to stand down and give himself up, but Davenport decided against that. Joyce had already shot at Davenport once.

Davenport threw caution to the wind, lunged for Joyce a second time, and tackled him away from the controls. The two men slammed down on the floor and Davenport scrambled to mount his enemy.

All sense of proportion vanished out of Davenport's head. This was the man who ruined Davenport's life.

This was the man who locked up Davenport at Terminus Anathema and then at Atlas Arcane Jail. This was the man who did all of this to Davenport's crew and then killed the Armageddon Core.

Davenport let his inner beast out of its cage and swung his fists to pound Joyce into next week, but once again, Joyce proved craftier than even Davenport could give him credit for.

Joyce bucked his hips once and dove for the gun he'd just used to shoot at Davenport. Davenport still had his fists raised to strike when the gun swung up and aimed at Davenport's face.

He dodged again, grabbed Joyce's wrist, and forced the gun up. Davenport pinned Joyce's arm to the floor, but Davenport couldn't hit Joyce like this.

Joyce laughed in Davenport's face and then head-butted Davenport in the nose. Davenport's head snapped back, but he didn't lose his grip.

Just then, another gunshot hit the Dagger from somewhere. The protective field blocked most of the impact, but that one small shudder gave Joyce a fraction of a second to recover.

He bucked again—a lot harder this time—and used his weight to throw Davenport into the control station Joyce had just been working on.

Joyce slammed Davenport against it and then Joyce lunged up again to throw Davenport off.

Davenport rolled to his feet, but not before Joyce got hold of the gun again. He fired and missed. Davenport charged him, ducked to avoid one more shot aimed at his head, and slammed Joyce back against the console.

Davenport hurled all his weight into Joyce to hold the bastard down, but for some reason, Joyce didn't fight back. He only laughed. That sound set off Davenport's deepest buried rage. He raised his fist to stuff that laughter back down Joyce's throat.

Joyce glanced up at Davenport's fist, and in one burst of desperate energy, Joyce yanked himself sideways, threw out one hand, and slapped it down on the controls.

Some kind of explosion went off in Davenport's face, ripped him away from Joyce and the controls, smashed Davenport against the back wall, and he collapsed on the floor unconscious.

He came to his senses sprawled in the same place. He hadn't moved.

No engines hummed through the floor beneath him. The ship was at a standstill and he didn't hear any gunfire anymore, either.

He dragged his head up with an effort. His whole body hurt, but his head hurt the worst. He couldn't stand. He could hardly think.

He could see just well enough to realize that something was very wrong with the world. Joyce stood against the wall by the bridge entrance. A bunch of big aliens crowded the bridge and three of them held Joyce at gunpoint.

These aliens had bony knobs all over their foreheads, along their eyebrow ridges, and even down their cheekbones. These knobs gave them a solid, brutal look somewhat like an Adik's horns, but these aliens didn't have any fangs.

They had pasty white skin, gleaming black merciless eyes, and sharp teeth that didn't extend outside their mouths. The rest of them appeared humanoid, but Davenport couldn't see much through their thick clothes.

The biggest alien held Joyce by his jacket lapel and aimed another smaller weapon in Joyce's face. Davenport didn't recognize the weapon nor did he recognize what species these aliens were. They'd boarded the ship and taken Joyce as a prisoner.

Where was the Wide Patrol? These aliens must have driven them off—which meant that Joyce and Davenport were all alone in Sacron Enigma.

"Shut the hell up!" the big alien snapped. "I'm asking the questions here, not you!"

"I was just trying to explain...." Joyce began.

The big alien punched his weapon hard into Joyce's face and made Joyce's eyelids flutter. "You explain when I ask you to explain, dumbass!"

"Okay, okay," Joyce stammered. "I was just...."

The big alien smashed him in the face a second time and blood gushed from Joyce's nose. "You aren't very bright, are you? What the hell were you doing trying to shoot a man while he's unconscious?" The big alien waved at Davenport without turning around. None of them turned around. They didn't see Davenport awake.

"Shoot the bastard, Eno," one of the alien's companions chimed in.

"Do you hear that, you piece of shit?" Eno snapped. "They say I should shoot you in the head right here for being a sniveling coward. Only a coward with no honor would shoot an unconscious man who can't defend himself. Is that what you are—a sniveling coward with no honor?"

"You don't understand...." Joyce began.

Eno cut him off. "I would kill you now if you weren't more valuable to me alive. Don't open your mouth and make me regret this or I might change my mind."

Eno dropped Joyce's jacket and snorted. "Get him out of here. Don't let me see his stinking face again."

The other aliens moved in, collared Joyce, and jerked him off the bridge. Davenport froze when Eno turned around and saw Davenport lying there with his head up and his eyes open.

Eno gave Davenport a hard scowl and then stalked over to the bridge controls. Eno didn't look at Davenport again.

Eno fired up the engines and put the ship in motion. He kept the speed easy. He flew away into space in no particular hurry to get wherever he was going.

Davenport put his throbbing head down on the floor. The engine noise sounded calm and soothing after all the screaming and streaking Davenport had been doing recently.

The sound eventually lulled him back into a stupor. He must have passed out again.

He woke with a start when someone touched his shoulder. Davenport jolted upright and instantly regretted it. His head reeled in pain, but he scrambled to sit up and get away from whoever was touching him.

"Calm down, Sheriff," a gruff voice snapped. "You're injured. I'm here to give you medical treatment."

Davenport gasped in alarm, looked right and left for someone to attack him, and then realized that the hideous creature in front of him was Eno, the alien pilot who threatened to shoot Admiral Joyce.

"Where......where......where's the.....the other man that was here.....Joyce?" Davenport stammered. "Where is he?"

"He's no concern of yours. Now keep still. I'm going to fuse the fractures in your head."

Eno gave Davenport a shot of painkillers and then did something to Davenport's head that made him pass out again.

His eyes opened staring up at the ceiling. Eno knelt over Davenport working on something on the floor next to him.

Davenport tried to remember where he was and how he got here. At least his head didn't hurt anymore.

Eno bent over and gave Davenport another injection. "Stay there and don't move, Sheriff," Eno ordered. "Try to sleep some more. We have a long journey ahead of us."

He stood up, put away his medical gear, and went back to the bridge station where he'd been flying the ship. He took the controls.

The engine noise through the floor under Davenport's back gave him a calm, peaceful feeling. He shouldn't feel that way. He was obviously these aliens' captive the same way Joyce was—if Joyce was even still alive.

Davenport was going to be extremely pissed off if Joyce had the bad taste to die somewhere other than under Davenport's own hand.

Davenport would have liked to see Dice, Emmett, and Fiddler get their revenge on Joyce, but Joyce was too far out in Sacron Enigma for that now.

Wherever Dice, Emmett, and Fiddler were, they weren't close enough to get their revenge whenever Davenport finally caught up with Joyce.

Davenport would just have to get revenge on behalf of the whole crew—and on his own behalf. No one wanted revenge more than Davenport did.

Joyce wasn't here, but some part of Davenport's being understood that Joyce was still alive. He had to be. He and Davenport weren't finished with each other yet.

Davenport did go to sleep—more than once. Eno stopped the ship a few times to check on Davenport and do different things to him. He left Davenport feeling better each time.

The last time Davenport woke up, he felt strong enough to sit up and then to push himself to his feet. Whatever that explosion did to him, he was all right now, thanks to Eno.

The minute Davenport stood up, he saw on the bridge controls that Eno was piloting the Dagger to some planet Davenport didn't recognize. Eno made no attempt to stop Davenport from seeing what he was doing.

Eno lowered the ship to some city and landed in a field full of other ships. Eno powered down the ship's engines, finally turned away from the controls, and waved toward the bridge entrance.

"We can do this the easy way or the hard way, Sheriff," Eno growled. "If you wouldn't mind stepping outside......"

Davenport didn't want to go through another several days of medical treatment when he'd only just gotten on his feet.

He walked off the Dagger and stopped when he stepped off the ramp onto the ground.

Dozens of different ships covered the field with hundreds of different aliens of all species mingling between them. Before Davenport could move, Eno stepped up and clamped a heavy iron manacle around Davenport's ankle.

Eno attached the manacle to a chain and chained Davenport to the side of the ship where he could see everything and everyone could see him.

All the aliens passed between ships, traded goods, pointed at the ships, and exchanged vessels for other vessels or goods depending on what they wanted.

Davenport's heart sank at the sight. He didn't recognize any of the species present or any of the ship types. This Dagger was the only Reserve Wing vessel on the whole field. He must be really deep in Sacron Enigma with no way to get back.

Eno sat down on the edge of the Dagger's hatch and observed all the aliens around him. He lounged there without a care in the world while dozens of different aliens came by and inspected Davenport like the product he was.

Some of the alien buyers even prodded Davenport with their appendages or even pushed back his lips to check his teeth. Davenport tolerated it all. He just couldn't bring himself to care anymore. He only cared about finding Joyce.

Hours passed. The sun crossed the sky and more aliens flew away in their newly purchased vessels while new aliens arrived with more bizarre creatures for sale. Davenport didn't see any other humans. He was a one-of-a-kind oddity.

The sun started to go down before a group of giant aliens approached Eno. He stood up to meet them and they conversed in some strange language.

Davenport should have realized that English wasn't Eno's first language. He spoke it so well, though, without a trace of an accent.

Davenport had somehow tricked himself into believing that Eno came from the Confederacy even though Davenport knew that wasn't possible. There were no aliens of Eno's species in the Confederacy.

This new species dwarfed Eno by at least a foot. They had huge, bulging muscles and a thick, overhanging upper lip that covered most of their mouth.

Their conical heads sloped down and barely curved inward to their necks. A matching downward curving skin flap covered their eyebrow ridges and surrounded their faces. These aliens would have looked stupid if they hadn't looked so brutal.

They spoke in squeaks, whistles, and growls, but that didn't seem to bother Eno. He answered in the same language in a normal tone of voice and waved at Davenport.

Davenport cringed when he thought about these aliens buying him, but some part of Davenport realized already that it was inevitable.

Sure enough, the giants gave Eno a bag of something. Davenport never even saw what it was. Then Eno started unbuckling the manacle from Davenport's leg.

"Hey!" Davenport protested. "You can't just sell me to these people! I'm a Confederate sheriff. You know that! I'm here to apprehend a fugitive who tried to destroy the whole Confederacy with a doomsday weapon. Interfering with my mission is a crime punishable by imprisonment."

Even as he said those words, he knew they didn't mean a thing out here. He got lucky by getting captured by someone who spoke English.

Davenport had been too injured to say this before, but he should have. He should have realized that Eno wasn't being so caring and considerate out of the kindness of his heart. That didn't happen in Sacron Enigma.

Eno only scoffed at Davenport and then shot a sneering glance at Davenport's star. "*That* doesn't mean anything out here, Sheriff. You know that." He dropped the chain into one of the giant aliens' hands. "Have a nice life, Sheriff."

Eno walked off into the market and left Davenport standing there with a load of butterflies in his stomach. Eno couldn't just leave. He couldn't turn Davenport over to these creatures.

One of them seized Davenport by the back of his shirt. The alien didn't give Davenport a chance to protest or even say a word.

The alien yanked Davenport toward the hatch. When he tried to struggle, they overpowered him with their strength, pitched him back on board the Dagger, and then all the other aliens climbed on board.

Davenport stood rooted to the spot and stared through the hatch until the giant aliens closed it in his face.

Davenport's desperate brain clung to the last sight of Eno disappearing into the market.....but he didn't disappear. He crossed the market to a different ship.

All the other aliens of Eno's species who had captured the Dagger stood around that ship. They must have traded it—or bought it.

Davenport's heart leapt when he saw some of Eno's companions holding another chain. It ran down to an identical manacle locked around Admiral Joyce's ankle.

His terrified eyes darted around the market and his features pinched in desperation at what he saw. He knew exactly where he was and what was happening to him.

Before he could move, Eno's companions grabbed a fistful of Joyce's clothes exactly the way Davenport's new captors grabbed him.

Eno and his crewmen dragged Joyce on board their new ship. Just before the hatch closed to cut off Davenport's view, he spotted a number printed on the ship's side—the ship that was carrying Joyce.

485702-XO. That was the ship's identifier. Davenport repeated it over and over in his mind to memorize it. *485702-XO.*

Then the hatch closed and Davenport lost sight of Joyce and everything else.

Chapter 32

The aliens who'd bought Davenport shoved him across the Dagger's lower deck to the corner. One of their crew carried a metal cage on board, anchored it to the bulkhead, and the others pushed Davenport into the cage.

He drew up his legs up to his chest to make room for himself. He had to huddle in a ball just to fit inside the cramped space.

Then all the aliens climbed up to the top deck and left Davenport alone. He curled up on the floor and listened to the engine noise coming through the floor. These aliens flew faster and made more course changes than Eno did, but at least Davenport didn't hear any gunfire.

He fell asleep more than once before any of the aliens came back downstairs to see him. One of them kicked the cage to wake him up and then growled at him while the alien unlocked the cage.

Davenport took a quick look at the lock. God knew why he was even thinking about escape. He would never be able to overcome these giant aliens and he had nowhere to run away to as long as the Dagger was flying through space.

They must be flying even deeper inside Sacron Enigma, which meant escape would be even more impossible than it already was.

The alien pulled the cage door open and didn't give Davenport a chance to crawl out on his own. The alien seized Davenport by the scruff of the neck again, dragged him out, and shook him to make him stand upright.

Davenport didn't protest and he tried not to struggle against the alien's grip. That would only make the creature mad and Davenport didn't want that.

The alien started barking at Davenport in his own language. The creature's growls and whistles got louder and more annoyed the longer this went on.

Davenport studied the alien from a distance. If Davenport spent enough time around these people, it would probably pay to learn their language.

Davenport didn't want to spend any time around them or learn their language. He wanted to leave—but how?

The creature became more and more enraged that Davenport didn't understand whatever the alien was saying. The more agitated the alien got, the more comical Davenport found the situation. He would have laughed if he didn't sense how much danger he was in here.

The alien finally grabbed Davenport again, marched him to the stairs, and shoved up them to the top deck.

The alien prodded Davenport down the corridor, past the crew quarters, and the alien kicked Davenport into a cabin at the far end.

Some large electronic device sat in the center of the cabin. There was nothing else in here.

The alien pointed at the device and launched into a long speech about something. The creature kept pointing at different parts of the device, but Davenport couldn't make out what the guy was talking about.

Davenport had definitely never seen any device like this before. It resembled a giant mound of tubes, wires, manifolds, and a bunch of other stuff Davenport couldn't for the life of him figure out.

The creature talked for ten minutes and then stopped to stare at Davenport. The creature barked a few more short statements and waited some more for Davenport to respond.

Davenport could only stare at him, and when Davenport still didn't answer, the creature clubbed him across the side of the head and stormed out.

Davenport huddled on the floor for a second, but when the creature didn't come back, Davenport stood up. What should he do? Should he start planning his escape now?

He was just about to walk out of the room and go explore the Dagger when the creature came back with a bucket and rag. There was nothing else in the bucket but the rag.

The creature pointed to the rag and then swept his arm up and down in front of the device to make a cleaning motion. Davenport nodded. He finally understood.

He picked up the rag and started wiping down the machine. That seemed to satisfy the creature at last. He scowled at Davenport for a while, watched him work, and then left.

Davenport settled into his task, now that he at least had something to do. If he made himself useful to these people, maybe they would let him live somewhere other than a cage.

He studied the device a little closer. He didn't see the aliens bring this device on board. They would have had to carry it past his cage. He would have seen that—and besides, the ship had been in flight ever since the market. When would they have been able to bring it on board?

He couldn't answer that and he didn't really care. He wiped down all the wires, tubes, and manifolds as best he could.

He didn't see anything else he ought to do with this thing, but before he could think about escape again, the same alien came back and swiped his arm toward the door.

He took Davenport back downstairs, locked him in his cage, and then pushed something through the bars. It was a rectangular square of some black substance as hard as molded plastic and it smelled awful.

It fell with a clunk onto the floor in front of Davenport. Davenport stared at it, and when he looked up, he discovered the alien glaring down at him. Was this creature waiting for another response?

The creature said something else and then got busy attaching some kind of hose to the side of the cage. Water dripped from the end of the hose. That must be for Davenport to drink, which meant that square of whatever it was must be the food Davenport was supposed to eat.

He was too hungry to turn up his nose at anything. He'd eaten more Universal Staples and Peanut Surprise in his life than he could even begin to remember. This couldn't be much different.

He managed to leave the square where it was until the alien left. Then Davenport picked it up and tried to bite off a corner of it.

It was much harder than Peanut Surprise and it tasted like a combination of tar and salt.

Davenport had also eaten plenty of Tarte Tatin, so he stuck the square in his mouth and sucked it. It started to dissolve, but that didn't improve the taste.

He sucked down the juice his saliva made of the melting square, and in a little while, he realized that it really did take the edge off his hunger.

The aliens left him where he was long enough that he managed to suck the whole square down his throat. It satisfied him enough that he fell back asleep.

He woke up in darkness. The engine noise told him that the ship was still flying at the same speed. Nothing had changed.

He sat up in the darkness and got himself a drink of water, but once he got upright, he started to think. He had to find Joyce which meant Davenport had to get off this ship somehow—or get the aliens off the ship.

485702-XO. That was the ship in which Eno took Joyce away. How long would Eno and his companions keep Joyce around before they sold him, too?

Davenport sat up for hours trying to puzzle a way to get off this ship, but nothing presented itself. He found the lock and felt it all over in the darkness.

A few hours later, the Dagger's internal lights came on and he studied the lock in detail. He thought he could work out a way to force it open without alerting the aliens to what he was doing, but that didn't help him get off the ship.

If even one of them saw him walking around unguarded, he would be a dead man. He couldn't take on even one of these aliens, much less the whole crew.

He didn't see them carrying weapons, but he didn't have any weapons himself. He wouldn't get them out in space, either.

He decided to stay where he was and watch and wait. Something would present itself. He needed to be patient and not think about the fact that Eno was taking Joyce farther and farther away from Davenport with every passing second.

He relaxed in his cell until the lights went off again. Whatever cycle they were on was much shorter than a human circadian cycle. He was still wide awake, so he started working on the cage lock again.

He managed to jam it open without making too much noise, eased the door back, and crawled out. He stood on the lower deck listening for a long time, but he didn't hear anything.

The aliens must all be asleep, but the ship was still in flight. At least one of them must be up on the bridge piloting the ship.

Davenport tiptoed to the stairs and groped his way up there in the dark. He didn't dare to turn on a light in case someone noticed. He was taking his life in his hands just by moving freely about the ship.

The lights from the controls shone out of the bridge. He froze on the threshold when he saw that the bridge was empty. There was no one here.

He crossed to the controls. The ship was flying on autopilot.

He attacked the controls trying in every way to find out how to take control of the ship. This was his one chance. He couldn't waste it.

He switched over to the ship's life support system praying to Almighty God that he would find something he could use against the aliens. He had to find a way to overcome them.

He rifled the life support controls, and without meaning to, he brought up a schematic he'd never seen before. It was a lighted diagram of the device he'd just spent so long cleaning.

The controls rotated the schematic in front of him and then showed him another image of twenty of these devices all lined up in one of the ship's larger crew compartments. The aliens had removed all the furniture and installed these devices instead.

The schematic rotated in a circle and showed an alien inside each one. Then the ship's controls returned some kind of biological data on each alien. They must be in some kind of hibernation cycle—a sleep cycle. That was the only explanation.

The ship reported each alien's circulation, blood gas composition, brain wave activity—the works. Each device formed a little pod that kept the alien in a state of perfect equilibrium.

The controls also showed an interface junction on the side of the device where the aliens had connected all these machines to the ship's systems. Davenport had cleaned that junction without realizing what it was.

Curiosity took hold of him and he paced down the hall to the compartment in question. He stepped across the threshold and stood there staring at the twenty devices.

The front section of each device had slid back to reveal a glass window showing the alien inside. A mask covered each alien's face and their eyes were closed.

His heart started racing. The whole damn crew was in here and they were utterly at his mercy. He could shut down all these devices and the ship would be his. It was so simple.

He had to control himself when he turned away to head back to the bridge. He just had to figure out how to shut these things down.

He made it out into the hall before all the lights switched on. He jumped out of his skin and glanced up at the ceiling when realized their sleep cycle was ending.

He sprinted down the stairs, scrambled back into the cage, and pulled the lock shut before anyone saw him.

A second later, he heard the aliens walking back and forth on the top deck. They talked to each other and then went about their business. None of them came downstairs to check on him.

Chapter 33

D avenport jolted out of a sound sleep when a deafening crash slammed into the wall right behind him. He tried to sit up, but this cage held him in a cramped, huddled position.

He could never mistake that sound, though. Gunfire bombarded the Dagger from all sides.

The crew's crazy language drifted to his ears from the bridge and then half the crew thundered down the stairs heading for the targeting cradles.

The ship crashed back and forth taking dozens of hits. Davenport cringed at every one of those blows. He would have given anything to get out of this cage and man the guns....or do something to defend the ship.

A punishing strike smashed the ship from above and it started venting breathable gas through a hull breach. More of the crew dashed here and there trying to fix the damage and then one of the engines exploded.

Davenport cowered lower in his cage and waited for the end. Every strike set his teeth on edge and threatened to snap his last nerve.

This was the last straw. If he survived until the crew's next sleep cycle, he had to get out of here at all costs. He couldn't die locked in a cage—not with freedom within his grasp.

He shut his eyes, but another brutal smash to the ship's other side startled him into opening them again. If whoever was attacking these aliens hit the other engine, the ship would be dead in the water. Escaping wouldn't do him any good then.

The ship would become a death trap if the crew didn't patch that hull breach. His mind spun in all kinds of directions imagining every disastrous thing that could possibly go wrong.

He couldn't do anything but lie here and wait for the crew to finish the battle one way or the other. What felt like hours passed and the shooting stopped eventually, but not the mayhem.

The crew kept charging back and forth, whistling, squeaking, and roaring at each other, and trying to fix everything that was wrong with this ship.

Davenport stayed where he was and didn't make a sound. He didn't want anyone on this crew to remember that he existed.

The craziness quieted down and Davenport and the crew didn't die, so that was a bonus.

None of the crew came to check on him. They really must have forgotten all about him which was exactly what he wanted.

They all went up to the top deck and he heard them arguing on the bridge. Their voices traveled down the hall to their sleep chamber and then the whole ship fell deadly silent. The engines weren't running anymore. The ship was at a standstill.

Davenport counted down the seconds before the lights switched off. He didn't waste a single second this time. He attacked the lock, pried it open, scrambled out of his cage, and sprinted up to the bridge.

He had to work on the controls for a while before he figured out how to cut power to all the sleep chambers. He felt absolutely no guilt at all when he finally shut them down and watched all the lights switch off. The life sign readings dropped to zero and they didn't move again.

He slumped against the controls and let out a shaky sigh of relief. It was done.

He was in control of this Dagger with no one coming after him, no one telling him what to do, no one keeping him locked up, and no one shooting at him.

He could use any of the normal crew cabins to sleep in. He couldn't wait to sleep in a regular bed again.

But first, he had to find Joyce.

Davenport straightened up and studied the controls. The ship only had one engine. That was going to slow him down considerably.

He transferred over to the scanners to find out where the hell in Sacron Enigma he was. The problem was that the Reserve Wing didn't have accurate charts of this part of space—or any charts at all of this part of space.

The alien crew had loaded some on, but when the scanners identified where the Dagger was, Davenport didn't recognize it. He had no clue where he was or how far he was from where he started.

He would just have to follow the route the crew took to get here. That should be simple enough.

He pulled up the navigation records for the last few days. They showed the Dagger's progress all the way from Vorax Suma. Davenport hadn't been gone as long as he thought.

The records also showed where the market was where Eno had sold Davenport. Davenport entered the identifier for Eno's ship into the scanners.

Davenport didn't expect much, but he got a pleasant surprise when the scanners revealed the ship's route heading away from the market in the opposite direction. Eno and his crew were on their way to another star system with three inhabited planets.

The scanners couldn't pick up any human life sign on board—not from this distance. Davenport would just have to track them down.

He turned the Dagger around and fired up the one remaining engine. He had to concentrate to keep the ship flying in a straight course, but at least he was going in the right direction now.

He flew for ten minutes before he passed a different planet and a bunch of other alien vessels launched from the surface to intercept him.

He couldn't outrun them, but he wasn't about to lie down and die. He made one check on the weapons systems and made up his mind. They were still fully operational.

He also discovered that Joyce's protective field was still intact. The aliens who most recently purchased this ship must not have realized the field was there.

Davenport activated it and then turned his weapons on the incoming enemy. They tried to communicate with him, but instead of running from them, he switched off his engine and brought the ship to a halt.

He fired first and he struck hard. He plastered three of their ships and blasted them to kingdom come before he took aim at the others.

They plunged for him and hammered his ship with epic gunfire, but none of it could touch him. He chuckled wickedly when he saw them swooping around him trying to punch their way through his field. Idiots.

He selected his next target with care. These ships were much smaller than the Dagger. They only had one seat for a single pilot with one heavy afterburner engine in the back. He wouldn't be able to disable one of them without blowing up the whole thing.

He fired up his engine, maneuvered himself into the very center of their grouping, and then fired at the ship he wanted.

He hit its underside and sent it toppling head over heel. The ship pitched out of the battle and he yanked the helm hard to starboard. He skidded the Dagger backward, threw the ship into reverse, and opened the Dagger's hatch to back up to the floundering ship.

He took it on board, slammed the hatch shut, fired his one remaining engine, and continued on his previous course.

The other attackers pounced on him, but they couldn't touch him. He flew for another half hour and completely ignored their continuing assault. They finally broke off and returned to their home planet.

Davenport kept flying for another four hours before he dared to leave the cockpit and go downstairs to the lower deck. The alien fighter craft sat there immobile. It hadn't extended its landing gear. Davenport sure hoped the ship still worked because, if it didn't, he and the alien pilot were both in big trouble.

Davenport stopped by the Dagger's weapons locker, but it was empty. Eno must have sold everything Joyce had on board—or else Eno and his crew must have taken everything for themselves.

Davenport went out onto the lower deck and strode around the ship to a spot where he could see the cockpit. The pilot still sat in his seat. He hadn't moved or tried to open his cockpit cover. He could probably tell from his controls that the Dagger's atmosphere would be deadly to him.

Davenport thought over how to communicate with the guy. Davenport didn't want to outright kill the pilot just to steal his ship. Killing the alien crew was one thing. They would have gotten Davenport killed if he didn't do something.

The pilot glared at him in open hatred. This pilot no doubt expected Davenport to kill him.

Davenport made up his mind, returned to the bridge, and scrolled back through the log records to the pilot and his comrades trying to communicate with Davenport. The Dagger couldn't translate their communications, but Davenport gambled that the pilot's ship might be able to.

He opened a communications link to the craft on the lower deck and patched his own voice through the Dagger's translation technology. It would translate his voice into dozens of languages. With any luck, the pilot's own translators would be able to change it into something pilot could understand.

"I don't want to kill you," Davenport told the pilot. "I just want your ship. You can have this one and you can use it to get back to your own planet. I'm reading a different atmospheric concentration in your cockpit. I'll make you a deal. I'll suit up in a protective suit, change my ship's atmospheric concentration to one that you can use, and then we'll switch ships. You can get out of your cockpit, I'll get into it, and then reconfigure your ship so I can fly in it. Do you agree? If we cooperate with each other, we can both survive this and go our separate ways. What do you say?"

The pilot glared at him for a minute and then a low, rasping voice came through the link. "Why are you doing this?"

"I told you I just want your ship. This ship's engines are crippled and I need something faster. I don't want to kill you. Just let me take your ship and we can both go home."

"Very well," the pilot rasped. "Do what you must."

Davenport cut the signal and got to work. He had to go back and forth between the lower deck and the bridge controls to put on his suit, change the atmospheric gas concentration of the Dagger, and to transmit *485702-XO's* course to the other vessel.

Davenport made sure to arm himself before he opened another channel to the pilot. "Okay. I'm coming downstairs. As soon as I get there, you can get out and we'll change places. You can see from your controls that the Dagger's atmospheric gas concentration is favorable to you. Get ready to get out of the cockpit."

Davenport went downstairs. The pilot played his part perfectly by staying where he was until Davenport appeared in front of the ship.

Davenport waved and the pilot popped the cockpit cover. He climbed down to the floor and walked up to Davenport. The pilot showed no sign of feeling threatened by Davenport's weapon.

The pilot said something in his own language that Davenport couldn't understand. Davenport nodded. "You, too. Have a safe trip home. I wish you all the best."

Davenport walked away, climbed into the cockpit, and shut the cover. He spent a few minutes reconfiguring the atmospheric gas concentration inside the cockpit before he could take off his helmet and suit.

Then he had to translate all the ship's controls into English. Fortunately, he was right about this ship having translation technology the Confederacy didn't have. The ship's computers took his previous transmissions and used them to translate and reprogram the vessel's systems so he could read the controls.

He fired up the engines and raised his head to fly out of the Dagger's hatch. He froze when he saw the pilot standing there watching him. Davenport couldn't read the alien's expression, but the guy raised his hand in farewell.

Davenport suffered a pang of regret when he raised his own hand to wave back. There had to be some good people in Sacron Enigma. He wouldn't stay here long enough to find out who they were or to get to know them. He had to keep on running.

He hit the throttle, blasted out into space, and left the crippled Dagger far behind.

Chapter 34

D avenport dropped his vessel out of orbit on some other planet far from where he started. *485702-XO* was down there in the middle of a giant city.

From what he could tell, the ship had landed in another market full of hundreds of ships and thousands of aliens. He also detected a dozen individuals from Eno's species hanging around *485702-XO*.

Davenport descended through the atmosphere and landed on the outskirts of the market where he would hopefully blend in with the crowd. He took his weapon and headed for *485702-XO*.

He found Eno and some of his friends hanging around the hatch. Eno raised his bony eyebrows when he saw Davenport. "Sheriff! What are you doing here?"

"I came back to find you."

"You aren't with the Darvis anymore," Eno remarked. "How did you get away from them."

"I can be very resourceful when I need to be. Now I need to know where the other man is—the man you captured at the same time you took me and my ship. Where is he? Do you still have him?"

"We just sold him a few minutes ago. He's right over there."

Eno pointed to a different ship across the market. A different group of aliens led Joyce by a chain attached to his ankle.

Joyce looked considerably worse for wear since he'd left the Confederacy. His face swelled up with bruising from all the times Eno had hit him in the nose. Blood and muck stained his uniform and rips in the fabric showed his shirt underneath.

Davenport's heart leapt. "I need to buy him back. I have skills that I can sell. I need you to translate for me, Eno. Will you tell those people that I want to buy Joyce? I have a ship I could trade or....."

Eno frowned. "I would have to charge you for that."

"I don't care!" Davenport blurted out. "Just help me get him back! I can't let those people take him away."

"Why do you want him so badly? He was about to kill you when we found you."

"I know that! Come on! Just help me get him back. Please. I'll pay you whatever you want—but I need to get some money....or whatever it is you want me to pay you with."

Eno furrowed his brow some more. Davenport squirmed while Eno thought it over.

"Fine," Eno finally growled. "Wait here. I'll be back in a minute and then I'll take you over there."

He went on board his new ship and left Davenport standing there with nothing to do but shift his weight and try to keep his nerves calm. Joyce was right there—right across the market in plain view.

Davenport kept an eye on Joyce while he waited for Eno to come back. The aliens who owned Joyce stopped off at a few different vendors on the way across the market. The aliens didn't seem to be in any big hurry to leave with their new prize.

Davenport also couldn't tell which ship belonged to them or if they even had a ship. They just meandered from vendor to vendor checking everything out like they had all the time in the world.

Joyce stood at the end of his chain each time while he waited for his new owners to finish what they were doing. Joyce glanced around the market, too, but he didn't see Davenport.

Davenport's grip tightened on his weapon. He could walk over there right now and shoot Joyce in the head.

It would all be over in a few seconds—but then Davenport would have to deal with Joyce's irate owners and anyone else around here who might decide to take revenge.

Davenport also didn't know if he'd be violating any local laws by doing that. He could wind up in hot water again. Buying Joyce outright would be the better course. Then Davenport could do what he wanted with the piece of shit and no one would be able to argue.

What would Davenport do with Joyce once he got his hands on the admiral? Davenport didn't let himself think that far in advance. Taking possession of Joyce was the first step.

Eno still didn't come back. Davenport was just about to turn away and look inside the ship to see what was taking Eno so long.

That was the moment Davenport noticed Joyce sitting down. He sat crosslegged on the ground while he waited for his new captors to finish talking to someone. Joyce pretended to scratch his ankle where the manacle clamped around his leg.

Davenport stiffened when Joyce looked down at the manacle and did something to it. Davenport had spent too much time these last few weeks dealing with Joyce's trickery not to recognize when the weasel was up to something.

None of his captors noticed anything unusual about his behavior. They didn't know Joyce the way Davenport did.

Davenport got a very bad feeling about this. He left *485702-XO* and set off across the market to intercept Joyce before......

Just then, the alien holding onto Joyce's chain finished talking, tugged the chain to signal Joyce to get up, and they set off walking through the market again.

The alien captor halted at another vendor. Joyce sat down immediately and did the same thing. He fiddled with the manacle behind his owner's back. Now Davenport knew for certain that Joyce was trying to escape.

Davenport picked up his pace. He had to get over there before Joyce made his move.

Joyce sat still and waited until his owner tugged the chain again. Joyce stood up and the owner turned away to continue his stroll through the market.

The minute he turned his back, Joyce kicked the manacle with his other foot. It came undone and Joyce took off running for the nearest ship with an open hatch.

It was a small fighter craft with gull-wing doors standing open so anyone could see inside the cockpit. Four seats filled the flight compartment—two in the front and two behind.

Joyce sprang inside before his owner or anyone else realized what he was doing. Joyce seized the controls and the doors started to close.

The owner alien took a second to realize what was happening. The craft's owner reacted quicker and rushed the vessel, but Joyce fired up the engines and started to lift off. The owner backed off waving his arms and yelling.

Davenport couldn't watch this. The idea that Joyce might get away gave Davenport superhuman strength and speed. He charged the craft just as the door was about to shut and he jammed his body under it just as the craft lifted off.

The door slammed down on top of him and crushed him against the fuselage. The ship kept rising as Joyce picked up speed. Davenport's legs dangled thirty feet off the ground, but his body stopped the door from closing.

It started to open again and he had to scramble to grab onto the rear seat safety harness. He dropped his weapon, but he grabbed it just in time to stop himself from falling to his death.

The ship's engines roared to life and the vessel rocketed into the atmosphere with Davenport's body flapping in the breeze. The door locked to its highest position and then started to close again. Now was his chance.

He hauled himself into the back seat and the door shut as the ship broke orbit. Now Davenport was alone in this vessel with no one but Joyce.

Joyce gunned the engines and blasted away from the planet. Davenport had to finish this now, but the vessel's configuration didn't help.

Davenport scrambled into the front passenger seat. Joyce sat at the controls with both hands on the helm and throttle. He didn't even look at Davenport.

Davenport punched Joyce across the jaw, and when that didn't work, Davenport lunged for Joyce and slammed Joyce's head against the window.

Joyce finally let go of the controls to fight back, but at that moment, the ship erupted into orbit and flew into a raging battle between two fleets of alien ships.

Davenport never got a good look at who they were, where they came from, nor did he ever find out what they were fighting over.

Joyce turned on Davenport and lunged back. Joyce tackled Davenport into the passenger seat and the two men wrestled, struggled, and fought for dominance.

Joyce landed a few good punches, but desperation and vengeance fueled Davenport to excesses he wouldn't otherwise have indulged in.

He punched Joyce in the body three times and Joyce winced. Davenport flung his weight up and tipped Joyce sideways.

Davenport tackled Joyce onto the ship's controls, grabbed for Joyce's throat, and slammed Joyce's head down on the dashboard.

That feeling of pounding Joyce to a pulp felt so good that Davenport reared off the seat to do it some more. Joyce fought to free himself and landed another blow on Davenport's jaw.

Davenport was too out of his mind with fury to care about that or anything else. He scrambled onto his knees still crushing Joyce's neck in both hands.

Davenport would have strangled the bastard then and there, but as soon as Davenport raised his head above the dashboard, the world went dark.

Flashes of gunfire and explosions had been flaring all around the ship and even bombarding the hull with fire. Now all of that died away.

Davenport froze when he saw a massive vessel moving in on Joyce's craft. The behemoth towered over the little ship and running lights led into a huge hold. The larger ship was taking the craft on board. Two dozen armed aliens lined the hold waiting to capture Joyce and Davenport—again.

Davenport wavered between finishing off Joyce right now or letting go of Joyce to steer the ship away, but it was too late. The larger vessel engulfed the little craft and some enormous rotating doors spiraled shut to lock the craft inside.

Joyce didn't see what was happening. He took advantage of Davenport's hesitation, exploded off the seat, and smashed Davenport against the opposite door.

The two men kicked and fought in a death struggle. Joyce managed to break Davenport's grip. Joyce's hand clamped around Davenport's face and smashed his head against the window while Joyce landed multiple punches to Davenport's ribs and stomach.

Davenport floundered trying to free himself. He flailed his arms trying to get some kind of grip on Joyce.

Davenport punched for the side of Joyce's head, but Joyce struck back with an elbow to Davenport's eye. Joyce threw so much weight against Davenport that Joyce toppled on top of Davenport.

That extra little bit of weight falling against the door popped it open and both men tumbled out onto the floor.

The aliens moved in with their weapons, but Davenport absolutely refused to let go of Joyce. No force in the universe could make Davenport release this asshole—not now—not ever.

They tumbled over each other kicking and scrapping. Joyce got the upper hand, pinned Davenport, and swung his fists to pound Davenport into the ground.

Davenport looked up at Joyce's contorted face. This had to end and it had to end now. Davenport couldn't let this bastard win. Hell no.

That thought gave Davenport the boost he needed to grab Joyce's ruined uniform, kick out with his legs, flip Joyce over his head, and Davenport body-slammed Joyce into the floor.

Davenport rocketed off the ground and whipped around, but he didn't take the time to mount Joyce.

Davenport grabbed the most available part of Joyce's body that Davenport could get hold of. He snatched a handful of Joyce's hair and smashed Joyce's head into the floor.

That feeling of finally getting the chance to really hurt Joyce where it counted—that feeling flooded Davenport with bloodthirsty exhilaration unlike anything he'd ever felt.

He yanked Joyce's head up and slammed it down into the floor again and again. Davenport straightened up higher to give himself more leverage.

He drilled Joyce's head into the floor harder. Davenport felt Joyce's skull give way, but Davenport couldn't stop. He would never be able to stop.

He kept slamming Joyce down again....and again.....and again.

He would have gone on beating Joyce's head into the floor forever, but Joyce's head dissolved. After the fifteenth blow, the skull didn't make the same satisfying crunching sensation in Davenport's hand.

He realized from a great distance that he was holding a fistful of hair and not much else. His arm collapsed and he let the body fall to the floor.

Davenport sank back on his heels panting hard. A puddle of gore surrounded what was left of Joyce's head. He was gone. It was over and finished at last.

Davenport buckled in exhaustion. Joyce was dead.

All of Davenport's energy evaporated. He fell back onto his seat, his chin dropped on his chest, and he shut his eyes.

He felt himself trembling all over. Blood and brains covered his arm up to the elbow and spattered his clothes and face.

He couldn't move as the full gravity of what he just did sank in. He had killed Admiral Killian Joyce. The nightmare was finally over.

Someone said something to him in a strange language. Davenport had to summon all his effort to open his eyes and raise his head.

The aliens surrounded him holding him at gunpoint. They all saw what he did and now Joyce lay dead on the floor next to Davenport.

Davenport couldn't bring himself to move. Nothing mattered anymore. The one driving factor that kept him going all this time was gone now.

Where would he go? What would he do with his life? He couldn't even think clearly enough to decide.

The same alien said something else to Davenport. Those words sounded like an order, but Davenport couldn't rally the energy even to care about that. He didn't care what anyone did to him after this.

Two of the aliens exchanged a snatch of conversation and one of them walked off somewhere. The others held Davenport at gunpoint—as if he could ever pose any threat to them.

He was unarmed and completely at their mercy, but even that somehow overwhelmed him with relief. He didn't have to go anywhere or do anything. He could finally just sit here and do nothing. He didn't even have to think.

The second alien came back with a different alien from a different species. The new-comer took one look at Davenport and burst into a flurry of remarks to those around him.

They inspected Davenport at close range and then the newcomer said in perfect English, "Who are you?"

"Davenport," Davenport husked. "My name.....is Davenport."

The alien jolted upright. "Davenport! I've heard of you! You work for Ekol Thaine, don't you?"

Davenport dragged his head up with another almighty effort. Ekol Thaine? These people obviously hadn't caught up with the times. Ekol was dead. Davenport's crew had been the ones to kill Ekol and take command of his forces.

Davenport hadn't worked for Ekol in years, but these people didn't need to know that.

The alien waited for Davenport to answer, and when he didn't, the alien's expression changed. "Did you run away from him?" the alien almost whispered. "Is he after you to punish you for something you did to him?"

Davenport still didn't answer. He couldn't go through the whole explanation—not now. He didn't even have the energy to explain why he just killed this man lying on the floor next to him.

None of these aliens even glanced at Davenport's star, not even the one who spoke English and knew about Ekol. Was it possible that these aliens didn't even know what the Confederate Sheriff's Service was?

The alien turned around and went through a rapid discussion with his comrades about Davenport's response and non-response. Davenport could just imagine what they were saying about him.

Fortunately, he didn't have to imagine it because the same alien turned around and waved toward the back of the deck. "Follow me. We're bound for the Confederacy. We'll take you with us and sell you back to Ekol, but don't resist or the crew will have to subdue you. Come with me and consider yourself our prisoner."

Davenport only nodded. What else was new? He needed to be someone's prisoner right now. He could barely drag himself off the floor, much less resist.

The alien led him into an elevator that raised both of them ten decks to another corridor. The alien escorted Davenport to a tiny crew cabin with one narrow berth and nothing else in it.

"I'm going to lock you in," the alien informed him. "We'll come and get you later. If you behave, you'll be able to move about the ship once the captain and crew see that you're willing to cooperate."

Davenport blinked at the cabin and then at the alien. "You're......you're taking me back to the Confederacy?"

"Ekol will pay a lot of money to get you back. He might even take us into his service as a reward for bringing you in. Ekol doesn't take kindly to people crossing him. You should know that."

"I do know that. I was just wondering....." Davenport frowned to himself. "Have you ever been to the Confederacy? Have any of you?"

"Oh, no! This is our first trip there." The alien brightened up. "We've heard a lot about it, though." He nodded toward the berth. "Stay here. Someone will check on you later."

He pulled the door shut and Davenport slumped onto the mattress. His whole body crumpled in aching exhaustion and he collapsed onto the bed with his eyes closed.

It was over and he was on his way back to the Confederacy. He didn't care about anything else.

Chapter 35

G unfire slammed into the hull next to Davenport's head and startled him out of a sound sleep. He stared at the ceiling for a split second before he remembered where he was.

The alien crew that captured him had been traveling through Sacron Enigma for a week. They stopped off at different planets to transact business and they long since let Davenport walk freely around the ship.

He didn't interfere with anything they did. He was too interested in getting back to the Confederacy.

He didn't even really care who the crew sold him to. Davenport would find his friends one way or the other. He had friends just about any place the crew did decide to sell him.

He couldn't have interfered with them even if he'd wanted to. He didn't speak their language and he rarely saw the one crewman who spoke English.

He ate with the crew and even showered with the crew, but they never tried to talk to him and he never tried to talk to them.

He'd drifted into some kind of purgatory where he wasn't even sure anymore if his memories of the past few weeks really happened. He remembered everything from a numb distance as though it had all happened to someone else.

Maybe he'd been on this ship all along and only dreamed about the Ithium and Joyce and even working for Ekol and changing his life to become a sheriff.

The star pinned to his vest was the only evidence that it really did happen—the star and Joyce's blood staining Davenport's clothes.

The aliens never gave him any new clothes to wear. Every time he took a shower, he put back on the same clothes he'd been wearing when he killed Joyce. Even that seemed somehow fitting.

Davenport wore that blood as a badge of honor. He'd finished the job. He could go home with his head up and his shoulders back because he'd finally brought justice to everyone who needed it.

This was the first time he'd heard gunfire on board this ship, though. The trip so far had been utterly uneventful. It shattered the illusion and Davenport sat up straight in bed.

Concussions hammered the vessel's sides and he heard yelling out in the corridor. He stood up, stuck his feet into his boots, and opened his cabin door.

He couldn't get outside right away. The crew raced passed him going in both directions. They yelled back and forth to each other and then another punishing boom bowled everyone into the opposite wall.

Davenport fell against the door frame and pushed himself up. "What's happening?" he yelled to those nearest him, but they didn't understand him. They all ran away in different directions.

He waited for a break in the traffic and staggered to the bridge. He'd only glanced into it before.

The captain and officers bellowed orders and reports back and forth in their own language. The controls showed the crew manning the ship's guns to return fire against a horde of other ships all attacking at once. There must have been a dozen attackers out there.

A gunshot smashed into the bridge and an explosion ripped out part of the wall. Some of the controls fried and the blast hurled the crewman onto the floor.

The captain roared something else to his people and then a familiar voice came through the communications system. "Alien vessel, you are in violation of Confederate law. You have crossed the Confederate boundary illegally and you are carrying a human prisoner on board. Hold your fire and prepare to be boarded. Hand over your prisoner or we will disable your ship by force."

Davenport charged onto the bridge and tried to get near the communications station. "Marshall Healey!" Davenport yelled. "Marshall Healey—I'm here! It's Davenport! I'm on board!"

Healey's tone changed. "Davenport! Are you all right? We've been looking everywhere for you......"

The alien crewman shoved Davenport away and sent him staggering. The bridge staff went through another flurry of orders and counter-conversation.

Davenport rushed over to the captain. "You have to let me talk to them! I know them! They're searching for me! Just let me talk to them and I can stop them from attacking!"

The captain spat something back and went back to what he was doing. Another crackle came through the communications system. It was Healey again.

"Alien vessel, you are in violation of Confederate law. This is your final warning. Hand over Davenport or we will disable your ship."

Davenport's skin prickled at the sound of that voice. Healey was right outside. These ships attacking the alien vessel must be Sheriff's Service ships.

Davenport stared at the controls in front of him, and right then, like something out of a distant dream, the *Vindicator* and all the other ships of the Wide Patrol zoomed past the bridge.

He gulped down a thrill of almost painful relief and then he spotted the *Aries Royal,* the Drifter the Chorion Team had adopted as their new ship. They were out there. They were all here. All his friends had come out to get him.

He tore his eyes away with a wrench and turned back to the captain. "Let me talk to them," Davenport told him. "You can't win. Just let me talk to them and tell them that I'm okay. It's your only chance."

The captain frowned at him and stepped away from the controls. Davenport had to control his shaking hands when he switched on the communications link.

He hailed Healey's Nitrol. "Marshall—it's me. I'm all right. These aliens don't speak English. They don't understand your ultimatum, but I think they're ready to hand me over."

"Tell them to cut their fire," Healey replied. "Tell them to give up peacefully. If they cooperate and hand you over without a fight, we can discuss letting them go."

Davenport glanced at the captain. The alien obviously didn't understand what Healey just said, but the captain got enough of the message. He barked an order over his shoulder and the alien vessel's guns shut off.

Davenport had to resist the urge to laugh in pure relief and excitement. He was going home.

Some bright spark must have passed the word to the crew. The only alien on board who spoke English hustled up to the bridge and translated Healey's orders to the captain and his staff.

The Wide Patrol revolved around the alien ships and escorted them to Macron Calypso, which was the nearest Sheriff's Service outpost.

The alien vessel landed on the tarmac and Davenport watched in wistful, emotional bliss as Reserve Wing soldiers surrounded the vessel in guns.

They rushed on board and held the crew at gunpoint. Four soldiers surrounded Davenport. "If you'll follow me, Sir, I'll take you to the infirmary for medical treatment!" one of the soldiers told Davenport. "Marshall Healey's orders."

Davenport only nodded. The soldiers escorted him inside the outpost and sat him in a chair next to the doctor's desk.

The doctor was busy with some other patients just then. Two soldiers stayed behind to guard Davenport, but he didn't even care about that.

Five minutes later, Healey came in by himself. His eyes blazed when he saw Davenport.

The two men stared at each other for what seemed like an eternity. Davenport didn't think he could explain even to Healey everything that happened in Sacron Enigma.

Healey finally croaked under his breath, "Is it over?"

Davenport nodded and Healey's hand fell on Davenport's shoulder. That touch said it all. Davenport didn't have to say a word. It was over. No one cared about the details.

A second later, Pritchard came in with the Chorions. The boys made a huge fuss over Davenport and Breeze made the doctor's life miserable by tripping over the doctor's chair, knocking over racks of supplies and equipment, and making the electronic testing equipment go haywire just by standing too close to it.

Rodeo finally pointed to the door. "Go back to the ship and wait for us there, boy. You're a walking doomsday device all by yourself."

"Let him stay," Davenport interrupted. "It's all right."

Rodeo angled his head the other way to listen. "Are you sure?"

"Yeah," Davenport murmured. "I missed you boys—all of you."

"What happened out there, Sir?" Bandit asked. "We lost you when those aliens attacked. They cut Admiral Joyce's Dagger away from us, and by the time we got back to your location, you were gone."

"It's a long story," Davenport replied. "Maybe I'll tell you sometime."

"Tell me you paid that bastard Joyce back good and mean," Axel growled. "The rest of the crew will want to hear that you did."

"I did," Davenport murmured.

No one asked any questions after that. Healey made the boys back off so the doctor could give Davenport a full medical examination, but he was fine except for a few bruises to his face that he suffered during his last fight against Joyce.

After the doctor finished with him, Healey ordered Pritchard to take Davenport to the Sheriff's Service office and record Davenport's full statement. Davenport followed Pritchard there in a daze.

All the other sheriffs and deputies in the office turned around to stare at Davenport when he walked past. He realized just how messy he looked, but at least he was still wearing his star. He could replace the rest of these clothes, but he would always have his star.

Pritchard took him into a private room, shut the door, and sat down behind the desk. Pritchard folded his hands on the desk and leaned forward to pierce Davenport with a hard stare.

"I'm going to turn on the recorder and you can tell me what happened after you boarded Joyce's ship. Just so you know, the details of this case are already being classified by the Confederate Corps, so the chances are high that no one in the service will ever see this statement. Understand? In all likelihood, this report will disappear and no one will find out what you did in Sacron Enigma. Do you understand?"

Davenport nodded. Pritchard didn't have to spell out exactly what he meant. No one would get any wacky ideas about charging Davenport with murder or anything like that because no one would ever find out that he killed Joyce or how he did it.

Pritchard switched on his computer and leaned back in his seat. "So what happened after you boarded Joyce's vessel?"

Davenport took a deep breath and started talking. He poured out the whole story ending with when he woke up just now to the sound of gunshots, went to the alien vessel's bridge, and heard Healey ordering the aliens to give up.

When Davenport finally stopped talking, Pritchard sat in his chair with his fingertips pressed together for a few silent minutes. He studied Davenport too closely.

Davenport didn't know what to say to break the silence, so he didn't say anything. He'd given his statement. What else was there to say?

Pritchard finally seemed to come to some decision, leaned forward, switched off his computer, and got to his feet. "Welp, that's all finished, then. Thank you for giving your statement, Sheriff. A ship will take you back to Ultra Meridian where you'll be free to return to duty."

Davenport's eyes popped. "You mean....now? I'm going back to Ultra Meridian....right now?"

"Whenever you're ready. You're all done here. There's nothing more you need to do.....unless you want to."

Davenport opened his mouth to say something, but no sound would come out. Go back to Ultra Meridian.....right now?

He'd been thinking about this for so long. He found it impossible to believe that he could just....go.

No one would be hunting him at Ultra Meridian anymore. He could go back to the jail.....and return to duty as though none of this ever happened.

What did he think would happen—that the Confederacy would throw a big party and organize a parade in his honor?

He didn't want that. Going back to Ultra Meridian and resuming his boring little life of inspecting every ship that passed through—that sounded like the sweetest reward anyone could possibly give him.

It was the fulfillment of a dream that started long before he found the Ithium on board the *Echo Omicron*. It was the fulfillment of a dream he'd had when he served his first stretch at Terminus Anathema—the dream he had when he decided to change his life.

Living and working at Ultra Meridian was all he'd ever wanted. He couldn't ask for more than that.

Pritchard sauntered around the desk. "Anyway, if you don't want to go back there right now, there are a few people down in the residential wing who'd like to see you before you go. If you come with me, I'll show you where they are."

Davenport stood up and followed Pritchard out of the room. Davenport couldn't feel his legs. Everything seemed to be happening outside of himself.

Pritchard left the Sheriff's Service office and the same thing happened. Sheriffs, deputies, and a few Reserve Wing officers stopped what they were doing and watched him pass. Silence fell over the office until after he left it.

Pritchard crossed the compound to the residential wing, climbed a set of stairs, passed down a corridor, and turned into a lounge where Lyons. Dice, Beauty, Fiddler, Emmett, Jace, and Jericho sat around at their leisure.

Lyons looked up and smiled at Davenport when he walked in. The others smiled at Davenport, too, but none of them stopped their conversation or whatever else they were doing. They treated his return as normal.

Healey and the Chorions turned up right after Davenport.

Pritchard turned to face him. "This is the key to your apartment. It's number twelve down the hall on the left." Pritchard put the key in Davenport's hand. "You can go down there, take a shower, change your clothes, get some sleep—do whatever you have to do. Don't worry about those aliens that brought you over the line. We'll deal with them."

He clamped Davenport on the shoulder and walked out. The Chorions went into the kitchen, helped themselves to the food, and then flopped on the couches and chairs.

The tide of conversation, laughter, and banging noises coming from the kitchen washed over Davenport in waves. This was really happening.

The whole crew was back together in one place and everything was okay—because Davenport made it okay. Joyce was gone because Davenport made Joyce gone.

Alla pulled a package of Nutra Noodles out of one of the kitchen cupboards and held it up. "Do you want some, Sir? We got some Aceros nuggets to add to it."

"Sure," Davenport replied. "Count me in."

"Aceros—seriously?" Lyons called across the room. "Is there anything you won't eat?"

"Marshall Healey said I could eat Ekol Thaine, but I didn't." Alla stuck out his tongue and grimaced. "That's just sick."

Everyone laughed and Davenport walked the rest of the way into the room. He found a seat for himself between Dice and Jericho. They were talking about some creature that was native to Chorion Osiris.

Davenport listened to all the crew's conversations, but none of them asked him anything else. None of them asked about where he'd been or what he'd been doing or even if he was okay.

Somehow, none of those questions applied to him anymore. Everyone here treated him as though he'd never left.....which, in a way, he hadn't.

Chapter 36

F iddler threw her arms around Dice's neck. She had to stand on her tiptoes to hug him. "I'm gonna miss you so much! I can't believe I won't see you again!"

He chuckled and hugged her back with one of his giant arms. "Aw. We'll see each other—sometime."

She let go of him and turned to hug Lyons. "You guys take care of each other, okay? I know you're gonna be just fine, but still."

"We will be fine," Lyons told her. "It's you I'm worried about."

"We'll be okay, too." Fiddler held her at arm's length, clasped both of Lyons's hands, and Fiddler sniffed back tears. "Oh, my God! I can't believe this is really goodbye."

Davenport looked away. He didn't want to think about Fiddler leaving—let alone watch her leaving.

Jace, Jericho, and Emmett stood off to one side watching, too. The Drifter that would take them to Chorion Osiris waited for them on the tarmac at the Macron Calypso Sheriff's Service outpost.

One of Jericho's copies sat in the Drifter's pilot's cradle waiting for the passengers to come on board.

Fiddler turned to Beauty. He stood next to Dice and Lyons and grinned up at Fiddler with an open, beaming smile of pure loving happiness.

Fiddler pressed her hand to her mouth. "I don't know how to thank you, Beauty!" she choked.

"You don't have to do that," he growled. "Just have a good life. That's all you have to do."

She bent down and hugged him. He blushed and looked away.

She tore herself off and rushed down the line hugging all the other Chorions. "You guys are gonna be great out there. I know you are. Just try to stay out of trouble, okay?"

"Maybe we'll see you on Chorion Osiris sometime," Bandit told her.

"I doubt that. We won't stay there long—just long enough for Jace to visit his family. Then we're going traveling. I don't really know where we'll go, but we'll definitely be going somewhere."

She came to the end of the row and hugged Healey. "Thank you so much for everything, Marshall. The world is a safer place with you in it."

"Thank you, darlin'," he murmured and hugged her back. "I'm happy for you. Have a safe trip and don't hesitate to contact me if you need anything—anything at all."

She beamed at him, but she went quiet when she got to the end of the line and came face to face with Davenport.

Tears brimmed in her eyes. Davenport had to swallow the lump in his throat when he looked at her. "Davenport...." she quavered.

"Don't say it," he husked. "Don't say anything. Just know you'll always have a home at Ultra Meridian."

She nodded fast and fought to control her lips. Then she threw herself at him and crushed him in a hug.

He felt her shaking in his arms, and when she pulled away, tears poured down her cheeks. She panted to control herself.

"You know where to find me if you need me," he murmured and let her go.

She turned away to hide her face and then hurried over to her father and the twins.

Jace came forward and shook Dice's hand. "Are you going to be okay?" Jace asked.

"Sure, pal," Dice growled. "Thanks to you. You be happy out there, okay? You deserve it."

Jace smiled back at him, shook his hair out of his eyes, and then shook hands with Davenport before all four of them headed for their ship.

Fiddler turned around once, waved, did her best to smile, and then all four of them went on board.

Jericho waved from the cockpit as the ship fired up and lifted off. Davenport looked away again. Those four were only the first batch. He had four more of these farewells to get through and he wasn't looking forward to a single one of them.

Lyons turned to the Chorion Team and hugged each of them one after another. "I don't know what to say to you boys except maybe, 'see you around'. I hate to admit it, but I'm sure our paths will cross soon."

"Let's make sure they cross in a nice way," Rodeo replied.

"Yes, absolutely," she agreed. "You're going back to take over Ekol's syndicate and I'm going back to Acrolith Diastema to take over my father's empire. We can form an alliance that will enrich both our organizations. We don't have to be enemies at each other's throats anymore."

"It's a deal."

She hugged Healey and then Davenport experienced a whole new dimension in agony when Lyons stopped in front of him.

Her features trembled, but she held it back better than Fiddler did. Lyons locked eyes with Davenport for a second and then hugged him without a word.

He found himself starting to unwind as he hugged her. All these people had become such an indispensable part of his life these past few weeks. He didn't like to think about his life without them in it.

They would all be better off going on with their lives. They could all put these past few weeks behind them and become human again.

This tearing sensation in his middle would pass. He knew that, but knowing it didn't make it any easier.

She stepped away and shook her hair out of her eyes. She didn't look at Davenport again.

Dice shook hands with all the Chorions and with Healey, but Dice stopped when he came to Davenport.

Davenport forced him to smile up at Dice. "Don't come around my outpost smuggling contraband, okay?" Davenport teased. "I couldn't stand it."

Dice laughed and then clasped his big, rough, warm palm against the side of Davenport's cheek. "You take care of yourself, porkchop. I'm gonna miss you."

Davenport tried to speak, but his throat hurt too much.

"You're one hell of a lawman, Davenport," Dice rasped. "The best I've ever seen. It feels good to know you'll be out there at Ultra Meridian keeping an eye on things for us."

Dice patted Davenport's cheek and then closed him in a crushing hug. Davenport shut his eyes and swallowed hard. He knew saying goodbye would be hard, but he didn't think it would be as hard as this.

Dice broke away and left Beauty standing in his place. Davenport couldn't speak.

Beauty smiled up at him. "Don't ever change, Davenport," Beauty told him. "Stay exactly the way you are. You're a good man."

"Thank you, Beauty," Davenport croaked. "Thank you for everything from the bottom of my heart."

Beauty smiled even more broadly, stretched out his hand once to squeeze Davenport's, and then walked away.

He, Dice, and Lyons strode out onto the tarmac to the Cyclone that would take them to Acrolith Diastema. Lyons's people had sent out a crew to pick her up and take her home.

All three of them waved before they went on board. Davenport couldn't watch that ship fly away, either.

As soon as it left, the Chorions turned to Davenport and Healey and everyone hugged both sheriffs.

Davenport felt the boys hugging him and he heard them saying all the right things, but he couldn't answer them.

He just wanted this to be over. He hated to lose even one of them. Now he was losing all of them at the same time.

Wolf hugged Davenport last of all. Davenport put his arms around Wolf, felt Wolf's fur, and couldn't let go. Davenport hugged Wolf a lot longer than he should have.

Wolf growled in his ear. It was a comforting growl—a growl that told Davenport that nothing would change between them, not even when they were on opposite sides of the galaxy.

Wolf and Davenport pulled away at the same time. Wolf gave one more growl and the boys went back and forth between Healey and Davenport a second time.

"Keep it real, Sir," Laub told Davenport.

"I will, man," Davenport choked. "You boys keep your noses clean. Don't make me have to come out to Nyx Anonyma to straighten you out."

Some of the Chorions laughed. "If you need anything, you let us know," Rodeo told him. "What's ours is yours—always."

"Thanks," Davenport husked. "Ekol's empire is in good hands."

The boys finally broke away, boarded the *Aries Royal,* and Bandit launched into the atmosphere at breakneck speed heading home.

That left Healey and Davenport alone. They both watched the Drifter out of sight before Healey bumped his knuckles against Davenport's shoulder. "Come on. Let's get going."

Davenport felt better once he started walking away. Things would get easier from here. He just had to keep moving.

Healey led the way to a brand-new Nitrol—the Nitrol the Sheriff's Service had assigned to the Confederate Marshall of Pandora's Needle.

Healey had already gone back there to straighten out the chaos the satellite had been plunged into since his absence. He'd only come back to Macron Calypso to say goodbye to the crew.

Healey and Davenport both went to the bridge and Healey powered up. Davenport read the controls, but there was nothing to do but sit here and watch while Healey flew out to Ultra Meridian.

The trip took a long time, but neither sheriff spoke on the way out there. Davenport allowed his mind to wander over everything that had happened since he came back from Sacron Enigma.

He and his crew had stayed at Macron Calypso for five days just relaxing and enjoying each other's company before they all parted ways.

True to Pritchard's word, no one had said a damn word to Davenport about anything that might or might not have appeared in his statement about what happened between him and Admiral Joyce.

In fact, everyone in the Sheriff's Service apart from Pritchard and Healey had given Davenport a wide berth.

Davenport had been called to one meeting with his superior officer, the Marshall of Macron Calypso, Andrew Fuller—the man Davenport had always reported to before the whole Ithium disaster began.

Marshall Fuller had given Davenport an update on Typhon Elexor's and Mount Refractory's activities at Ultra Meridian along with some other known criminal activity in the surrounding space.

Fuller had also given Davenport the manifest of weapons, supplies, the new Skimmer, and all the other goods the Sheriff's Service had shipped out to Ultra Meridian to prepare the jail for Davenport's return.

Fuller didn't say a word about the Ithium, Davenport's crew's activities on the planet, or anything else. Fuller kept the meeting strictly business.

It was exactly the same kind of meeting Davenport had always had with Fuller since Davenport first became Sheriff of Ultra Meridian.

Davenport had expected to get either excited or emotional when he finally returned to Ultra Meridian to resume his duties at the outpost.

He surprised himself by feeling nothing when the planet came in sight. His heart didn't skip a beat nor did his pulse quicken.

Coming back here felt perfectly normal and natural. It didn't arouse any excitement or nostalgia.

Ultra Meridian didn't change. It would always be here and it would always stay the same, just waiting for him to come back home where he belonged.

Healey landed on the planes and he and Davenport both stepped to the edge of the hatch. Stinging, sandy wind bit Davenport in the face. The smell flooded his nostrils. He could never mistake that smell for any other place.

The jail sat alone in the distance. The Sheriff's Service had rebuilt it one last time. They wouldn't have to rebuild it again because he would be here to make sure no scavengers stole anything out of it.

Healey got Davenport's attention by gripping Davenport's shoulder. Davenport had to concentrate to tear his eyes off the jail. His whole being wanted to be out there. He belonged there.

He turned to face Healey, but neither man got emotional or showed any sign of distress. This was all in the natural order of things.

It had been coming for a long, long time. It had always been inevitable that Davenport would come back here. He had nowhere else in the world to be.

Healey held out something. "Take this. You'll need it."

Davenport looked down at a mask and a pair of goggles in his hands. "Yeah," he whispered. "Thanks."

Healey smiled at him. Healey's eyes glowed with understanding, admiration, and that deep knowing that he and Davenport would meet again. That part was inevitable, too.

Healey jerked his chin at the jail. "Get out of here. You're making me late."

Davenport laughed. "See you around sometime."

"You betcha."

Uncontrollable laughter bubbled out of Davenport's deepest being when he turned away, pulled the mask and goggles over his head, stepped through the hatch, and set off across the planes toward the jail in the distance.

He didn't turn around to watch Healey fly away. Davenport had work to do.

His heart lifted as he got nearer to the jail. It looked exactly the way he remembered. Damn, it was good to be home.

The End.

Keep Reading

Battlefleet Series

Ellis "Sailor" English used to be the most decorated, most highly-respected captain in the whole United Space Force. Now he's nothing but a grunt gunnery sergeant in charge of the worst fighter wing on board the USS Lightning Rod and the captain is NOT happy to have him around. Loud-mouth disciplinary cases, ex-criminals, nobodies from the streets, and even a few who can't fly at all—it will be a miracle if English can whip this lackluster bunch of punks into shape before the captain dumps him out of the service along with his pilots.

But when war breaks out and threatens everything the crew holds dear, everyone in the whole United Space Force will have to change their ideas about who and what Sailor English is. Can the most unlikely hero save what's left of Earth before disaster brings humanity to its knees?

You can find it at your favorite book retailer.

Sign Up Once--Get all Theo Mann's free books including brand new releases

Sign Up Once--Get all Theo Mann's free books including brand new releases

Humanity on the brink of annihilation.

A mysterious package, a corrupt officer, and a conspiracy that goes all the way to the top? What could possibly go wrong?

When a routine mission goes horribly wrong, Warrant Officer Ewing Archer and a handful of faithful friends get trapped in a battle to save the last survivors of Earth.

The human race has abandoned the ecological disaster of Earth. Now all that remains is a network of interconnected ships, stations, and satellites surrounding the planet.

But when war breaks out, Archer becomes a firebrand that could destroy it all....or save it.

Sign up at www.theomann.com to read it for free

About Theo Mann

I write 70 books per year—and yes, before you ask, all these books are my original creative work. Nothing written under my name is AI-generated or ghostwritten because I write better than AI and any ghostwriter out there.

People don't read fiction for entertainment or to escape from reality. People read fiction to see their humanity reflected in another person's character and story.

This is my promise to you. When you read my books, you'll see your own humanity reflected in the characters and stories. I take this commitment to my readers very seriously. My books are an intimate form of communication between us. I would never disrespect my readers by turning that over to a machine or another writer. This is my bond between me and you as my reader.

I write 20,000 words per day as my daily work output. If anyone with a public platform would like to challenge me to prove this in a controlled environment, feel free to contact me on this website's contact page.

I worked as a professional ghostwriter for fifteen years. Now I'm on a mission to set a Guinness World Record by writing 700 books over the next ten years and 1400 books over the next twenty years, all originally written by me. See my website for the full book list.

I'm also the author of *Proof for the Existence of God* and the *Crimes Against Fiction* blog. You can find all my nonfiction work at www.crimes-against-fiction.com.

If you have a story idea, or if you would like me to explore a series in more depth, or if you'd like me to explore a character by writing a spinoff series about that character or world, leave me a message on my website's contact page. I answer all reader emails, so ask me anything, tell me what you liked and didn't like, and let me know where you'd like your favorite series to go. I would love to hear your ideas and find out what you'd like to read next.

Find out more at www.theomann.com.

Also by Theo Mann (so far)

www.ingramcontent.com/pod-product-compliance
Lightning Source LLC
Chambersburg PA
CBHW070519030726
47503CB00004B/1314